The Little Comedy
and Other Stories

ARTHUR SCHNITZLER

The Little Comedy

AND OTHER STORIES

FOREWORD BY FREDERICK UNGAR

FREDERICK UNGAR PUBLISHING CO.
NEW YORK

Translated from the original German
Arthur Schnitzler, *Gesammelte Werke in Einzelbänden. Die Erzählenden Schriften*. Zwei Bände.

Printed in the United States of America
Designed by Edith Fowler

Library of Congress Cataloging in Publication Data

Schnitzler, Arthur, 1862–1931.
The little comedy and other stories.

CONTENTS: The little comedy.—Riches.—The son. [etc.]
I. Title.
PZ3.S3598Lg 1977 [PT2638.N5] 833'.8 77-6952
ISBN 0-8044-2802-6
ISBN 0-8044-6839-7 pbk.

· CONTENTS ·

· FOREWORD ·

Though you bemoan your crit'cal need again,
I can but sing for you the old refrain,
That well-known song of love and play and death—
Be comforted: The sense, the soul, the breath
Of all things earthly are within these three,
As is all truth and what but seems to be.

—*Arthur Schnitzler*

Arthur Schnitzler was one of the most famous men of his day. Americans who visited Vienna in the first quarter of this century were eager to meet him. In a congratulatory letter sent on the occasion of Schnitzler's sixtieth birthday in 1922, Sigmund Freud wrote: "I think I have avoided you from a kind of reluctance to meet my double . . . whenever I get deeply absorbed in your beautiful creations I invariably seem to find beneath their poetic surface the very presuppositions, interests and conclusions which I know to be my own. . . . So I have formed the impression that you know through intuition—or rather from detailed self-observation—everything that I have discovered by laborious work on other people."

Schnitzler was born May 12, 1862 in Vienna, the still glamorous capital of the Austrian-Hungarian monarchy and a cultural center. He was the son of Dr. Johann Schnitzler, a renowned laryngologist and university professor, and a Jew. Young Arthur studied medicine at his father's wish and

Note: The above lines by Schnitzler are given in a translation by Lowell A. Bangerter.

started to practice. He soon became disillusioned with the medical establishment of his day and stopped accepting new patients. He also felt that he had chosen the wrong speciality, laryngology; his real medical interest lay in psychiatry. Finally he gave up his practice altogether in order to devote himself to his writing, which had been his other lively interest almost since childhood, when he wrote his first drama.

Schnitzler's early reputation as playwright and novelist was gained largely through his plays *Anatol* (1893), *Light-O'-Love* (*Liebelei,* 1896), and *Hands Around* (*Reigen,* 1900), which later caused an international stir as the film *La Ronde. Hands Around* also triggered a famous court case on the freedom of the theater. This celebrity mixed with controversy soon made Schnitzler appear to be the dramatist of love. And that in turn prompted his detractors—largely motivated by their anti-semitism—to call him an immoral, near-pornographic writer. Nothing could be further from the truth. What Schnitzler did, with a subtle hand, was to portray the decadent, frivolous, upper-class Vienna society of his time. Many characters in Schnitzler's plays were indeed unprincipled and bored pleasure seekers, but only a rather unsophisticated reader would take the opinions of a dramatist's characters as those of the author himself. Even in *Hands Around,* a masterpiece of satire, in which each of the ten scenes ends with the intimated sexual act, the dialogue is handled with utmost discreetness. The subject of the scenes may make them appear at first to be nothing but subdued pornography, but the play is in fact the work of a moralist. The repetitiousness of each scene's ending has the effect of emptiness, if not revulsion. No wonder, considering the time and place of the first staging, that riots occurred at the theater. Yet the court's final verdict vindicated the drama, describing it as "a moral deed" and in the interest of the preservation of public morality.

As a member of a more or less subtly persecuted minority, Schnitzler felt throughout his life the pervasive hostility of many Austrian journalists and writers. The following distich gives voice to his reaction:

"You who are as yet unborn, a friend I could cheerfully call you.
Were you alive today, one hater more would I count."

A man of deep compassion and a humanist with a high sense of social responsibility, Arthur Schnitzler attacked long-standing prejudices, such as those surrounding the institution of the duel in *None but the Brave* (*Leutnant Gustl,* 1901). For this the Imperial Army High Command found him guilty of insulting the honor of the military and deemed him no longer worthy of being an officer in the medical corps of the Imperial Army. In *Professor Bernhardi* (1912), Schnitzler explores another delicate question: should the final hours of a dying person, unaware that she is close to death, be disturbed by the last rites a priest wishes to administer? A decision against such rites is made by the Jewish clinic director, who acts according to his conscience. The incident is distorted into interference with religion. Professor Bernhardi is suspended from his position, accused of having hastened the patient's death, and sentenced to jail. Although this play was staged in many countries (it was presented in New York in 1936 under the direction of Schnitzler's son Heinrich), production in Vienna was possible only after the collapse of the monarchy in 1918, at the end of World War I.

Distortions and denunciations by the Vienna press proved so effective that a Schnitzler stereotype was soon created, picturing the writer as a frivolous erotomaniac, an atheistic relativist who denied stable moral values. The opposite, in fact, was true. The deeply ethical note in his work can hardly be overlooked. In his philosophical search for enduring ethical values Schnitzler clearly distinguished between relative virtues, which are only expressions of a certain cultural epoch, and absolute virtues, which remain valid for all time under all circumstances. He defined both in his *Buch der Sprüche und Bedenken** (Book of Sayings and Reflections). Schnitzler was

* *This work has not been translated into English, but many of its reflections are included in* Practical Wisdom: A Treasury of Aphorisms and Reflections from the German, *Ungar, 1977.*

anything but a detached observer; he was a man of profound humanity and deep concern. And his warning is unambiguous: moral relativism leads to a desiccated life and to spiritual death.

Schnitzler was not religious in the normal sense of the word; he remained highly skeptical toward organized religion. Yet he was not an atheist, as his detractors called him. He believed that neither irreligion nor atheism actually exist; rather, in place of what others call God, even the most unspiritual person sets another concept, another idea, another assumption. The chaotic diversity of life, the cryptic nature of fate and its inscrutability filled him with wonder, with awe, with a feeling close to or identical with religiosity. If that wonderment before life's mystery is a basic religious experience, then Schnitzler may be called a religious poet. "As far as my doubts are concerned," he wrote, "there is so much devotion in them that they are probably closer to piety than what you call your religion."

Although he hated politics and was not tied to any party, Schnitzler raised his voice as an individual in support of ethical principles and against the corruption of political parties, the fickleness of public opinion, and society's pervasive materialism.

Despite his skepticism, and even though such concepts as patriotism, eternal love, and the constancy of emotions were revealed under his penetrating glance to be the stirrings of selfishness or unmasked as self-deception, Schnitzler had faith in the possibilities of the human condition and hope that life can be made worthwhile.

As a man of letters, Schnitzler's importance is his introduction of the psychological play into modern drama (as Ibsen and Hauptmann created the social play). His dramatic work focused mainly on the relationship between the sexes, but his significance transcends this narrow categorization. He was not only one of the great literary figures of his time, a writer of technical virtuosity and innovative ingenuity—he also introduced the interior monologue to German literature long before James Joyce and Virginia Woolf brought that innovation to English writing.

Schnitzler's work also gives a matchless cultural-historical picture of the era of Emperor Franz Josef's reign in Austria. An entire epoch takes form in Schnitzler's work, in his stories as well as his plays. In particular, he presents a classic portrait of the turn-of-the-century Vienna that he knew so well and that came to an end in 1914 with World War I. That world he portrayed with inimitable charm. Nothing he wrote after those cataclysmic years went beyond that era. The period that followed held no interest for him.

Although Schnitzler is regarded as the poet of the Vienna of a certain era, it would be incorrect to think of him as a regional writer. As one who dealt with the essence of human existence, he has transcended the limitations of time and place. His work has the validity of what is eternally human. Even though the world he captured with such charm and refinement has long since disappeared, Schnitzler's characters are still very much alive; they are true and original. And this is so because the questions he posed are timeless, as are the topics of his stories and plays—the lure of love, man's transitoriness, the incomprehensibility of fate. Nothing has gone stale—his work still speaks to us today.

Schnitzler's great contemporaries paid the highest tribute to his achievements. Thomas Mann, for one, praised "his virile knowledge of people and the world, the fascination of the problems he poses, the graceful purity of his style . . . and best of all, the personal charm that emerges from everything he has created." Franz Wedekind called him a German classic. "No one deserves the name of master more than he does." Heinrich Mann and Hugo von Hofmannsthal admired his witty sophistication, delicate irony, and subtlety of style, as did many others.

The five stories included in this volume show Schnitzler at his peak; they have never before been translated into English.

Regrettably, most of the earlier Schnitzler translations published in English do not do justice to the writer's achievement and, indeed, are sometimes inaccurate. The translations here have been prepared with the utmost care to convey the full flavor of the original text.

The first selection, "The Little Comedy," is a masterpiece of characterization, providing deep insights into two people involved in a lighthearted romance. This charming story fully captures the atmosphere of Schnitzler's Vienna and shows his subtle social criticism and sophisticated wit at their best.

In "Dying," a brilliant account of a young man's last months of life, as in the others that complete this volume, Schnitzler proves himself to be a dramatic storyteller with a profound knowledge of the human soul.

In this foreword the writer has aimed to show the range of Schnitzler's life work and his exemplary qualities as a human being. It is not often that a great literary artist can also be admired for his humanity. We can all rejoice that this is true of Arthur Schnitzler.

FREDERICK UNGAR

The Little Comedy
and Other Stories

The Little Comedy

ALFRED VON WILMERS TO THEODOR DIELING IN NAPLES

My dear Theodor,

Many thanks for your letter. Man, how I envy you! How the life you are living sparkled and glowed at me from your lines! You understand how to enjoy solitude, and when you gaze into the blue for an hour you get more out of it than people like us get out of a year of wandering in search of adventure.

I beg of you not to call my condition Weltschmerz—it's a quite ordinary state of weariness with myself, but no, not even that, it's boredom—nothing more. I cannot hide the fact that the world and its troubles are a matter of total indifference to me. The other evening while writing I was interrupted by Fritz. Lord in Heaven, that was another one of those nights! And that time I wanted to be gay. It was meant to be a last attempt. I drank and I got a headache instead of getting drunk. His girlfriend flirted with me, it angered me instead of amusing me. An emptiness, an emptiness, I tell you!

It's clear that something very special will have to come along to arouse me. It's a question whether I'll still be able to recognize this very special thing should it have the goodness to appear! And then even so I'll be plagued by doubt as to whether this special thing is something ordinary in disguise which I am too stupid to see through. — You see, now's the time I regret that I have no talent, no talent whatsoever for anything! I remember now, with something like shame, the time I used to sneer at you because you had talent. I didn't consider it chic—and I had lofty contempt for anybody who wanted to achieve anything. And now, I tell you, if I could only paint portraits, that would be enough to make me happy.

You know I have given up photography completely. Not even there could I get anywhere. My last two works of art were the Kahlenberg as seen from the Leopoldsberg and the Leopoldsberg as seen from the Kahlenberg. You see, now my one single modest talent, the ability to entertain myself, has been lost. I scrupulously avoid any occasion where it might still be possible—because my last disappointments have soured me. Headache instead of rapture—that's the hallmark of my whole existence. So it's only natural that I stay away from wine.

Today is Sunday; and now, while I'm lounging on my divan and scratching these lines with a pencil, they are all down at the races. At two Fritz sent up word to ask whether I wouldn't perhaps like to come down after all; I went to the window and waved him away. And then he raced off with his carriage, and Stangelberger, his coachman, when he saw me leaning out the window in my dressing gown, winked at me, thinking to himself: Aha, a nocturnal adventure that has been prolonged to the middle of the next day! — Oh, long gone are the times when Stangelberger would have been right!! Now it's five. Still rather hot and my blinds are down. And quite still, quite still. After lunch I slept for an hour, and now I'll get dressed and go down to the Prater as a common pedestrian and watch the people coming back from the races.

Do you still remember the first of May with the two sweet little creatures down there! — That was ten years ago. We trailed the two little darlings that time for a good hour and a half before Mama got lost. And then didn't we show them the way! — Do you remember? — Of course, they knew the way already! — Today let anyone propose running after a female creature for an hour and a half! Where is she for whom I would be capable of such a sacrifice?

I have made a rendezvous with Fritz, Weidenthaler, and the others on Constantine Hill.* Including the women, of course! — I'm not going. Mitzi should cheat Fritz with somebody else; for her the act of cheating is certainly more important than I am! — No, not to Constantine Hill, I'm going to the amusement park in the Prater today, to mix properly with the rabble. First of all I'll plant myself in front of the puppet show, watch it, and when they kill the villainous Jew, I'll be as happy as a tailor's apprentice! Then I'll go to the velocipede circus where the ladies for sale ride around with seven-colored stockings—and then I'll go to the fortune teller and to Präuscher† with the separate booths. And on to Calafatti's.**

Cheerio, old chap, write me something, and greet the pretty Neapolitans for me.

Yours,
Alfred

Josefine Weninger to Helene Beier in Paris

My dear, good Helene,

Well, I have big news. You can guess what it is already, i.e., that it's all over with Emil. Of course, it always makes one a bit sad, for a parting is after all still a parting; and saying goodbye, goodbye forever, as I said above, is very depressing. But, when I don't brood about it, I find that I'm really better off than I've been the whole time lately. You know, these last days were very unpleasant before the break came. I had al-

* *A section of the Prater with an open-air restaurant.*

† *Waxworks combined with peep show.*

** *Popular merry-go-round.*

ready noticed it for a long time, as I recently wrote you, my dear Helene. When he was supposed to come to me in the evenings, he sent word he couldn't come, twice in one week, and then he often let me go to the Prater alone and even sent me to the theater without him being there! Well, we know all about that, that's no longer true love! I don't hold it against him; since lately I haven't honestly been enthusiastic about him at all any more. But I must tell you the whole story of how it finally came about.

Last Tuesday, just a week ago, one of those little notes came from him, at half past seven in the evening, saying he can't come. The next day at noon he will take the liberty of inquiring how I have rested. You know he always used these courteous phrases, which I liked very much, never any crudeness, never—always as if he were allowed only to kiss my hand at the most. — It was a nice evening, too, and me faced with terrible boredom—then I thought to myself—you're going to take a cab and go for a ride. It was half dark already so I simply put my coat over my shoulders and ran downstairs. Then as I'm driving around the Ring, I begin to feel awfully happy, the air was so pleasant, so mild, and I got to thinking, it's quite a good thing that the whole affair is finally ending. In that moment I felt quite indifferent toward all men—completely; not only toward him as I was already used to being.

I order the cab driver to go slowly, I get out at the Stadtpark and have him follow me, get in again at the Museum and then the whole way around the whole Quay and the Ring and when I get home it's well after nine. I go cheerfully upstairs, then Lina tells me, "Fräulein, the gentleman has been here for an hour already." What? I think to myself and go into the sitting room but it's dark in there, and then into the red room. — There he is, sitting properly on the divan in his overcoat, and tapping about on the floor with his walking stick. He looks up as I come in and asks, "Where have you been, my Fräulein?" Quite calmly. I answer him with the truth since there was no reason to lie, "After you wrote that you weren't coming, I took a cab and drove around the Ring because the weather was so nice." — "So," he says, stands up, and with his overcoat still on, walks back and forth in the room without looking at me. — "What's the matter?" I ask him. No answer. I leave him alone and go into the sitting room and hear him still walking back and forth the whole time. I give Lina my coat and send her out for cigarettes because mine have run out, and go back in to Emil again, because I've had enough of it. "Dear Emil," I say, "I can't stand it. If you don't like me to go out for a ride then just say so straight out, it makes no difference to me anyway. Moreover when you write me that you're not coming, then I am not obliged to lock myself in my room and mope. If that were the case I'd be a sight by this time, going through that as many as three times a week," and so on. — Now he suddenly starts to talk, stands still in the middle of the room with his hands crossed behind his overcoat so that his walking stick is poking up into the air above his head. "You're right," he says, "it can't go on like this, and I really can't take it upon myself to demand of you that you stay home alone three days a week, I see that."

Aha! I think to myself and ask him, "So what do you want and why do you make a face and why do you come after you sent word that you're not coming, and why do you send word if you're coming after all?" At that he said, "There was a time, Pepi, when you were very happy if I came unexpectedly—of course that's past now." I wrinkle my nose. He continues, "That's the way things go in the world, I have known that for a long time now, and if I didn't know that it bothers you very little, I would probably send word less frequently that I'm not coming. But I assume that you don't miss me too terribly much." — That's about the way it was, and I only know that I then said, "I'm not going to run after you." — "I don't expect that either," he explained, "on the contrary." — Now it was really almost spelled out, and I say, "On the contrary? Does that mean that it's quite agreeable to you if I don't run after you?" — Now he makes an impatient gesture and stands near the window with his back to me. Then he murmurs, "Don't twist the words in my mouth." At that I go up to him quietly and say, "Well, it's better if you say it straight out, what you have to tell me—there's certainly a reason why first you send word that you're not coming and then come up after all and are so contrary now!" While I'm standing there beside him, he suddenly takes my head between his hands and kisses me on the brow, right there by the window, but the blinds were down. He kisses me once, and once again, and again and finally very, very long. I don't move, just let it happen and only say quietly while he's still kissing me, "You're coming today to say goodbye to me?" Then he lets go of me. "What kind of idea is that?" he asks with a forced smile. I take his two hands and say, "So be glad that I'm making it so easy for you. You might not have been able to hit it so well another time!" — "Yes, of course," he bursts out, "because you're glad about it yourself and want to get rid of me yourself." And now he starts to reproach me, how he has noticed for a long time that I don't really love him and that my caress is a comedy and I don't know what else. And it needn't have come to this, not at all, but a man notices such things and it's really no mystery if one is then pushed by the other party to the point of longing for true love and so on.

I kept calm. "You're quite right," I say, "but I don't believe that I'm the guilty one and probably you aren't either, but it just had to come to this in the end and that's because of the circumstances. I can only tell you that I have always been very fond of you and hope you will find a creature who is as fond of you as I have been, and who makes you happy"—and so on, what one says in such cases, but in that moment I felt that I really did like him very much and that such a parting always has something touching about it, even if one has been looking forward to it for a long time. Then we sat down on the divan and he finally takes off his overcoat and then we get to chatting away. And I tell him how I have been faithful to him for the whole two years, and how nice it really was, and he says he will be thankful to me for life for all the kindness and tenderness which I showed toward him, and it is really not true at all that one ever stops loving someone and that it is really only the circumstances, and he will remain my friend no matter what, and, just because he's a true friend, he is honest and has to say goodbye to me. And he pulls me toward him and strokes my hair and starts kissing me again, but not only on the forehead. I must confess I even cried a little bit, my dear Helene, you do understand, don't you?

And so finally it gets to be twelve o'clock just from saying goodbye and it was touching, how he kneeled beside the divan afterward and kissed my hand. That's my last memory of him for I fell asleep during the hand kissing and when I wake up in the middle of the night, the lamp is turned down and he's gone—up and away.

Well, I haven't seen him since then and haven't heard anything and the affair is over and done with. — What do you say to that?? And if you ask me what I'm doing or what I'm going to do, I don't know myself. For the time being I'm quite content. I rest, sleep famously, smoke my twenty cigarettes a day and think to myself, if only it would stay like this forever! It's all just a matter of habit. Of course, it's only eight days, but if it's up to me, I'll live like this the whole summer. Now I'm reading novels all day long, one recently which I truly recommend to you. There's something in it which I have believed for a long time, that is, that *we* are the really honest women. We're not less than the others at all, the novel says, we're more, because we're natural, and he proves it too in the novel. You must read it. Wait, I'll have Lina pack it up for you and send it to you.

Now I'm curious whether you will write me such a long letter! How are you spending your time, you two? Going often to the theater? Are you behaving nicely and not flirting a lot with the gentlemen of Paris?

What would we have thought, my good Helene, if someone

had told us what would happen to us? Good Lord, when I think of it, in the early days of this gay life, how earnestly I went to the theater because I was thinking how much I needed the fifty gulden a month. And how Anton came for me every night and we went to a restaurant and ate Swiss steak and hash-brown potatoes! My mother, who you ask about, is fine by the way, she also came to see me this past week and sends you her best. But now it's really enough, I think. Please kindly send me an equally long answer. Say hello to your fellow for me.

Have you made up your minds already about your summer plans? Be good and don't do anything rash. I have a sort of feeling that you're on the right track. That is, you might be able to become a proper wife. So save any good-looking Parisian men for later. Or even not at all.

You don't need to be conceited if he marries you, you'll read soon enough in the novel that actually you'll be much less then than you were before.

So, once again, love and kisses from

Your old friend,
Josefine

Alfred von Wilmers to Theodor Dieling in Naples

Dear Friend and Poet,

I thought so! Not without reason does one stay on into the summer in Naples. You express yourself so discreetly, to be sure, that I have no idea whether you're talking about a princess or an orange vendor or whether the moon shining through olive branches or the light of a blue crystal lamp is the "witness to your rapture," but that is really beside the point. And these love affairs abroad have such a special charm! The end comes along so easily—one morning you just depart after having, the night before, not taken leave. They certainly don't run after you, first it's too expensive, and secondly the traitor isn't worth it, and thirdly there are certainly plenty of other men nearby after all. As for me, my honorable poet, I can hardly give you any news. Unless it is that I am still lonelier than I was on the day of the races when I wrote you the last time. You know, I really did go to the amusement park in the Prater but—it was disgusting. Until steam baths and perfume have penetrated to the lower classes I shall hardly be able to make friends with them. That is probably mean of me but I can't help myself. I should like so much to see all people prosper, but I just ask you, if the lucky ones were continuously unhappy because there are unlucky people, where would the lucky people be then, for goodness sake?

Happy—that's just a manner of speaking. I belong to the kind who are considered thus. In reality those who can buy themselves four kreuzers worth of rum and get a kick out of life in doing so, are better off. You see, after the Prater I went up to Constantine Hill* after all. Ah yes! I thought at first the contrast must have an effect. I explained that to myself as best I could. You see, now you have just been among people who all have shabby trousers, greasy hats, coarse voices—who smoke little cigarettes, who have been sweating and straining all week and carry the musty odor of their low class dwellings in their hair—among women who've been toiling in the kitchen and with all kinds of "domestics"—among whores who will let themselves be loved tonight on the greens of the Prater—and now you are joining the well-groomed gentlemen in elegant summer suits—who speak softly, took their baths this morning, smoke Egyptian cigarettes or Pfosten for 2.50 each and drink twelve glasses of cognac without getting a shade redder in the face—the ladies with manicured, rosy nails who wear black silk stockings, some even with silk chemises (Fritz claims they do and Weidenthaler smiles to himself at Fritz's claim)—who are fragrant with Violette de Parme and are evil only in their souls! — How lovely, how discreet that is! Since I don't bother myself with their souls, they are simply enchanting. — So, as I said, I'm looking forward to it, and walk up, and there, in one of the tents, they're all sitting properly together, Fritz and his girl, Malkowsky and his girl, Weidenthaler alone—and in addition they've brought along Fellner, you know him, who imitates Girardi and sings limericks and is generally much more comical than his fellows realize. He owes each of them, according to rank and age, between five and two hundred gulden.

So there I am suddenly amongst them and soak up the contrast. I inhale the aroma given off by the rustling dresses of the ladies and by their hair, I touch with my foot the exquisitely shod little feet, everything, so to speak, out of scientific interest. I listen to Fellner singing limericks and laugh with the others and explain to myself, "He is really a dear fellow." Our arms linked together, I drink with Fritz's little one, while he keeps telling me, "Go on, give each other a little kiss—why not among friends?"—and I let her give me a little kiss and feel her little teeth on my lips, which is not exactly a matter of indifference any more, not even among friends—I drink four glasses of cognac, Prunier with six stars, and smoke a Pfosten costing 2.50—and the whole time, the whole time I have the confounded feeling that none of it is amusing at all! And it gets later, and the carriages are waiting down below, and Weidenthaler and Malkowsky with his girl get into one of them and Fellner gets up on the driver's seat in the meantime as if in jest while in truth he would otherwise have had to walk back to the city, and Fritz and his donna pull me into the second, she sits between us. So now, since it was so much fun and such a nice evening, we race back down to the pavilion, through the dark avenues, so dark that one cannot see his own lover, which Mitzi naturally takes advantage of, and then back again, and Fellner up in the driver's seat sings "The Heart of a True Viennese"—and Malkowsky's little one wants to switch, that is, Weidenthaler should get in the other carriage and I should go to them, and Fritz's little one won't let me go. In short, it was immensely jolly! And now out to the Prater. Where next? Back to the Sacher, we decide, to a separate room, to play the piano a bit and dance. All right, so off to the Sacher. Fellner jumps down from the driver's seat, plays the footman, opens the carriage doors, the women hop out, we find the little salon free, the one with the piano, champagne and cognac are brought, Weidenthaler sits down at the piano, plays a waltz, Fritz insists that I dance with Mitzi. "Dance cheek to cheek! Dance cheek to cheek!" and so we waltz, Malkowsky's noble lady feels ill, lies on the sofa, Weidenthaler unbuttons her bodice and her pink corset is admired by all. — Suddenly she says, "I feel better again, kids," and we waltz some more, and Fellner performs magnificent pirouettes, invents a solo dance over which we split our sides with laughter. He mimics Cereale, Rathner, and finally Girardi. Fritz lounges in a corner, opens his eyes only from time to time, Weidenthaler pounds away on the keys like a madman, a worried waiter appears in the door. — There is silence, we sit in an artistic grouping around the table, Malkowsky, colossally elegant, leaves and settles the bill behind the door. Champagne was drunk, cognac too, so now more champagne with cognac and the feast comes to an end. — And now we all go out. The two couples graciously wave farewell to us from the fiacres, and Weidenthaler, Fellner, and I are left standing there.

We want to go on to Scheidl's, but the chairs are already standing on the tables, the waiters are sweeping up and the lights have been partly turned off. So there's only an all night café left. Weidenthaler and Fellner are in no condition to go anywhere else, I shake hands with them. — Then follows a long, lonely walk around the whole Ring. Morning dawned, the air was marvelous, and I felt things have to change. Things can't go on like this any longer, this society, this tone, this hollowness, this imbecility, no, no, no! — The women and the men are equally repugnant to me. Perfume and silk stockings are not everything after all, even if they are all there is! — I walked along the edge of the Stadtpark, the first, gray light of day lay over it already. Then came the memories. Of what I call young love. I don't mean the platonic, when you promenade under the windows and they're married out from under you because you're only seventeen years old. No, the other, which is not sufficiently appreciated, the first serious love, for some little girl from the outskirts who works in a store by day, whom you wait for on a street corner in the evening and whom you then accompany to Mariahilf or Fünfhaus—and who doesn't want anything but a Sunday outing or an evening at the music hall or a seat in the third tier at the latest operetta or a one-gulden bracelet and very, very, very much love. No, how nice it was in those days! Bus trips from Hietzing into the city. Long walks in Weidlingau in the forest, deep in the forest. — Yes, that's what I need. It is incredible how my taste has been spoiled since I became so terribly elegant and have the ambition to possess the best-dressed woman in Vienna. Who knows how many exquisite creatures I have blindly passed up? And who knows whether I would still mean something to them, to them who need much, very, very much love and who, with the fine instinct of natural womanhood, wouldn't mind looking at the fatigue and overwrought state of my eyes and my brow. Oh, to be a fresh, young man once again, cheerful, in love, longing for the fragrance of honeysuckle, spring and tenderness. Oh, they can see that in you, the sweet girls who want springtime and love, and suddenly one of the sweet things is hanging on your arm and you've got a lover instead of a mistress. — This longing shows me that I'm younger than I thought I was and that makes me actually feel better than I have recently. Who knows whether you, with your Neapolitan love, may not be partly guilty for this insight? — It's getting late, my dear friend, I've been writing you for three hours. Now I'm going down to wander around the streets. Who knows? There's adventure in the air! The fragrance of evening wafts in through my open window and makes me ten years younger and dumber! And now—now, in Fünfhaus or in Alser a sixteen-year-old maiden is perhaps pinning a flower on her breast in front of a simple mirror with a wooden frame without suspecting that she is destined for me!

If only I knew whether in Alser or in Fünfhaus! Thus to be without any fixed destination! Farewell!

Yours faithfully,
Alfred

Josefine Weninger to Helene Beier in Paris

My dear Helene,

You ask me if there's any news. Well, since the last time I wrote you I have hardly been out the door at all. I went for a walk a couple of times and I was also in the theater, just yesterday in fact. Do you know where? Balcony, first row, where you're really more at ease, after all, than down below. And the comedy is such a great attraction and even though they've been running it for six weeks it was still sold out. Yes, even a really fine audience. Many friends, down in the first row some nice people, and I used the occasion to take a good look at myself, to see how things are with me. You know, I made them sort of pass by in review, the whole first row. And it was quite remarkable. Toward the end of Emil's time I liked this or that one quite a lot, once, in fact, as I can now tell you in confidence, one of your former ones, Karl Zabelberger, who really has a nice face even if there isn't much to him apart from that. And among others in the orchestra seats was Karl Zabelberger who, however, this time, left me cold in a way I cannot really describe to you. Next to him sat a friend of his whom I've also known though I don't know his name, very chic, more chic than Karl actually, then a soldier in the dragoons, not bad, then Baron Zenger, tall, boring, slept during the play, then two strangers, apparently Rumanians or Italians, dark with very white teeth and very elegant. Then another older gentleman whom I know by sight and whom I also liked quite well in other respects. But why should I tell you all this? I put the question to myself, "Who from among all these would now have a chance with you?" And the answer, to my own amazement, was none.

And I didn't have much more luck with the people in the loges.

I tell you I looked forward so much to my evening meal at home alone, which I had ordered for myself, with the *one* place setting and falling asleep quietly afterward.

Girardi was magnificent, I had the feeling moreover that he was looking up and greeting me. Otherwise I remained more or less unnoticed. So when it was over, I go down like everybody else and it's a beautiful warm evening. And then I couldn't help remembering again so clearly how I sort of crawled out the stage door in the back and how Anton called for me about—well, a few years ago. It's really incredible, all the things one thinks of on such evenings when one comes out into the fresh air after the theater. I can imagine so well having such an adventure as in the old days when I could actually have wept for joy. God knows I'm not too old for one. It can't be my fault. Something new just has to happen, that's all there is to it, a sort of youthful experience, then I'll be young again and ready to try my hand against all the little trollops of sixteen and seventeen. It has to be an interesting man. Emil brought one a couple of months ago, that is, a so-called interesting artist, but he was a bore! Looked exactly like the others, except that he talked less and said over and over that he had a headache. I don't mean such an artist either but I'm thinking of a real one without a headache, terribly lively, with very long hair and without money for all I care. In short, an artist as in the earlier novels, such a one would have had a chance last night, but ask the artists where they all were yesterday evening! And who knows whether one of them might have dared to speak to me, one of those I'm talking about, if he had seen me with all my finery and the blue stones in my ears. And I was powdered, too, and even had a bit of makeup on.

And now when I look at myself in the mirror, when I'm in my negligee, I must admit to myself that I'm really not exactly without what it takes, even without makeup and powder. —

Would've been a nice experiment, to go out once for a conquest, wouldn't it? I mean it. I don't give a hoot about being good. In truth I'm longing for some kind of magnificent change. Do you know that I've even thought of coming to Paris? But alone! — How would that look? And to take the first fellow that comes along? No! No! And really the very ones who are able to travel to Paris are just the ones I'm not the least bit interested in at the moment.

Have you read the novel Lina packed up for you? Write and tell me this and lots of other things.

Your faithful
Pepi

ALFRED VON WILMERS TO THEODOR DIELING IN NAPLES

Good morning, my dear friend,

Today I've got something to tell you! I'm young again! I've put an end to my problem, hurrah! — I won't be annoyed with you if you don't understand me. It was Sunday. That's at least a beginning. So it was Sunday, at two or three o'clock in the afternoon. Very warm and the sun lay over the city. And the people from the outskirts were all going past the city line, they all had an enormous desire to get out into the green, into the open, and they were happy. At the time at which our little story takes place (what do you say to my style?) there was no longer much going on in the streets. Among the pedestrians who were good naturedly wending their way toward the city limits there was one . . . no, I can't, I can't write a novella. I'll limit myself to the factual. To be brief, I had a great idea. I had an urge to disguise myself. I wanted once to be somebody else because I was bored with myself. So I dressed in a velvet jacket, took a flat collar, a loose, flowing tie, put on a soft hat, left my gloves at home, and set out for a walk. You have no idea, how disguised I felt. I looked like a house painter.

Of course, it wasn't only for the fun of the masquerade. I

had a specific purpose in mind. I wanted to have the assurance that I wouldn't have to thank the faith in my ability to pay and in my tailor for any conquest I might make. I changed my way of walking too. I sauntered, I put something naïve, carefree, devil-may-care into it. I was damn well not to be recognized. Just imagine, a completely crumpled soft hat and a loose tie! At three o'clock I come to the city line and I lean there against a lamp post for a couple of minutes, light myself a cigarette and take a look at the good citizens and the lovers who are walking by. I even let some young girls in pairs or in threes walk by, very pretty, very nice. Then two more come by, they wave up at a window where a fat old woman is happily looking down. And I see how at so many windows there are people looking down, men in their shirtsleeves and slovenly women. Here where I'm standing the sun is shining and a couple of children are playing on the embankment. Suddenly my mood becomes somewhat gloomy again. I hardly know why. This Sunday bourgeois life suddenly poured its whole repulsive dreariness over me. The two girls who walked past me long since I can imagine in their home, very busy in the kitchen and with the laundry and reading the local scandal sheet for amusement. And Herr Papa complaining about the taxes and everything else under the sun. This difference that they are all feeling, that today is Sunday and not six other days—in short, very repulsive!

Then suddenly I see something quite enchanting. A girl, no longer quite young, who is twenty-two or twenty-three. Wonderful and quite alone. Simple flowered dress, beautifully made, nice wide straw hat, wonderful eyes, slim, willowy figure, not tall, parasol open. As she walks past me she looks at me with wide eyes and smiles. Then she turns around, actually goes back past me without looking at me. Only about twenty steps and then she turns around again. — Aha! A rendezvous. I have time and wait too. The unbelievable happens—and this creature is waiting in vain! — I take a better look at her, really charming! So nice! Past the very earliest youth and, God be praised, also the very first innocence. Small tell-tale folds around the eyes and a trace around the mouth that comes only when one has kissed and bitten many times. The figure willowy and used to cuddling up. But something naïve in this conscious fulfillment of her womanly fate. So sweet! — And *he*, he didn't come! I watch her, walking back and forth, she hardly takes any notice of me, in which indeed there was an element of coquetry, and finally after about ten minutes she draws her mouth tight, half in annoyance, half in contempt, and sets out at a rapid pace, not back toward the city, but rather out toward the Währinger Hauptstrasse. Then I go after her and without losing a second, try my luck. I say a few meaningless words and she responds, turning toward me, almost sternly. "What do *you* want?" I don't let her scare me off and a conversation was soon in progress. She had the intention of "just" going out into the country because the good air was certainly more important than he and, as far as she was concerned, I could walk along beside her if it gave me pleasure.

It was remarkable how rapidly we settled into a pleasant chat. I must really compliment myself on how well I played my role. When she asked me, "What are you actually, anyway?" I answered, "Guess." "Well, what do you want to be, an artist?" she guesses. "What kind?" I ask. I was truly curious. "Poet," she says suddenly, with great certainty. I regard her with a look that tells her, you are not only a very pretty, but also a very clever girl. "Well, did I guess it?" she says smiling. And then she asks me further whether I have already been writing poetry for a long time, whether I write very beautiful poetry and whether I enjoy it and so on. — Oh what a merry string of lies I began now! It is unbelievable, all that I told her—it must, however, have been not only interesting but also credible. For she listened raptly. Well, yes, the struggles of my youth up to the point where, with great difficulty, I managed to break through, and my little mother, far away in a little town, and then the women and the great pains and the buried love—it was really touching and I am only sorry that I didn't keep track carefully of all I experienced. And all at once we were out in the open air. Really out in beautiful nature, and we walked through the woods and it became lonely and more quiet. We sat on a bench. Now and again people came by and through the shrubbery we could see a meadow, beyond it forest again and there, in the distance, in the shadow under opened parasols, the good Sunday picnickers were lying. Sometimes we heard loud cries and laughter carrying over to us. Then again it became quite still—a close, quiet afternoon.

Now she too began to tell about herself—the old story, but it suited her well. She is a seamstress, no longer has her parents, until recently lived with her aunt, but that was not permanent. She implied that some love story or other—certainly not her first—had played a role. But that too seemed to be ending. "Do you love him very much?" I asked. She looked at the ground. "Oh, yes," she said, "of course, it is also very much a question of habit," she added. And then, suddenly, "But surely you have a sweetheart too?" I didn't want to disavow a sweetheart, that would have decisively damaged my case—but in my case too the affair was in the process of dying slowly. I didn't want to say anything more—she didn't even ask many questions. In any case, we soon found that whatever led us together could not really be called simply a coincidence. The similarity of our fates, the special moment of our meeting, both so tired from a dying love at that very time, well, if that isn't destiny! — And so we chattered in the green forest and it was so close, so close! Finally, after chattering for a long time, came the silence. She moved so she was sitting quite close to me—and the pleasant aroma that floated from this sweet body of a girl was truly quite wonderful. It is so nice of these girls from the outskirts that they are always so soignée. The little dear had let someone give her a very good perfume for her name's day. But from her wavy hair there came a quite unique fragrance. I pulled her to me. "Sleepy?" I asked. She nodded and leaned her head on my breast and actually closed her eyes. Now I really had to kiss those charming closed eyes, she let it happen, then I kissed her cheeks, her mouth. She said, "But!" and kissed me too. People came by and we stood up.

Now it was completely clear that it was the mysterious hand of fate that had led us together, which, as fate so often does, wanted nothing but our happiness. In any case we said "du" to each other . . . How well we felt cannot be described. She claimed that her secret longing had always been for a poet. And mine? I was marvelous and claimed that she alone had been the object of my longing, just exactly she, just this little, sweet Pepi who, on Sunday, June the whatever it was, came strolling across the Währinger city line with a parasol and a straw hat. And how the time passed! It was already starting to get dark. So what now! Have supper together, naturally! But she wanted to be home before ten for sure. So now we went to an inn that lay right at the end of the path leading out of the woods. One of those petty bourgeois inns I normally always flee from. But how nice all that was today. We walked in through the garden where the tables stood under the large trees with the garden lamps fixed to them, and where tall lanterns stood at measured intervals. It was not very full, whole families sat at some tables, terribly tired and thirsty, at others amorous couples who held each other by the hand, here and there little bourgeois parties. And as I looked around more closely, there were also more stylish people, summer parties at their own regular tables. We sat at a smaller table somewhat to one side, I ordered a frugal supper (haha!)—we both had a famous appetite and were enormously happy.

By now it was quite dark and we sat in deep shadows. I was overcome by a sort of tenderness. I could even call it a sort of compassion, which is really always hiding in tenderness. She told me about her home. Imagine, a little room on the third floor looking out on the courtyards, a very simple room, of course, only one thing always had to be there, flowers. Earlier *he* had always sent the flowers, recently he became negligent about them. Then she bought violets or lilacs for herself and put them in a little vase, which stands on the windowsill of her room. — Finally we left, she took my arm. "How late is it?" she asked. It was half-past ten. Hackney cabs stood at the garden gate, we climbed in. She wanted absolutely only to be driven to the Währinger city line near which she lived, absolutely did not want to drive into the little street with the cab because of the neighbors and the concierge—and probably also because of Emil, I thought. She sort of lay in the cab as she sat holding her straw hat on her lap and her head with its fragrant hair lay on my shoulder. "It's all over with Emil," she said. "It's really been over for weeks. He doesn't want to know anything about me anymore. And it's better this way too. And if you want to see me again at all then don't talk any more about Emil. I won't ask you anything either." And now she was silent and we drove on and I stroked her cheeks. In a quarter of an hour we were at the line. Then we got out. I wanted to accompany her to the entrance to her house. "What are you thinking of?" she cried. "Every child knows me there!" And she gives me a kiss and leaves me standing and runs off.

In great good humor I walk home. First, though, I sit down in a café out there to have my cup of black coffee—I certainly couldn't go to the Kremser or the Imperial the way I was dressed. So there I sat and had a comfortable feeling, the way one does at the beginning of a new love affair, and looked forward to tomorrow's kisses and to everything else that tomorrow or, in the worst case, the day after, will bring. That tomorrow is today and since it is now high time for me to put on my disguise, dear friend and poet, I close this long letter and look forward to hearing from you soon again.

Alfred
youthful lover

Josefine Weninger to Helene Beier in Paris

My dear Helene,

I have let the blinds down, I'm sitting here in my negligee so that I can write you some big news in peace and quiet.

Did you get my letter? Well then, you too know what has been going through my mind lately and how I suddenly have no more taste for high living. No, I've been thinking to myself, the next one should be handsome but, for heaven's sake, just not a big spender. And I would like once again to have such a nice, little adventure as in the old days. So just imagine, little by little I get the idea to dress like the old Pepi and take out of my chest a calico dress I wore a couple of years ago once when I played the part of a parlormaid, put on a simple straw hat, in short, deck myself out sort of à la "girl from the outskirts." Lina exclaimed over and over again, "No! So pretty! Oh, how pretty!" — And I myself was quite satisfied when I looked at myself in the mirror. I'll have myself photographed in the whole costume and send you a picture. I'll be putting it on a couple of times again as you will soon hear. Yesterday, Sunday, I had it on for the first time. And my firm intention was, today I'll pick myself a fellow just because I like him. I go along Währingerstrasse—purely by chance, it could just as easily have been the Alserstrasse—and from under my parasol I take a good look at the people. Well, I must confess I almost lost interest in the whole scheme right at the beginning.

Finally I reach the city line, actually very ill-humored. There a young man is standing near a lamppost who is looking at me with a sort of naïve, admiring look. My first impression was, he's waiting for someone. My second, he is a handsome fellow. Artist, that was quite clear. Brown velvet jacket, loose flowing tie, absolutely not elegant, but a nice, well-groomed complexion, small mustache, very nice way of standing. — That's just what I would need! — Anyway I decide he's worth a try. So I act as if I am waiting for someone too, walk back and forth, finally go on. He comes after me and speaks to me. I have to admit that it was very pleasant. I was just a little, teeny bit gruff, then I let him walk beside me and the rest took care of itself. Naturally I was right in my guess, and he was greatly amazed when I told him to his face that he was a poet. He has a wonderfully agreeable way of talking, so gentle, so flattering, at the same time always with a certain respect. He has surely had much experience already and some girl must have made an awful fool of him recently—or I'm no longer a good judge of men. — Wealth? — I need have no fear of wealth with him, and suppers at the Sacher as well as sparkling gifts are out of the question. And he was very touched by what I told him. But you should have heard it yourself! A cock-and-bull story about a lover who doesn't like me any more, and about an old aunt with whom I have had a falling out and about a little room and what a nice, poor person I am and everything else under the sun. Just think, we went on foot way out to Pötzleinsdorf and sat in the woods for hours and I wasn't bored for a minute, and when he held me in his arms and kissed me on the bench, I had a cozy feeling that I haven't had for a long, long time. I don't know what all I might have been capable of doing if it hadn't been a bright and clear afternoon with people going by every minute. I really felt sort of touched. It occurred to me what such a poor writer has to put up with who, on top of everything else, spends half his income on his mother and is, of course, persecuted and treated with hostility by his competitors.

In the evening we were in a little restaurant garden and then he showed such tenderness! — And his eyes! — His glance alone made me years younger. And this modesty the whole time. I was so happy that he remained modest and quiet all evening, it was really nice. I don't think he could have been more considerate of his fiancée than he was of me. It was also lovely the way we rode home in the hackney. Believe it or not, it would have been terrible for me if he had made advances at that point. But not a word of it. He only asked me for a rendezvous for the next day, that was all. At the city line I jumped out of the cab. You see, for him I live somewhere there in a side street on the fourth floor. — I had to run for at least a quarter of an hour before I could find a fiacre! Once I got home I was in quite a strange mood. As if I had changed completely. And then, the special luck that he is not only a poor devil but also a poet! An artist! You see, for once I'll have something for myself out of a comic role. I have to stop writing, I go on again in an hour.

Many kisses from your faithful
Josefine

Alfred von Wilmers to Theodor Dieling in Naples

My dear Theodor,

How long since I last wrote to you? A day or a week? Or a month? Or for the length of half my youth? And why do I now take pen in hand? Why aren't I lying down on my divan as I so often am these days for whole hours reliving in my fantasy the beautiful moments whose memory I bring home with me? If someone had told me a week ago this would happen. . . ! Well, at least I've regained my sense of time. Today is Sunday again. Yes, yes, it's not more than a week since it began. So you see, my dear Theodor, I'm living in an amorous idyll, in the course of which one day is like another, which seems to have no end and for which it is barely possible to imagine a beginning. Yes, I'm living it, for I no longer feel that I am playing it. When I put on the wide, soft hat and the velvet jacket in the evening, I feel as if it could not possibly be any other way, and when I go out walking in the open air with the sweet creature and stroll around arm in arm with her far out on the outskirts of the city or in the woods, then I hardly know any more that it is only lies that I'm telling her about myself for the main point is true, that is, that I haven't felt so well for an unspeakably long time.

Yes, it's young love once again, the first love, if you like, which one can relive now and again if one is born under a lucky star or if fate wants to reward one for a good idea. — Do you know that I sometimes believe that I have been going through the world in a disguise for the last few years and have now laid the mask aside? I don't understand myself what kind of words pass through my lips when I am with her, and what kind of moods envelope me. The hours in the evening in the country! And once, the other day, in the morning when we awoke in a little inn somewhere in one of those places not far from Vienna where Viennese never go and a heavenly blue sky laughed in through the window! How we had the table moved into the little fruit garden and drank our coffee while the morning breeze rustled gently through the trees. — When we are separated and she goes back to her work just as I supposedly go back to mine—then I have a childish need to walk back and forth in front of her window just to be near her. And the funny thing about it is that I have only known since yesterday where her window is. The street she lives in I knew. But I should find out for myself the window behind which she works—that was one of the sweet ideas which tumble about in her childlike head—and I was sure to find it if I really loved her. And so I walked back and forth in front of the seventy-six third-floor windows which are in that street, and, you can laugh if you want, correctly sought out hers from among the seventy-six (I counted them). She was overjoyed when I told her. I recognized it from the flowers.

And now I have to confess to you that I even walked back and forth in that street and stood in front of the window in the moonlight like a dumb kid! That's what makes the affair so special and new for me, this intertwining of moods of chaste young love and mature voluptuousness. And just think, I am loved completely for myself. The violets that I bring her she kisses a thousand times. And our evenings in the little restaurant gardens in the suburbs! And how I tell her then of my earlier life as we sit together in front of our glass of wine and soda water. Surely you won't object when I confess that I make use of some of your biography, and quite especially of your student and love years in Munich, with those changes my weak memory makes necessary, and also take the liberty of adapting for my use your hiking trips through Thüringen and Switzerland and especially your adventure in Geneva with the English lady painter. Oh, how she hangs on my lips when I do this! How visible her emotion!

And then I let her tell me about herself again, and tears sometimes actually come into my eyes. How much sadness and sweetness we ignore for the sake of gaiety and the insipid. For, my being in love doesn't make me altogether blind, and I am convinced that there are a hundred more such creatures like my little Josefine. But sometimes I feel as if the little one was just beginning to understand what has been happening to her up to now and I feel how thankful she is for the way I treat her. And I am filled with a peculiar nostalgia when I think of her future for, you see, I know full well already that I shall leave her! And perhaps it won't even be especially sad. — But just that fact hurts me—isn't that strange?

Sometimes I wonder what would happen to her if I suddenly appeared before her in my true form. Whether the whole magic wouldn't be over? Whether it isn't precisely my mask that she loves? It would be painful for her if she were to discover how far apart we really stand in life, for she has grown fond of many experiences in my past. There are things that she likes to be told over and over. Thus I have told her three or four times a quite unbelievable story about a couple of desperate days when I was close to suicide because I was almost dead from hunger. For it is our poverty that brings us close. Now, I believe, she's earning enough and doesn't need to suffer any lack. But you have no idea how frantically the urge sometimes takes hold of me to create a rich and carefree life for this poor, sweet creature and how I would still not dare to give her even a hint of this. Certainly, everything would be over then. She lets me give her flowers. Next time I'll try once with a little thing, for example, a tiny little heart made of gold which she can hang around her neck. But now it's enough, for I can't tell you the real story after all. Young love, I find no other word! I no longer envy you your Naples and your Neapolitan girls.

This evening we want to go out in the country again. I really don't know which is more enchanting, the amorous hours in the woods or the trip home. Up to now we have come back from the country with the omnibus—naturally—because it's cheaper—and I shouldn't spend so much money, she said recently when I wanted to take a hackney cab again. I ask her little about her experience before me. It's enough for me to feel that I signify a sort of salvation for her. I wouldn't at all want her to have nothing to forget! Then she certainly wouldn't be the one I was really looking for. No, I didn't want a girl whom I seduce and who cries after me, no, I want to be for her one of her mature affairs, the best one though, one for which she need never reproach either herself or me. One day I'll disappear from her existence as I came. When I feel that the end is coming I'll go away on a trip and write her from here or there but without telling her that I was actually acting out a comedy. It will have been a beautiful dream for her.

But enough, enough. You'll be hearing from me soon again, perhaps not from Vienna. For we intend to withdraw to the country for a couple of days, to a completely secluded place—under trees, to dream sweetly, as the poet says to Countess Melanie.

Farewell for today and do write me soon again.

Yours,
Alfred

Josefine Weninger to Helene Beier in Paris

Dearest Helene,

Really, how I had to laugh at your letter! You know, if you're going to worry about me so much then I'll hardly dare to write you anything any more. — But I'll risk it.

I'm in love, yes, yes, awfully, in fact. He is such a sweet fellow. Have you ever had an affair with a poet? I mean with a real one, not with one whose plays or operattas are performed, but with one of those who are nothing and have nothing and probably never will amount to anything, with one of those genuine poets who makes poems and is crazy about you. Oh, that's a race apart! I won't even talk about love but the respect! When we go walking together in the evening then it's exactly like a bride with her fiancé. A couple of days ago we spent the night together out in the country, and we had such a good time there that we have decided to withdraw to a completely secluded place for a week or two. I hope that something will come of it, I'm just worried about one thing, that he will have to borrow the money for the trip somewhere. For it's downright funny how little money the man has. I can see how much good it does him when I hold him back from making big expenditures like, for example—now you're going to laugh—for a hackney cab! It would be a mistake, of course, if I were to offer him anything. Me the poor seamstress. Oh, you'd be astounded if you knew the story of my life. Yes, I have been in love before and have often lied—but never have I lied so much or been so much in love! Naturally I can't tell him such moving things as he can tell me—such things can't be invented!

I'm too lazy to write very much but when we're together again I must tell you the story of what happened to him in Berlin. I am so truly glad to be able to bring him a little happiness after the way people, especially the women, have played with him so shamefully. And he is thankful to me and tells me how he recognizes that I am quite a different girl. Quite a few girls could have had different lives . . . So, dear little Helene, don't worry, he is also much too conscientious to tie my fate to his "uncertainty." For he often speaks of his uncertain fate and becomes quite sad. And up to now I certainly haven't been in love forever, so your fears, dear Helene, are groundless. Of course, it would be nice but one can't spend one's entire life riding back from the country in an omnibus after all.

So farewell for today and say hello to Lixl for me. But don't tell him anything about my affair! On account of what might happen later.

Yours,
Josefine

Alfred von Wilmers to Theodor Dieling in Naples

My dear Theodor,

Take a good look at the postmark—you don't know yet where the letter's from. First of all there is no post office here. A messenger fetches the letter. We are barely two hours from Vienna and still so well hidden as if we were a hundred miles away. A cozy inn, set back from the highway, in the woods, really belonging to a mill. Secluded, country people come here sometimes, but usually we are quite alone, and at noon at most the innkeeper sits down at our table. We get up at God's daybreak, and then the whole magnificent fragrance of morning comes in from the forest, which starts right behind the house. Half or all the morning we are up in the woods, lying together on a gray, plaid blanket, looking up at the sky and breathing in the sweet peace. Yes, we love each other very much to tolerate such solitude. But it is really nice and I can't even complain about the food.

In the afternoons we are usually in our room for a long time and then she sleeps. Now, for example, is such a moment. And I have seated myself on the windowsill and let the fragrance of the forest waft down toward me, which is really the only entertainment you can have here. But the nice part is that you don't really feel the need for anything else. When she wakes up we will take another walk in the woods, of course, because there are no other walks here. A nice shaded path leads to the next village, which is quite poor with nothing but one-and-a-half story houses—without summer visitors. But that's just the nice part about it. Far and wide, not a human soul, nothing but peasants, country people, and so on. And after we have gone through the forest, then at dusk when it is very shadowy we come back on the highway to our inn. On the highway we encounter mail carts and haywagons and mostly miller's apprentices. Then we have our evening meal in the garden. — They say that excursioners from Vienna stray here by accident only on Sundays. Then we will flee, of course, since we came here only to be completely alone. That really has a wonderful charm! Especially on the first and second days it was indescribably charming. When you're in love you can take anything. The fact that our room is painted and not papered bothered me a little bit. It is unpleasant when you pass your hand over it. But it is rustic and also we are so seldom in the room—we have the forest after all. In a word, we are having a very happy time here, and my sweet darling is loving and beautiful. When I look at her now as she is lying there smiling in her slumber—it actually hurts when you think that there will come an end, a farewell.

She's stirring, I must close this letter. In a couple of minutes she will be awake and ask me what I have written today. For while she's sleeping I'm supposed to be writing poetry. You know, I actually tried it on the first day, to give her pleasure—but you know that is really hard. — And I chose myself a very popular theme at that—love. But it's no use. She is already quite offended that she has a poet for a lover and still doesn't —she's opening her eyes. Farewell!

Yours,
Alfred

Josefine Weninger to Helene Beier in Paris

Dearest Helene,

Only in haste because I'm never alone for a second. We are out in the country, quite isolated. We still like each other immensely and that's really why we came out to the country where we can be quite undisturbed and live our love. It's not even countryside. We live in an inn, deep in the forest, a hundred miles from everybody. The surroundings are beautiful. Excellent air, only a bit oppressive, I sleep for half days at a stretch. But for people who are in love, it's perfect. It's unbelievable how undisturbed we are. It is a real piece of luck that we love each other so much, otherwise we would be bound to go crazy with boredom. But he is truly a sweet fellow. And I feel it's good for him, after all his sufferings, to be able to recuperate in the forest solitude. I only feel sorry for him that he has no money at all. Because, as a matter of fact I fancy it would be wonderful to take a trip with him. That would be such a surprise if I were to suddenly turn up at your place in Dieppe with my poet! But it's impossible I'm afraid.

It's a genuine stroke of luck that I like him so much, otherwise I might have come to Dieppe in the summer after all. No, it's good this way. To be loved and to love, that is true happiness. — Then you're happy everywhere. Then you can get along in the desert, I'm firmly convinced of that. Only it shouldn't rain, I have to say that—because here it must be hopeless when it rains. Write me again in Vienna because we won't stay here for long—we're such poor devils.

Farewell, many kisses,
Yours,
Pepi

Alfred von Wilmers to Theodor Dieling in Naples

My dear Theodor,

Back in Vienna, for two days in fact. We were out in the country for a whole week and now, when I think back on it, I really must admit that it was very nice. Only on the last day it was somewhat unpleasant, just imagine—a downpour from morning till night—that's why it was probably also the last day. Otherwise, who knows? Just imagine standing by the window in the miserable room for hours, not being able to budge outdoors because you sink in the mud. Dreadful! Then we reached the decision to come home.

I tell you, I don't think we were actually so cheerful throughout the whole week as we were when we were packing up our things. Generally speaking it seems that too much loving precludes gaiety. There is certainly something to be said for sadness in love, and I was right after all to yearn once again for this kind. You can't really call it sadness. Well, what's the use of theory? It was lovely, that's a fact. It was? Hmm, no, it is, and will, what's more, I hope, continue to be for a long time, as you will immediately understand. You see, one thing became clear to me while we were out there, that the story with the soft collars and the omnibus and the attempts at poetry would be impossible to keep up for ever. — Even traveling third class is not exactly my weakness. So just listen. As we were coming back to Vienna in the evening I take the risk and buy first-class tickets. You should have seen the girl's face! When the train stops and I calmly lead her past all the cars to the first class, which was, of course, empty . . . "What do you think you're doing?" she cries. I, in somewhat the same tone as if I wanted to give her a feast: "Just come along, just come along." And now all of a sudden we're sitting in the comfortable velvet seats with the white lace coverlets and she just looks around. In that moment she was the genuine girl of the outskirts, who comes into the drawing room. "Well, what are you thinking of?" she exclaims. But instead of pouting as I actually expected for the first moments, she falls on my neck, kisses me and jumps about to and fro in the compartment like a little child, and when the train makes a sudden jerk, she sinks into my arms. It was one of the nicest hours we have spent together. Now I could be more courageous in Vienna at the station—I risk it and take a fiacre. She looked at me and said, "Well, have you gone mad?" — I thought I had to try to explain, we had, after all, saved a couple of days in the country by leaving early. — At the corner of her street she bade me a tender farewell; naturally the fiacre couldn't drive up to her house.

That was yesterday. And today the following is going to happen. In one hour I shall take my stand before her—that is to say, this time in my true form. I'll risk it because she loves me. We have our rendezvous out near the city line as usual.

But today I'm not coming on foot with a loose, flowing tie and with an adoring look about me, no, I'll come riding up in the fiacre and an unspeakably elegant summer suit, an eight-gulden scarf, and an English straw hat and will invite Fräulein Pepi with a friendly nod of the head to take a seat at my side and confess to her that I have played a shameful trick on her and that I am a man of means who, unfortunately, cannot write poetry at all. It will be a hard blow for her, but her conduct in the first-class compartment lets me hope that I will succeed in consoling her. Everything's in readiness—you know, I'm actually happy that tonight I'll be able to walk on the street like a reasonable man again.

But now she is putting down her work and getting ready to go out for a walk. Poor child! It actually does me good that I can now hope to be placed in a position where I can improve her situation a little. And for a whole period of time, fourteen days in fact, I have been loved for my own sake. What have I got to lose? It's getting late, Theodor, tomorrow I'll write you again.

Yours,
Alfred

Josefine Weninger to Helene Beier in Paris

My dear Helene,

First of all let me ask you very nicely for one favor: don't look at the last page of this letter before you have read the first one, otherwise the whole fun will be spoiled. But wait, first I have to think what I wrote to you the last time. Oh yes, about the countryside. Well, just think, after we are out in the country for a week, it starts to rain hard. Just imagine our despair. But, thank goodness—there are carriages and trains and on the same evening we decide to go back to Vienna. Now, imagine though—when we get to the station, my poor poet buys first-class tickets. I naturally assume he means it as a treat so that we are sure to be alone and behaved accordingly in the compartment. When we get off he signals for a fiacre. Well, I was dumbfounded. But I must say it was amazing how good I felt to enjoy these better circumstances again. So when I get out near the city line and have to take another carriage as usual in order to drive home and when I am finally at home again in my dear, nice, papered, cheerful room with the canopied four-poster, an idea occurs to me. This can't go on like this, I thought to myself. The comedy has to come to an end, that's certain—but why necessarily the true part of the comedy? And the truth was, of course, that I was actually still very much in love with my poet, which I noticed especially when, after one week, I was suddenly so totally and completely alone in my own room. — So then I decided I must take my mask off some time or other, sooner rather than later. And the idea kept bothering me that I would indeed have to have him once at my place, right in my own cheerful room, in order to show him properly how much I love him. Well, finally before I even went to sleep I was firmly determined to explain everything to him the next day.

So what does your Pepi do on the next day, or rather evening? She doesn't put on the chambermaid's dress again but an elegant street dress (the dark green one you know), puts on a chic hat (one you don't know, I bought it for myself in June), takes the parasol with the tortoise-shell handle from Baron Lenghausen, gets into a fiacre and drives to the city line—out to where I had the rendezvous with him. It was half past seven, almost dark already, and I stop the carriage but stay seated inside. You know, my heart pounded, I have to admit it, because it could also have gone sour. I imagined he might come around the corner there in his velvet jacket and, when he recognized me, look at me angrily and despise me—or at least make a row. . . . So I'm sitting there and waiting. He doesn't come. It's already almost completely dark. I don't understand, I start to think perhaps he has already seen me and immediately run away. For it never happened that he kept me waiting. Then I notice that some twenty paces away from me another carriage is standing—it must have been there some time already because I didn't notice one coming up in the last few minutes. And a man steps out of the carriage. An elegant gentleman, a very elegant gentleman. He walks up and down the sidewalk, at first I can't properly make out his face, but when he comes by right in front of my carriage—I just can't believe my eyes, it's him! — Him, my poet, the elegant gentleman! And he got out of the fiacre over there. Well, at first I'm speechless and I let him go by. But then he turns around immediately as if he had only forgotten to look into the carriage I'm sitting in and makes big eyes—and only says— "Well, Pepi!" And I, "Alfred! Alfred!" And then we both start laughing out loud, but laugh so hard that people stopped and looked. — And then he says, "Well, is it really possible? Pepi! Pepi!"

You know, Helene, we were both glad. I can't begin to describe it. Then he makes me get out, sends my carriage away, and we get into his without actually saying another sensible word. When we are sitting in the fiacre—meanwhile it's gotten quite dark—he says, "Haha! That's pure operetta! Haha! That's pure operetta!" And he repeats it ten times. The driver looks in at us with a questioning face. — "But, of course," exclaims my false poet, "where are we going then?" And without waiting to hear what I say, "To the Prater!" — And now, on the way, we start telling each other everything. Just imagine, he played the same comedy with me as I did with him. We paid each other the nicest mutual compliments. To be sure, I always was just a little suspicious of him. It was lovely in the Prater. We went as far as the Pavilion. Then we went through the whole story again, starting with that Sunday when we first met, just for the fun of it. And then, at nine, we drove up to the Constantine Hill.

By then there were few people left in Vienna, most of those who were sitting up there were from elsewhere. We had an expensive supper served in a tent such as we hadn't had for a long time. And we became very gay. When we had the champagne, he promised me that we would go to Dieppe together. — That's the important news for you—since I'm hoping that you're sure to be going there too with your man. Then we will certainly also go to Paris. — Above all, I believe he's a good acquisition and if you stop and think now how I truly love him too, then I have really gotten my money's worth out of my little comedy. Oh, when I think back, just the day before yesterday I still thought he was a poet!

I'll close my letter with the supper on the Constantine Hill, because when we drove home I nearly fell asleep on his breast after all the champagne.

So farewell, my dear Helene, don't expect a letter from me, I'll let you know by telegram when I leave.

With many kisses,

Yours,
Josefine

Alfred von Wilmers to Theodor Dieling in Naples

My dear Friend,

The bags are packed—I'm leaving. Not alone. Send your letters to Dieppe, I just want to tell you that in haste. From there you will learn what has happened to me the last five days. Today I have no time for that. The adventure with the little seamstress is all over. On that evening when I cast my mask aside it came to an end. We laughed a lot at the time, because she played the same comedy on me as I played on her. Oh, Theodor, she has done just as little sewing as I have poetry. She's accustomed to gowns worth five hundred to a thousand gulden and hats costing eighty. She had diamonds and pearls. She has a very active past behind her. I'm going to Dieppe with her and will pay her bills. She will be kept by me, and the day after tomorrow she'll cheat on me. Don't think I'm an optimist because I say "the day after tomorrow," there's really no opportunity on the train.

The little comedy is finished, as you see, but from the tragedy that could develop I'll know how to flee in timely fashion. At the end of the first act (scene—Dieppe) I'll smilingly disappear behind the scenes.

Yours,
Alfred

—*Translated by George Edward Reynolds*

Riches

· I ·

Early one morning Weldein dimly heard his wife's voice through his sleep. She was standing next to his bed, dressed and ready to leave, and said, "Good morning, Carl, I must be off to work." She did sewing, but not at home. Weldein pulled the covers up to his chin, vaguely remembering that he had fallen into bed with his clothes on. "Good morning," he replied. She glanced at him with compassion, resignation.

"Our little son is at school already . . . what will you be doing?"

"I've no work today. Let me sleep."

She left. None of this was anything new for her. At the door she turned around. "Don't forget the rent is due today. I've left the money in the drawer, already counted out." And she looked at her husband again, seeming to have second thoughts. Then she went over to the linen closet, opened a drawer and took out some money. "I think I'd better pay it myself."

"Fine, pay it yourself then," he said with a laugh.

Glancing at him sadly, she left. And Carl Weldein lay there, alone, barely awake, with his eyes open. The room looked shabby, but well kept. The early morning rays of the spring sun shone in through the two sparkling windows. On the wall the clock ticked monotonously.

Suddenly Weldein sprang out of bed. There he stood in white tie and tails, his shirt rumpled, shoes dusty, his short hair tousled, his eyes red-rimmed. He went over to the simple mirror hanging above the dresser, looked at himself and smiled. "Good morning, Mr. Weldein," he said, "good morning." Then he skipped about the room, whistling a song. Then he sat down on the edge of the bed, crossed his legs and began to think hard. Only gradually did it all come back to him. It wasn't a dream, that much was certain, for how else could he have ended up in bed in these clothes? So it had to be real and true.

And he saw himself sitting in the tavern again where his adventure had begun. He saw himself sitting with those shabbily dressed people and playing cards, as he had done so often. He could even smell the smoking lamp that stood on the table as usual, and before his eyes appeared the plump shape of the innkeeper slouching at the door, when those strangers walked in. It had happened last night! Was that possible?

He had lost his money, all of it! And the strangers, watching the game with amusement and curiosity, had given him some money so that he could continue to play, and—it was then that he began to have luck, mysterious, incredible good luck.

Weldein got up from the edge of the bed and began to pace back and forth in the room. His eyes glowed as he relived his experiences in his mind. He saw himself leaving the dismal tavern with the two strangers when he had no further business there; the other players had departed in ill humor after he had won all their money.

And he recalled how he then stood in the narrow street on the outskirts of the city and looked more closely at the two strangers who had appeared like good spirits in a fairy tale! They made him tell them who it was they had helped. Who, indeed! A poor house painter who had hoped to become an artist and for whom everything he had ever undertaken had gone wrong . . . really everything! Now he had a wife and child to take care of and managed to make ends meet, with difficulty, but honestly. Once in a while, however, a kind of evil spirit took hold of him; those were the weeks when he was driven, really driven! to drinking and playing cards, whether he willed it or not. And even when he played cards, his usual bad luck plagued him! Today too, as always!

But who were the strangers? He had asked them, and they had simply given their names: the one Count Spaun, the other Baron von Reutern. There was nothing strange about that, for he realized at first glance that they were young aristocrats.

And then, as they walked through the quiet streets that evening, the die was cast for Weldein! The two men at his side were merry and bold, full of imaginative ideas. Would such a peculiar plan have otherwise crossed their minds? Would they otherwise have thought up the prank they staged with him?

And now the strange scenes of last night went through his mind, one after the other. He found himself in the barber shop where his shaggy hair and beard were neatly trimmed; he saw himself in the count's dressing room where he was fitted with the elegant attire still clothing his body. And then—then he saw himself sitting at the green table right in the midst of all those wealthy and distinguished gentlemen, in the magnificent great gambling hall of the aristocratic casino with its many glittering mirrors. He remembered how, as agreed, he had played the role of a taciturn American whose travels happened to bring him to this city, so he could look up some old friends he had met . . . where was it again? . . . in Moscow . . . or in Paris. The two gentlemen who had led him to this table had probably not imagined how their prank would turn out. With burning clarity Weldein could recall every detail; he seemed to feel the smooth cards in his hands again; his glance again fell on the pieces of gold, the bank notes piling up in front of him; he remembered how a bottle of champagne stood in its cooler on a chair next to him and how he downed glass after glass of the intoxicating drink. He also recalled exactly the peculiar expressions on the faces of the other players: how they first were amazed at his never-ending luck and then how the amazement turned into consternation, as he won with every card . . . and finally got up, with shining eyes, but speechless and dumbfounded by his adventure—a rich man!

And then, without saying a word, the count had led him down the wide carpeted stairs. They stood below in the open entryway. The street before them was deserted. The street lamps burned brightly, and a marvelous gentle breeze wafted through the night. "Go, Mr. Weldein . . . go home now," the count said. And Weldein stood in the street, alone—with a fortune in his pocket. He turned around to see his well-born friend just disappearing on the stairs without looking back. The flames in the street lamps flickered, and Weldein staggered away.

And when he now tried to recall what had happened after that, his memory failed him. He hardly knew how he had found his way home. No matter. But he had experienced all of this, truly experienced it, and he was a rich man, there was no doubt of that . . . And as he paced back and forth around the room, he murmured to himself:

"What do I do now? Last night shall remain my secret . . . for that night is only the beginning of a new life. . . . In a few days I'll disappear from town, yes, that's it, I'll disappear from town. . . . My wife needn't worry, I'll write her where she should follow me to. To the South—to Monte Carlo . . . where I'm not the house painter Weldein, where no one knows me!" He became engrossed in thought.

"Good, very good. . . ." He pulled off his formal suit and put it in a bundle along with all the other accessories of yesterday's elegant role. Soon he stood in his working clothes before the mirror. He laughed again. "Good morning, Mr. Weldein," he cried out, almost rejoicing. He went over to the window and looked down at the street. It was a sunny spring day! He opened the window wide. Gently the morning breeze touched his forehead. He took a deep breath and, with the glance of a conquering hero, looked toward the heavens. In the building across the street everything was as usual; at some of the windows the curtains were still drawn; at others he saw women in housecoats cleaning and dusting, then disappearing back into the rooms. Down below the shoemaker was hammering at the open door of his shop. All of them were busy, were at work.

Carl Weldein stepped back from the window, lit a cigar and stretched out on his bed. He was rich, he was happy. He lay there for perhaps an hour. When he woke up, he found the burned out cigar next to the bed on the floor. His head pounded dully when he got up . . . Something important had occurred to him. Where was his money? He had done something with it. But what? Yes, of course . . . as he staggered away from the casino through the dark streets, the thought had suddenly struck him that he could not take the money home with him . . . it was too much! Then he had come upon the crazy idea of hiding his riches. . . .

At night it had seemed so logical—in those moments when his head felt flushed and giddy from the bubbly wine—that he had better hide the money from his wife, from the neighbors, from everyone! . . . As he tottered through the streets last night, he had been seized by a curious sense of fear, bordering on guilt. That feeling seemed almost stranger to him now than his whole adventure.

But what did it matter? In the end his wife would undoubtedly have found the money too soon . . . and then . . . it would have stayed in the drawer and gotten moldy. . . . Well, he couldn't change things any more . . . he had hidden his riches . . . and all he had to do was go get it. Not right away, of course . . . not before nightfall. At night he would go there . . . go there . . . go there. . . . He put his hand to his forehead. . . . Go where? . . . Well, sure . . . starting from the casino through that long street . . . and then . . . well, then where. . . oh yes, to the left . . . and then. . . . Well, where? Where had he gone? To the left . . . left . . . left. . . . And Weldein racked his brains. He ran his fingers through his hair. He stamped on the floor. He mumbled. . . . Where. . . ? He screamed. . . . Where? With head hanging, he paced around the room in circles. He began to recite in a singsong: Where . . . where . . . where?

He found himself once more before the open window. Coaches rattled past. He slammed the window shut. The rattling of coaches. He had heard that sound last night, shortly before. . . . "Just calm down," he told himself. "So the coaches rattled down the street . . . fine . . . and then I went to the left." With his forehead to the window, he stood motionless and brooded. He remembered exactly the long dark street . . . then there was an intersection—he had gone on to the left—and from there . . . where? . . .

He stood there for many horrible minutes, white as a sheet, with sweat on his brow. It was enough to drive him out of his mind! He grabbed his hat from the table, put in on and dashed out the door, down the stairs and away, away—to that place!

• II •

There it was, the long, long street, lying before him in the bright morning sunshine, and he rushed on down it past the buildings. There was the intersection, at last—and then . . . then he had gone to the left, down another splendid, but much longer street! He knew the street, of course, but he could not remember having been there last night. Well, naturally, it had been very dark. And now an important detail came back to him . . . he had bent down. He knew it quite clearly . . . but when had he bent down? How far had he gone on? For a few minutes? For an hour? Calm down, calm down, he told himself again and stopped. He stood there and let the life of the city flow past him. Young and old, they walked by, dressed as if for summer, and all of them were enjoying the beautiful new day. No one paid any attention to him. He tried to whistle, anything that would come to his lips. He could not do it, his throat was too tight and dry. "Why are you so upset?" he said to himself, "you went to the left—for quite some time . . . and then bent down. So it's down below, somewhere down below I'll find it . . . that's a lot already . . . to know so much . . . for yesterday at this time you were still penniless. . . . But . . . why does anyone bend down? To bury something. . . . So I buried it . . . oh . . . now I know more . . . the wind was murmuring through the trees. . . . So I buried it in a garden. . . . No . . . it wasn't a garden . . . there was an echo . . . it was a fountain . . . sure, a fountain, that's why there was a murmuring sound . . . and I climbed down, and that's why there was an echo." He walked up and down the same street, repeating close to a hundred times, "A murmuring sound . . . and an echo. . . ." After a while he stopped. "And if it was a fountain . . . where . . . where? But no, that's ridiculous, it wasn't a fountain . . . most certainly not! And it's good it wasn't a fountain because then I surely couldn't find the right one, that's good. . . ." He laughed. His teeth chattered; he thought he was losing his mind. Then he started all over: "A murmuring sound and an echo. . . ." He was standing in front of a bar. He went in and ordered a brandy. Through the windows he looked out at the street where the people were passing by, not caring, in good spirits. He drank and drank. . . . "It just has to occur to me now . . . a man sees more clearly when he's drunk. . . . Sure . . . last night I found the way in the dark . . . only because I was drunk . . . Now I'll find it again." When he went out his steps were unsteady, but his heart felt lighter. "Now I'm happy," he mumbled. "Lala, tralala . . . happy. . . . And why am I happy? Because I feel my memory returning. To the left . . . sure, to the left! I was here . . . and I went . . . somewhere, where there was a murmuring sound and an echo. . . . Just be happy. . . . Don't worry, Weldein, you'll find it!"

He had come to the end of the street and was standing at the entrance to a large park; a slight breeze rustled through the leaves.

"You see, Weldein . . . there's your murmuring sound. . . ."

He staggered on . . . along a broad gravel path with tall trees in full leaf at both sides. Nannies and young mothers sat on the green benches; elderly gentlemen, students strolled by; children played with hoops and pebbles. Weldein turned into a side path; he came upon an open meadow shimmering in the hot sun. The grass was not fenced in; at dusk children usually played here; right now a few boys were lying there asleep. Weldein lurched on across this meadow. The bushes swayed gently; the leaves rustled almost imperceptibly. "There's a murmuring sound, murmuring . . ," Weldein babbled with heavy tongue. Then he sank down on the hot grass and fell into a leaden sleep. After only a brief time he sat up and stared into space. His head was clearer now, and he tried again to collect his thoughts. "It's probably past noon already, and yesterday I was still penniless. The main thing . . . sure, of course, the main thing is that I calm down enough to remember it all. Nonsense! I'll have to remember eventually. . . . But it's too hot now . . . it's impossible to think with the hot midday sun pounding down on your head. So calm down . . . and wait until it's cooler." He got up and strolled at a leisurely pace along the broad paths of the park. Sometimes he felt like throwing himself down and digging his fingers into the sand. He ground his teeth and bit at his lips. A few times he sat down on a bench, but he just couldn't stay put for long. He felt like screaming and cursing. Suddenly he dashed away —away from this park where the trees rustled incessantly. He couldn't understand what he'd been doing there so long. He wandered through the streets and alleyways, sometimes slowly, sometimes hurriedly; it never occurred to him that he'd not yet eaten a single bite. . . . With tears of rage in his eyes, he rushed back and forth through the city, and at nightfall, totally exhausted, he stood again in that long street in front of the bar. And again he went in, sat down at a small table and ordered a glass of the strongest brandy. But when it was in front of him and he wanted to take it to his lips, he could not do so; tears rolled down his cheeks, and with his face in his hands he sobbed and wept like a man who had lost his beloved! At first people looked at him—the pretty girl standing at the bar, and the people who had come to renew their strength or get drunk again—but no one really cared, and they simply let the poor man weep in peace.

After a long time Weldein wiped the tears from his face and drank his brandy. He ordered another one, and then another, drinking for about an hour. Outside the street lamps were burning; darkness had come. A light warm rain was falling. The rattling of coaches died down; fewer people streamed by. And Weldein went out again, taking his hat off so the rain would fall on his hair. The night air cooled his forehead. Slowly he walked on . . . not since morning had he felt so calm. "Now to work," he said to himself. "Now you'll find it." And for the hundredth time he repeated, "to the left—there was a murmuring sound and an echo. . . ." He shook his head. "That's not everything . . . that's not enough." He stared blankly . . . and suddenly a ray of hope appeared on his face . . . "I started out at the casino. I'll wait a bit and then do everything just like last night. Sure, sure, that will work, just calm down now . . . calm down." And again he paced back and forth, took out his short pipe, filled it and lit it. "The time will pass somehow. . . ." And Weldein again roamed the city. "I should probably look in at home. No, I'd better not. . . . Hm . . . but something to eat. . . . In the tavern where I met those gentlemen yesterday? No, no, later when I get hungry. . . ."

The minutes and quarter hours crept by . . . time stretched out endlessly before him. Occasionally Weldein rested on a bench for a while, but then got up again; midnight just would not arrive. The streets were empty. The rain began to fall more heavily. Then the city came alive again, coaches drove past in greater numbers, there were more people in the streets, the theaters had let out. So it was past ten. . . . Two more hours. And what should he do until twelve. . . ? Irresistibly he was drawn back to that long street. Something to eat? No, he couldn't. But to drink! That would calm him down a bit. Back to the bar! But no, not to that one, where people knew him. Rather to some tavern where he could get a bite to eat. Drinking tastes better that way. So . . . here. And he went into a small tavern, ordered some food and drank wine with it. He ate slowly, pausing between bites. There was a clock above the door . . . it seemed to have stopped. No, no, the hands were just moving so slowly. Outside he heard the clock strike in the tower. He counted . . . nine . . . ten . . . eleven. Oh . . . eleven o'clock! and there it says quarter to . . . That innkeeper! Naturally. So that people will stay longer and eat and drink more. He asked for a newspaper and read it from front to back, with his eyes burning, firmly intending to think only of what he was reading; but he could not comprehend a single word. He paid his bill and left. The clock said quarter past eleven, so it was eleven thirty. Alone, not a soul in the streets. Slowly he walked back to the casino. There it was, lying before him, its doors wide open, its windows bright with light, a glittering jewel set amidst poorly lit streets with their dim, flickering lanterns. His heart pounded when he looked at the building from across the street. It impressed him as something gigantic, a mighty fortress of stone. It stared back at him as he stared at it. The shining windows were a hundred glowing eyes that devoured him. And he recalled that moment again. . . . The great moment when he broke the bank and was an equal to all those distinguished gentlemen sitting with him at the same table. . . . It was up there, sure. . . . Those were the windows. And away now . . . to win the money once more, once more!

He walked with measured step, went around the corner, the long, long street . . . farther, still farther . . . to the left . . . he tried to make his mind blank . . . so . . . good. It must have been here . . . and now another street, good . . . it was here . . . here something was drawing him onward, so . . . and now . . . sure . . . there . . . there was a murmuring sound, there is a murmuring sound . . . really . . . what is it? . . . oh, the river . . . was it perhaps here? . . . certainly . . . no . . . yes! There he stood. Before him, foaming slightly, sparkling in the light of the lanterns on its banks, lay the river that flowed through the city. And across on the other side rows of houses . . . and above them the cloudy night sky from which the warm rain fell incessantly. The sound of the rain drops blended strangely with the sluggish lapping of the waves. So it was here? . . . and he went along the river bank, to the left . . . then he turned around . . . to the right . . . and then he stopped next to a mighty stone lion, a statue at the end of a bridge. He stepped onto the bridge, over which a heavy coach was just rolling.

The sound died out. Silence everywhere, just the rain and the river below. Leaning over the balustrade, he gazed down, helpless, trembling. . . . "What led me here? Wasn't I drawn here? And now?" He continued to stare down . . . he became dizzy. Suddenly he was seized by a horrifying thought. "Perhaps . . . I threw it into the water!" And he began to whine like a child. "Into the water . . . because I was drunk . . . I got drunk! And whatever for? Up there! And why did I want to hide it? From my wife? From my child? Would they have stolen it from me? Was I really out of my mind? What have I done? . . . What have I done? . . . I know, after all, that drinking muddles my thoughts. . . . In there, down there the money! Jump in after it, Weldein, you idiot, you drunkard, you wretch!"

And he held onto the balustrade as he ranted and raved. "Hide it! I had to hide it. . . . In the river. . . . On the bottom? . . . No! I just can't have thrown it in! Even the worst fool is not that foolish! But where is it? . . . Where? Where? Where? . . ."

The rain let up. In the sky there were dark blue streaks, and a few stars could be seen. The dark city lay deep in sleep; now and then there was a muffled sound from the distance; once the fading noise of carousers singing as they went home, then all was quiet again; and down beneath him, rushing away from him toward the veiled mountains, the regular murmuring of the waves. For a long, long time he leaned there against the balustrade, his eyes had dried and he had calmed down again. And the sound of life once more. . . . It was coming from the other end of the bridge . . . carts drawn by sturdy horses; first one, then two or three at a time, the farmers were coming from the country to market. A nearby clock chimed in its tower . . . one . . . two . . . And once more deep, deep peace. Weldein left the bridge, and gradually the murmuring sound grew faint behind him. When he could no longer hear it at all, he wanted to return. But he shook his head and went on his way . . . his mind blank. He looked down at the cobblestones beneath his feet . . . he began to count his steps. He continued to count, reaching one hundred—three hundred—six hundred. Then he gave up. Again he was overwhelmed; he just had to think of it again. . . . "And can I possibly go on living this way?" he wondered. "And where do I stand? Am I rich? Am I poor? Will I find it? Won't I have to find it eventually? Of course, I have to. . . . The time will come when I'll know again. When I'm in bed . . . or tomorrow . . . in a few days . . . when I've calmed down. . . ."

And onward . . . toward the outskirts of the city where he lived. A gray streak of light in the east. Soon everyone will wake up to a new day, to new work. "And I?" thought Weldein. "Must I go to work again—? I, the millionaire? Climb on a ladder again and paint walls? When only this morning the whole world belonged to me? . . ." In front of him was the house where he lived. Fear took hold of him when he came upon it so suddenly . . . up above his window was open, the drawn curtains swayed gently. And Weldein leaned for a while against the wall of the entryway, then he took out his key and unlocked the door. It made a horrible sound when it clicked shut. Behind him lay all hope, all happiness! Slowly he climbed the stairs . . . back to his old miserable existence.

· III ·

And the years went past. Carl Weldein painted ceilings and walls, sometimes got drunk and played cards no more. He, a rich man, should play for pennies! Once in a while, when the brandy had gone to his head, in a flash of inspiration he thought he'd found it. Then suddenly everything was dark again. Sometimes he was amazed that he had not given in to despair. But after he had managed to get through the first few days, his lot became bearable. At first he retraced his steps every night . . . each time more and more calmly, occasionally thinking only how nice a walk it was. On other evenings, however, and for entire days and nights he felt he was close to losing his mind. Then . . . brandy! A few moments of hope, the illusion of happiness. At times, when he stood on the ladder with the wide paintbrush in his hand throwing the paint on the ceiling, he wished he would fall so that his dreary life would at last be over! What kind of a life was it anyway! A sickly wife at home, who earned only a pittance with her sewing and was ruining her health, growing paler and thinner by the day. His son in patched clothes who stormed home after school and was always hungry. And then the meager meal in the shabby room with barely a word spoken. His friends in the tavern, all of whom thought only of themselves. And outside in the world all that happiness and the wonderful things he had to pass by—he, a rich man! And he had to keep his sorrows to himself. If he had announced to the world: "I'm very rich . . . incredibly rich. . . . I just don't know where my money is!"—how people would have laughed! Laughed? They'd have had him put away as insane!

One day he read in the newspaper of Baron von Reutern's death. Somehow that was a consolation for him. Yes, death comes eventually to us all. It seemed as if he had forgotten that pleasant solution. Now there was only one more person alive who knew the story of that night, Count Spaun. Weldein hated him. Once a shocking idea occurred to him—what would happen if Count Spaun, suddenly a pauper, remembered him and came to him with the words: My dear Weldein, I made you rich, now give me part of your wealth. . . . He became obsessed with the idea. He trembled at the very thought of Count Spaun. And what if on some merry occasion the count told his friends the story! And they would come to him—all of them—merry, full of scorn! Hey, painter friend, don't be so stingy! No decent human being lets his wife and children go hungry when he has money stashed away! And he, what could he say? I don't have it stashed away, I have it—I don't know where? Who would believe such nonsense! Then he wondered if it might not be best to seek out the count and tell him about his misfortune! His misfortune! It was more than that! The most awful bad luck that ever happened to anyone.

But what did the world or the times care about him! He stood on his ladder and slapped on paint. The hair at his temples turned gray; he became fat and began to suffer from shortness of breath and a cough. Drinkers age prematurely.

When his son was twelve years old, his mother died. She had not taken to bed for long; she lay down only when she knew the end was near. She was gentle and kind during her last days; she kissed the hand of her husband who sat next to her bed; she stroked her son's hair.

"You know, Carl," she said on her last day, "let the boy choose to work at something he'll enjoy . . . he'll be luckier than you and I." Both of them quietly wept at her bedside, the boy kneeling and the husband sitting on a wobbly chair that sometimes creaked. And evening came, a spring evening just as mild and as fragrant as that fateful May evening six years before. Weldein thought about it. He saw himself standing on that bridge again and heard the waves murmuring, the rain falling. He had been awake for two nights in a row . . . now he fell asleep. It was pitch dark when he woke up; the boy had shaken him gently, but anxiously. "What is it?" Weldein asked . . . No breathing from the pillow. "Light a lamp," he said in a subdued voice, jumping up and leaning down over the sick woman. He called out to her, "Dear . . . dear . . . do you hear me?" The boy came with the lamp. He was afraid to move any closer. His father took the lamp from his hand and held it up at the head of the bed. For perhaps a minute he gazed at the pale face lying on the white pillow. Behind him his son wept. Weldein put the lamp down on the night table, turned around and said softly, "It's right to cry, Franz; your mother is dead."

· IV ·

Young Weldein wanted to become an artist, and his father was proud of that fact. He'll succeed where I failed, he thought. But from the start it was not easy! The boy's career as an artist began with his being thrown out of school. He was a good-for-nothing; he sketched during his classes and had no interest in learning what he was being taught. And at home! There he would sometimes sit with a piece of paper in front of him and practice his talent, but most of time he would stand idly at the window and stare into space. Then he would go down to the yard and romp with the children. His father usually did not get home until late in the evening; after work the tavern came first, then the family. And on those evenings when he did not have the money for a drink, he took the boy along for a walk through the streets of the city. And almost every time they took the same route: past the casino, down the long street . . . to the left . . . to the left . . . and toward the river. And the father thought: "How much my son could achieve if I had the money! But now he'll have to struggle to win any notice at all . . . he'll starve before achieving anything great." And together they walked back and forth on the banks of the river, both of them poor, the aging father with eyes grown dim in his puffy face and the youth at his side with eyes full of longing. And sometimes his father glanced at him, remembering how he himself had once aspired to greatness and how the world then lay spread out before him in richness and splendor. And once more, later, on the evening that brought him riches, once more it lay before him in richness and splendor. Silent despair seized him anew . . . would it never be over? And yet, again and again he was drawn along the same route to the same bridge. Oh, it was better to get drunk than to have to think of it all the time! Franz continued to sketch and paint, mostly faces expressing a certain passionate emotion; his father thought he saw talent in them and even said a few times, "Go on, present them at the Art Academy, maybe they'll admit you!" But the youth could not bring himself to do so; the drawings got scattered, and he fell idle, doing nothing at all for weeks, months on end. Then at some point he began to help his father out with his work. And sometimes it could happen that while he was occupied with the dreary painting job he suddenly felt his true talent awaken; then he threw away the wide brush, the paint and his pay, rushed home and locked himself in his room in order to draw or to paint. Then he sat there for hours, with the feeling he would create something great, something magnificent. And when he was finished, it turned out to be another failure. He threw everything in a corner, and a time of idleness set in again, when he squandered his money by drinking and playing cards in frivolous company.

The months and the years went past in this way, and the household of Weldein, father and son, managed to eke out a wretched existence. Then, when Franz was twenty, he once came home early in the morning when the sunlight already streamed in at the windows. His father was not in bed; he lay on the floor with a red face, breathing heavily; his tousled gray hair hung down over his forehead. Franz looked at him for a long time. He had a headache; he too had returned from an all-night spree and had gambled away his last few pennies, as his father had drunk his away. A slight shiver ran through the young man. What kind of a life could he look forward to! What an empty, miserable existence! And after a while he pushed the table over to the window, took out some paper and began to sketch. At first he made little progress, but as the hours passed his hand quickened. He felt it would become something really good. And he worked on, as if there were nothing that could matter to him. The sheet of paper was too small . . . he tore it up, took a larger sheet and began anew. And the miracle of inspiration came over him. His work became so easy that it was almost effortless. And the hours flew past, it was late afternoon. The drawing was finished. A small table in a tavern, gathered around it were a few drinkers and card players, that was all. And, as usual, he was most successful at rendering the expression of passion on the people's faces. He gazed at his work with shining eyes. He at least had achieved part of what he had intended. He turned around; his father was standing behind him.

"Good morning . . . Franz," he mumbled.

"Good evening," Franz replied.

"Ah—it's evening already . . . that was a nice sound sleep." He laughed. "I enjoyed myself last night. I really did. . . . And you've been working on something again? Let's see . . . Hm . . ." He looked closely at the drawing. "Hm . . ." His mood turned solemn, feelings of fatherly pride welled up in him. "Franz, that's good, very good. . . . I . . . Franz . . ." He stopped.

"What are you trying to say, Father?"

"I never could do anything that good . . . not even in better times!"

And both of them, father and son, looked at the drawing for a long time.

After a while the father took the picture from the table and, handing it to his son, he said, "Franz, this one you've got to take there . . . in any case. Take it to the Academy."

• V •

A few years later a small painting by young Weldein was displayed in an exhibit. People were starting to talk about his unusual and genuine talent. One characteristic appeared strange, however: it seemed that he could only paint card players and drinkers. It was like a curse. He did, in fact, use his artistry on other subjects, but he was never really successful with any of them. At times he sat at his easel desperately trying to conjure up his own vision of love, of bliss; ridiculous, grotesque masks stared back at him, not the faces of angels. Finally he had to give up; some ineffable power had control over him. "Am I out of my mind," he sometimes wondered, "or is it because I seem to be addicted to that vice myself?" And he tried to become master over himself, to escape from wine, from cards. But he could not do it; indeed, as soon as he had withdrawn for a few days from the circle of friends that lured him with drink and cards, he felt broken in spirit and tired to death. He lacked all creative urge. And then he rushed back to the card table, to the bottle. And then, when he came home in the light of morning, just like the time he had found his father lying on the floor, then he was the great artist again, inspired by genuine creativity and real ability. He had no choice but to accept his lot. His father had become a sick old man. He remained in his old apartment, while his son rented a small sunny room, closer to the sky and the light, on the fifth floor of a building in the same district. Sometimes old Weldein visited his son; exhausted from climbing the stairs, he would sit down at the window and stay there while Franz painted or lay on the sofa smoking. Occasionally they would talk and complain. The old man earned very little, and fame and wealth did not come fast enough for the young man.

A few times the father said, "I'm to blame that you can only paint such things. My blood is altogether poisoned, really poisoned." His son did not reply, but went on painting.

In the quiet of the studio, when Weldein sat there for hours, he became deeply and painfully aware of his age. Before his eyes he saw someone whose fate would not be better than his own. And where was it, that which could have made both of them happy? That night of long ago sometimes went through his mind like a dream.

And then his son interrupted his brooding and told him what he was painting. Now . . . a group of card players in a disreputable establishment . . . a few women standing among the tables holding champagne glasses in their hands. He finished that one quickly. Then a small painting. At the fireplace. . . . He and she. . . . They're playing bezique, smiling at each other across the cards. Another picture stood half finished in the corner . . . a medieval scene . . . soldiers of fortune playing dice. . . . He had trouble with that one, it was not modern enough. The old man listened while darkness began to fall. And the young painter joined his father at the window, which he opened wide to let in some fresh air.

It was a summer evening, muggy and oppressive. The street noises echoed up to them; with dull regularity life took its course. Always the same monotonous sound. Whatever they're doing down there, up above just the same sluggish hum can be heard. And the last rays of the sun moved slowly up the slanted roofs and then faded away, shadows spread, wisps of clouds appeared in the sky, casually drawn; a pattern of white streaks emerged. The twilight lingered on. Old Weldein gazed at the sky where another of his bleak days was waning.

More often than before he thought: will it soon be over? And he felt many a symptom of the old age that had come to him prematurely.

They had been staring out into the evening for a while when the father broke the silence.

"Do you have a new idea?"

"A new idea?"

"Yes, I mean, for a great picture."

"In outline—yes."

"Oh? What are you planning?"

"I want to paint the casino."

"The casino?"

"Yes, the gambling hall at the casino of the aristocratic club."

Old Weldein suddenly got up. "You would want to do that?"

"Do you think it's too difficult?"

"Oh no! But where will you get the right models?"

"Well, I'll simply get them at the casino—"

"But you've never been there!"

"Oh yes, I have, twice already."

"There? In the gambling hall? How did you manage that?"

"One of the club members introduced me. It's the gentleman who bought my last picture. . . ."

"The Black Ball?"

"Yes. At the exhibit recently he himself approached me and said he was interested in my talent . . . then he came up here and looked at my drawings. That's when I asked him for the favor of introducing me at the casino so that I could get first-hand impressions for my new painting."

"—Ah hah . . . How did he find out about you?"

"Well, obviously because of my picture in the exhibit."

"What's the man's name?"

"Count Spaun."

Weldein cringed and dropped into his chair. As it was quite dark, the son did not notice the expression on his father's face.

"Spaun . . . you say. . . ."

"Yes, a man of about fifty, very knowledgeable about art and with quite some imagination."

"Imagination . . . that's for sure. Did he ask about me? . . ."

"About you, Father?" the son replied, smiling.

"Well, I mean about your family."

"Well yes, in passing. He wanted to know whether my parents were still alive, whether I came from a wealthy family. . . ."

"And what did you answer?"

"You're asking me strange questions! I told him the truth."

"The count undoubtedly was quite surprised, wasn't he?"

"Surprised? Why?"

"Well, that a young man from such a poor family had gotten so far."

"So far! Do you really believe that, Father?"

"Well, yes! Your name is known, after all. People say: Weldein the painter."

The young man smiled again. He had become slightly melancholy from what he took to be fatherly pride. He went away from the window and, abruptly breaking off the conversation, he said, "I'm going to light a candle now."

"Oh? You're staying home?"

"I have to wait for a while."

"For whom?"

"Well, for the count."

Old Weldein got up. "He's coming? Count Spaun?" It sounded like a cry of fear.

"What's wrong with you, Father?"

"Nothing. But I . . . can't deal with such gentlemen. . . . No, no, let me go. . . . I'm very glad . . . he'll be very useful to you. Good bye, Franz."

"What's wrong with you?" Somewhat disturbed, he tried to see the old man's face in the dim candle light.

"Nothing . . . Franz. You're acting so strangely. What should be wrong with me? I'm leaving, as I do every evening. Have I ever stayed so long before? My friends at the tavern are waiting for me! You'll be going . . ."

"I'm going with Count Spaun to the casino." Laughing, he added, "It's good that I can't participate in the gambling. The stakes are so high, Father . . . to watch that. . . . But you've never gambled, have you?"

"No, never . . ."

And both of them stared out the window into the empty darkness. And the same scene appeared to them both. The brilliant glow of many lights. . . . In the middle the large green table; and the cards fall, and fortunes roll back and forth. . . . A sense of excitement and intoxication came over them . . . the intoxication of gamblers who remember. The intoxication of people who know that a mere quirk of fate could make them rich and happy. There was a sudden gust of wind, the candle flickered. The green table vanished, the glow of lights faded abruptly.

The old man took his hat and left. "Good bye, my son," he

said at the door. And he rushed down the stairs as fast as he could. It was high time. He had hardly gone out the front door when he saw, approaching from the other direction, the figure of the man he had not seen since that evening long ago, but had never forgotten. Opening his eyes wide, Weldein stood still. And he watched the count go into the building, climb the first few steps and disappear from view—just as he had on the stairs of the casino that night long ago, leaving Weldein alone in the street with all his wealth. And Weldein went away from the building, looked up at his son's window and waited. Moving shadows appeared on the opposite wall. His son and Count Spaun. . . . He shuddered. Why in the world? A thought suddenly came to his mind. He'll bring him bad luck! And he wanted to go back upstairs and save his Franz. . . . The bright lights in the hallway brought him back to his senses. He stopped. "Fool," he mumbled. And he went off to the tavern.

• VI •

Early the next morning Franz Weldein returned home. Overwhelmed with impressions, he sat down with some enthusiasm to make a few sketches. And yet something bothered him. "I know what it is," he cried, "I know what's lacking. It would be different if I could sit down in the midst of those people and feel what they feel! That could turn out to be some picture! Yes, then—"

And he went on sketching. After an hour he became tired. "I'll lie down for a while," he mused, "not in bed . . . I just want to think all this over." And he stretched out on the sofa. He closed his eyes, and a picture took shape in his mind. There is the hall in all its haughty simplicity. The four large mirrors with gold frames. Singular images reflected from one to the other. A tall gentleman with a blond moustache standing at the door with a gardenia on his lapel. A group of casual bystanders at one of the large windows, chatting and smoking cigarettes. And then the players around the table . . . The gentleman with the black beard. But no . . . they should not be recognizable. Just a slight touch of individuality . . . On each of their faces the passion of gambling finds its own characteristic expression. Almost all of them seem calm, but he, the artist, can see what others cannot . . . At the lips of the one, in the eyes of the other, on the brow of a third he detects the reflection of the very same fervor.

And Franz Weldein lay there with his eyes closed, sensing that he was coming closer to the true image. The sound of heavy steps startled him. Someone had come into the room. The painter opened his eyes. "Who is there?" It was a boy he didn't know. Weldein got up quickly.

The boy spoke in haste, holding his cap in his hand. "Please . . . Mr. Weldein, your father. . . . I live in the same house . . . he is sick. . . . He'd like you to come."

"Sick? What? What happened?"

"Last night when your father got home. . . ."

"Well, what?"

"He sang and screamed all night, and now he has a high fever."

"A fever? Is the doctor there?"

"No, people thought I should get to you first. . . ."

"Come along then."

And both of them hurried down the stairs. Then Franz Weldein said, "A doctor lives in the house next door. Bring him along, do you understand?"

"Yes."

And the young artist ran toward his father's house, which was scarcely a hundred paces away. After a few minutes he stood at the sick man's bedside. A woman from the neighborhood had watched over him in the meantime.

Old Weldein lay stretched out on the bed with eyes half closed, moaning. His face was quite flushed. He did not recognize his son. Franz called out, "Father, Father!" The neighbor, a kind old woman, tried to console the young man. "He's quieter now," she said. — "I see . . ." Franz said. Both of them stood there for a while, looking at the old man helplessly. "There's the doctor," the neighbor said.

"Oh, at last!" Franz cried and went toward the door to greet the doctor, a young man whom he had sometimes consulted himself.

"Well, what's wrong?" the doctor asked. "Your father, I hear."

"Yes, doctor, my father. . . ." and he turned toward the woman . . . "Thank you very much. Perhaps you might be so kind as to stop by again later!" The woman left.

The doctor had gone over to the bed, and he examined the old man thoroughly and solemnly. The son stood next to him, watching anxiously. He saw the doctor put his ear to the patient's chest, listen, feel his pulse, count his breaths. After several minutes the examination seemed to be over . . .

"Is it serious?" the son asked.

"Your father has pneumonia."

"Pneumonia . . . it's possible to recover from that."

"Certainly. It seems, however . . . your father was fond of alcohol, wasn't he?"

"Yes, he was, in fact. Does that matter?"

"I'm sorry to say it does, Mr. Weldein. But there's really no reason to fear the worst. Well—we'll see how things go."

"So it's serious," Franz whispered.

The doctor did not reply, but instead gave advice and instructions. Sadly and attentively, the young man listened. With a few heartfelt words the doctor took his leave, and Franz remained alone with the patient. A moment had come when the old man seemed partially to regain consciousness, and as in a dream he took his son's outstretched hand in his own. "Do you want something? Father. . . . Do you want something?" The old man moved his lips. His son leaned down so he could read what the lips were trying to say. But old Weldein got the words out quite audibly, though hoarsely,

"Something to drink!" Then he began to cough, tortuously and endlessly.

• VII •

The first few days had been tolerable; during the third night, however, the coughing got worse, the moans became frightened, the facial expression sunken. And the patient talked in his sleep and tried to jump out of bed. Not just once, but perhaps ten times. He calmed down only toward morning. The next day was bad, too. On the evening of the fifth day the doctor said to the son, "Dear Mr. Weldein, things do not look good. You must be prepared for the worst; it is my duty to tell you."

"Prepared for the worst," Franz repeated, highly upset, "prepared . . ."

"Do be calm, my friend, you're a grown man, after all." And the doctor left. Young Weldein stood rooted to the spot, staring after him for many long minutes. The candle above the sick man's head flickered; the smoking oil lamp on the table in the middle of the room cast a dim light.

Franz paced back and forth in the room, as if he had to look for something, then he stopped at the foot of the bed, bracing his arms on the footboard. He was exhausted, close to falling asleep . . . then his arms got tired, and the bed creaked. He trembled and moved away. He went out into the hall for a while where he could breathe the fresh air coming in through an open window. The light of a full moon shone on the tile floor. There was something so gentle and consoling about the soft radiance. Then the young man had the idea of letting this light shine in on the sick man, and so he went back into the room and pulled open the curtains. And the gentle radiance flooded the room, over the window sill, the floor, the bed; and the white sheets took on a blue shimmer. Out of them the old man's emaciated face shone pale—so pale. And his lips were quite white . . . On the night table the empty medicine bottles glistened. Young Weldein stood at the window, tired, sad, listless. And now, strangely enough, for the first time since his father became ill, he thought of something other than the patient. His picture came back to his mind, and he saw himself sitting in front of his easel, painting. And he could imagine stroke after stroke . . . And for a few moments he forgot everything else. Suddenly he heard his father's voice. He was awake! He was speaking! Was that possible? And again he heard, "Franz! My son!"

"You're calling me, Father? Father!" And he rushed over to the bed, clasping the hand of the patient who stared at him with wide open eyes, but no longer spoke. "Do you want something, Father?"

Old Weldein nodded his head. "What? What are you trying to tell me?" Franz asked. And he sat down on the bed, looking anxiously at the patient. "A miracle, my son, a miracle," the old man said.

"What? Do you feel better again?"

"No . . . oh, no. I'm going to die . . . but . . . oh . . . if only I can say it." And closing his eyes, he took a deep breath, as if he were trying with all his might to hold onto the fading spark of life.

"My son . . . come closer . . . closer to my mouth. A miracle . . . for twenty years I just could not remember, and suddenly in this very hour it all comes back to me. Listen . . ."

"I'm listening."

"Franz, you're rich. . . . A buried treasure lies waiting for you."

Startled, the son looked at his father with sympathy . . . it was clear that the patient was delirious. But the old man noticed the expression on his son's face and said, "I'm telling the truth . . . a treasure . . . near the bridge . . . the Lion's Bridge. I won some money . . . and buried it; I won it at the casino and then hid it.

"At the casino? You, money?"

"Yes, Count Spaun. . . . You ask him . . . he'll tell you how one night he took me with him and I won so much money. And I drank—a lot—too much. . . . And then I hid the money. I forgot where. . . . It was sheer misery. . . . You know what misery my life was. My entire life. . . . And now—now. . . ."

He had sat up in bed; his voice had become steadier; stronger was the hand clutching that of his breathlessly listening son.

"Now—suddenly—as I was lying here I finally remembered. Everything about that night! The bridge! Yes, the bridge. . . . It was there, I knew it all the time! Under the bridge—beneath the stones—a hammer was lying there. I dug up the earth . . . buried the money and then hammered it down . . . that's why I heard a murmuring sound and an echo."

"Father! Where is it? I don't understand you! A treasure . . . under the bridge, where?"

"The Lion's Bridge . . . the path under the bridge on this side, right next to the water . . . at this time of year two feet from the water. There's a narrow path leading to the dock . . . paved with cobblestones. At the time it was still being worked on, it wasn't finished yet. With a hammer I dug up the stones. The money is there!"

"But . . . !"

"You don't believe it, but it's true. . . ."

"Under the Lion's Bridge?"

"Beneath the pavement. I'm sure it's there! I see it. I can see, too, how I put it under the stones. It can't have been carried off, no . . . you'll find it, you'll be rich and happy."

"Father! You're still dreaming."

"No! I'm not dreaming! I know it."

"Well, fine, but the path under the bridge is long."

"Oh no, not long at all . . . at the second pier you'll find it with a single blow of the hammer."

Franz put his hand to his forehead; he still could not quite understand the whole thing.

"My son . . . quickly . . . go there!"

"Now?"

"Yes, now, because it's night. Take my work coat . . . and the hammer lying outside . . . next to the stove. Yes . . . go right away . . . I want to see it yet . . . it's wrapped in a cloth, paper money and gold. Go . . . go!"

The son got up, completely bewildered, and rushed out. In the hall he took his father's white work coat from the hook, found the hammer and hid it under the coat. At that moment he could not think of anything else but the treasure—not a thought of the dying man. The money danced and whirled in his head, the money . . . bright sparkling gold! And he dashed away. The streets were empty as he raced through them. Then he reached the long street through which so many years ago old Weldein had carried the money he'd won . . . and then the bridge where he had stood the following day, lamenting and desperate, while all the riches that could have made him happy lay beneath his feet. Here's the place . . . and he already stood at the second pier. The bridge arched above him, next to him the waves murmured, carrying the moonbeams downstream.

And Franz Weldein set to work. After a few minutes he had pried loose two stones. Nothing . . . nothing. Now a coach rolled over the bridge above him . . . with a dull, heavy sound. Franz began anew. And here . . . yes . . . something that looks like the end of a piece of cloth . . . and now . . . another stone. There was a murmuring sound and an echo . . . and this? What's this! It was dark under the bridge, with both hands Franz tugged at something white lying there. A cloth . . . tied together. Open it up. . . . He tore open the knot. Gold . . . bank notes. . . . Yes! he'd found it! The treasure! Wealth! Happiness! And Franz put everything beneath his coat, with trembling hands. Could it be true? And when he came out from under the bridge and the friendly light of the night shone upon him, he could have fallen to his knees, to weep . . . with joy . . . with happiness. He began to run. Suddenly he stopped. He looked around. Anyone there? Yes, a few harmless people taking a walk. But running in the middle of the night could look suspicious. Suspicious? Had he done anything wrong? Well . . . in any case. . . . And so he went on with measured step, his left hand placed casually in his pants pocket, his right one protecting the wealth under his coat.

A feeling of infinite peace gradually came over him. Now everything would be all right. And his picture was as good as finished. . . . Peace, wealth . . . all the bliss of the world! And the old man who was going to die? Young Weldein began to run again . . . who knows whether the sight of the money would not help the old man recover. What had made him sick in the first place? Poverty, despair, misery. Get back to him quickly, then, to bring him happiness and the certainty of a happy future. When he entered the hall, everything was quiet. Just don't be overzealous. He calmly took off the work coat and hung it in its usual place. Then he shoved the cloth with the money under his shirt. Into the room now. "Father," he called out, "here it is! I have it!" And he rushed over to the bed. The sick man was unconscious, breathing in uneven gasps. Cold sweat stood on his brow. Undoubtedly the end was near.

"Father!" Franz cried. No answer!

In vain Franz attempted to arouse the old man. He called out to him, shouted, smoothed his tousled hair. He breathed on him. He massaged his cold arms and legs with his own warm hands. Once he thought he noticed his eyelids moving. Nothing . . . nothing . . . the old man's breathing grew ever fainter. Not a stir, not an answer. time passed, Franz sat there, completely helpless. "Father! . . . The money! I have it with me."

Toward morning the doctor arrived. He went over to the bed with scarcely a greeting. He tested the pulse. "Can no longer be felt . . ." he said.

"What . . . do you mean?"

"Please—" the doctor whispered, putting his finger to his lips. He wanted absolute quiet so he could observe the breathing. He stood erect, then he bent down to the old man's chest and put his ear to it. After ten, twenty seconds he rose slowly and silently gave his right hand to the son who stood at the foot of the bed looking anxiously at the doctor. "Is he dead?" Franz burst out . . . taking the hand.

"His suffering is over," the doctor said with compassion.

Franz sank into a chair, hearing as he did so the clink of the pieces of gold at his chest. Cringing, he put his hand against them. Then he looked up to see whether the doctor had noticed . . . no! He had gone over to the window. As he opened it, he said quietly, "It's so stuffy in here." The morning sun shone over the rooftops.

• VIII •

Two men walked up the stairs of the casino together—Count Spaun and Franz Weldein.

"Are you really in the right mood?" the count asked.

"You're surprised?"

"Of course I am! Just consider: you come running to me straight from your father's freshly dug grave and plead that I take you to this house of joy and glitter."

"But for me it means something quite different! For me it's a place of study. And this particular picture is close to my heart. I must paint it, must paint it soon. . . ."

"You've already finished much of it, haven't you?"

"Sketches . . . yes . . . but something's still lacking . . . something."

They had reached the foyer in the meantime and went directly into the great gambling hall.

"And what is it that you lack?" the count asked.

"You'll probably laugh at me."

"My dear fellow, I never laugh at the whims of an artist." Both of them had gone through the door to the gambling hall and now stood right next to the green table where the card players were sitting.

"Well, Count Spaun," young Weldein continued as his eyes fell on the cards, "I still lack true inspiration for the picture!"

"Oh? That's not so strange, is it? You'll find the right moment sometime!"

"When?"

"How could I possibly know that!" the count said with a smile.

"But I know it!" the artist cried out so vehemently that the count looked at him in astonishment.

"Well?" he asked.

"I myself, Count Spaun, at least once I myself must feel what these people here feel when they play."

"What?"

"You shouldn't misunderstand me, Count Spaun! Unfortunately—I'm aware of it myself—there's something not quite normal about my artistic talent. . . . You know—I'm only able to paint certain kinds of things, and that's not quite as it should be, after all."

"Yes," the count said, "perhaps that really is a bit crazy."

"Crazy," Weldein said emphatically, "yes, that's the right word—and I am crazy enough," he spat out the syllables, "indeed, crazy enough to want to play along with the others here in their game. . . ."

Count Spaun looked at him steadily and calmly. "Here?"

"Yes. . . ."

"Hm!"

"I must be able to carry off with me the glowing sparks of their fervor . . . please understand me. I need . . . I need these very sparks to inspire me!"

"Your idea, my friend, is not really feasible. I don't actually find it so crazy. Yes . . . there's even logic to it. . . . Nevertheless you know that, no matter how welcome you are here as the talented artist, whom people know to be seeking the breath of life for his work, still. . . ."

"What, Count? Wouldn't a word from you be enough—to gain a welcome for me at this table for a single evening. . . ."

"Well, I'm sure I could not be refused that . . . but. . . ."

"Then what's stopping you?" As he spoke, the painter watched with shining eyes how the enormous sums staked on the cards flew back and forth.

"You can see for yourself, my young friend, what the stakes are here. . . ."

"Oh, Count Spaun. That's no problem."

"No problem? It certainly is."

"I have in my possession just as much money . . ." and he looked the count straight in the eye, "just as much as my father won at this very table." For a moment the count was speechless. Then he stepped back and said to young Weldein quietly and hastily, "How long have you known?"

"Just since the hour of his death!"

"So it's true. That's what I thought! At first I suspected he had lost it all gambling. But he hoarded it! Turned into a miser!"

"No, Count Spaun . . . that's not the way things were . . . quite different, in fact . . . I'll tell you all about it later. It's enough for now that I inherited it and have it in my possession."

Without another word the count took the artist over to the gambling table and said, "Gentlemen, our young friend, Weldein the painter, whom all of you know . . . would like to request the honor of joining you for once in your game."

"Of course . . . with pleasure, glad to have you, over here," he could hear the voices say. And there he sat! It was true!

There at the green table! A feeling of giddy excitement surged through him. He took out his bank notes and lay them out in front of him. There . . . something flew at him . . . a card. He wanted to take it. "Excuse me," the dealer said, "it's for the man next to you."

Naturally, of course . . . it wasn't his turn yet . . . the man next to him lost. That was lucky for him, for Weldein. Now he could stake a higher sum, as the probability of his winning had become greater. So . . . there before him was his card.

He lost. . . . Oh, well, it was only the first deal! He could easily win back that much. He put down a second, somewhat higher sum than the first. The card lost again. A third stake . . . higher yet . . . and he lost again.

The other players looked at the young man in astonishment; they had not thought him to be so wealthy.

Weldein himself sat there with a smile on his face, yet staring with a strangely fixed expression. Count Spaun quietly said to him, "You've had enough inspiration by now, don't you think?"

But the young man would not move . . . he played on and on and lost continuously. Some people had come over to watch; they were astonished at the artist's daring game. Soon everyone realized that he had come into a large inheritance and had lost a good part of it. Then Count Spaun said, "Won't you rest for a while?"

But Weldein played on. He lost one stake after the other. People began to feel sorry for him and shook their heads over the risks he took. His bad luck was inconceivable. Only at one point did things seem to take a turn for the better. But no. Bad luck prevailed. And the smile never left his face, in the end he even burst out laughing! And now he got up. It was all over. "Good night, gentlemen," he said. People made way for him, as if for someone whose incredible misfortune demanded respect. He went toward the door. Everyone watched him go. The count followed him. Weldein rushed down the stairs, along the street. The count caught up with him at the corner.

"Weldein . . . Weldein!"

'Oh, it's you, Count Spaun!"

"Where are you running?"

"I don't know. . . ."

"Don't do anything rash, do you hear? I want nothing rash. You've lost nothing really important."

"Oh no, nothing at all!"

"Money won at gambling! If it had been earned, saved up after years of hard work. . . ."

The young artist did not answer, but rushed on, taking the

route through the long street . . . as his father had done long ago. The count could hardly keep up with him. He repeated, "Where are you running? Come with me instead . . . let's go drink something."

"You are very kind, Count Spaun, but if you insist on following me. . . . I must go to a particular place, I just have to."

"Where?"

"Where? To the place where my father buried the money that evening."

"So he buried it after all!"

"Yes . . . and he forgot where."

"Forgot?"

"Yes—he forgot where. For twenty years he lived on, a rich man who just did not know where his money was. That's a pretty good joke, isn't it? And he remembered on his deathbed."

"What? What kind of a tall tale is that?"

"No, it's the truth, Count Spaun! What a miserable life! Constant torture . . . as a rich man to have to go hungry. . . . And I! Suddenly it all fell to me! And there I stood, independently wealthy . . ."

"Where are you taking me?"

"Just come along, we'll be there soon!"

"But why do you want to go there?"

"A whim."

For a while they hurried on in silence. They had come to the river bank.

"There—the bridge."

"Well?" the count asked.

"Just follow me now!" And he hurried down the path under the bridge. He threw himself to the ground next to the pier, crying: "There! There!"

"What—?"

"It was here . . . I dug it up here. And . . . just look . . . don't you see?"

"Well, what? I see that the stones are wet from the water splashing up."

"What? Just look right here!" He had gotten down to his knees, clutching at the stones with his hands.

"Well, what am I supposed to see?"

"There's money here again!"

"What?"

"Oh, what an amount! What enormous piles of money!"

"Where do you get that idea?"

"Oh—" and with his finger nails he dug in the sand between the stones, "I'm rich again."

"Weldein! Come to your senses!"

"Oh my, what luck—what great luck!" and he put sand and small stones into his pockets.

"But . . . Weldein! You're not in your right mind! Come to your senses! Consider what the world still expects from you! Get hold of yourself! Think of your mission as an artist! Your great picture."

But the painter did not listen. He dug up stones and shoved them into his pockets. The count seized him by the shoulders and cried, "Stop! Come with me! Come along!"

Slowly Weldein got up. "Oh, I'm coming. . . . Take me back there . . . Count Spaun!"

"Where?"

"Well, back to the casino! Now I can play again!"

The count stood there in complete dismay. Could it be true? Had such great losses really driven the man insane? They had gone up the path together and were standing next to the bridge. The count took the young artist's hand and said, "Please calm down."

"It's late . . . we'll have to go back quickly," Weldein replied.

"But—!"

With a sudden burst of energy Weldein tore himself loose and ran off with frantic speed through the empty streets. Shouting and pleading, the count followed him. After a few minutes the young man had covered such a distance that his pursuer could not catch up with him. Where had the madman gone? Could he actually be running to the casino. . ? The count hastened his pace. "The fit is probably over by now," he thought on the way. "His sudden agitation is certainly understandable. But where has he gone? I hope I can find him again! If he's rash enough to . . . No!" And he hurried on. As he approached the casino, the other man came up to meet him.

"There you are, Weldein. Well?"

"Oh, Count Spaun, oh!" And his voice had a whining tone.

"What's the matter? You've calmed down, haven't you?"

"Oh, Count Spaun! Just look!" And he emptied the sand and stones from his pockets.

"Well?" the other asked anxiously.

"Don't you see? Stones . . . sand!"

"Yes. . . . Now you realize it! You do, don't you? I'm so relieved! I was really worried about you! Now everything will be all right."

"Oh, Count Spaun!"—and he moaned and wailed—"My money, my money!"

"Well, yes—it's terrible, of course—it's all gone!"

"Gone!"

"But you have other things, better than money."

"My money!"

"Be quiet, won't you?" Some people were walking past through the dark street and looked around.

"I've buried it! I've buried it!"

"What? What's come over you again?"

"Buried! Hidden, and I don't know where!"

"You've gambled it away! Weldein . . . just listen to me, you lost it at the casino!"

"Oh no, oh no, I won so much, so much money! And then I hid it and don't know where. Oh, my poor wife! My child! My Franz!"

The count stared at him, horrified. . . . It seemed as if all of a sudden the painter's features were strangely transformed, as if it really were the elder Weldein who stood there gazing dry-eyed into space and whimpering softly, "My son, my poor son!"

—*Translated by Helene Scher*

The Son

Taken from a Doctor's Papers

It is midnight and I am still sitting at my desk. I can't get that unhappy woman out of my mind. I think of the gloomy back room with the old-fashioned pictures, of the bed with the blood-stained pillow where she lay, her face pale, her eyes half closed. It was such a cloudy, rainy morning, too. In the corner of the room, sitting on a chair with his legs crossed and a defiant look on his face, was the wretch, the son, who had taken a hatchet to his mother's head. Yet, there are such people, and they are not always demented. I looked at this defiant face, trying to read what was in it. It was an angry, pallid face, not ugly, not stupid, with bloodless lips and somber eyes, the chin buried in a rumpled shirt collar. His tie hung loose at his neck, and he twisted one end of it back and forth in his slender fingers. He was waiting for the police, who were to come and take him away. Meanwhile, someone stood watch outside the door. I had bandaged the unfortunate mother's temple; the poor woman was unconscious. After a neighbor offered to stay with her, I left. On the stairs I met the police, coming to get the matricide. The residents of the apartment house were quite agitated; they stood outside their doors in groups, talking about the sad incident. Some of them questioned me about the situation upstairs—whether there was any hope that the injured woman would live. I could give no definite answer.

A woman I knew, no longer young, the wife of an office clerk whom I had attended as physician, detained me a while longer. She was leaning against the stair railing, looking quite devastated. "This thing is even more terrible than you think, doctor," she said, shaking her head. "More terrible?" I asked. "Yes, doctor. If you only knew how much she loved him!" "She loved him?" "Yes, she doted on him, spoiled him." "This fellow? Why?" "That's just it—why? You see, doctor, the boy was troublesome from his earliest childhood. But she let him get away with anything. She would forgive him the worst kind of misdeeds. We who live here often had to warn her about him. The good-for-nothing used to get drunk even as a boy, and as soon as he got a little older—oh, those things!" "What things?" "For a short time he had a job in a store, but he had to leave." "Had to?" "Yes, he got into all sorts of trouble there. He even stole from his boss. His mother replaced the money, even though the poor woman had barely enough to live on herself!"

"What does she do for a living?"

"She did sewing and embroidery. It was hard for her to make ends meet. And the boy, instead of supporting her, took the little bit she earned and spent it in the tavern and God knows where else. But that wasn't enough. The silverware, two or three pictures, the clock, almost everything that wasn't nailed down, ended up in the pawnshop!"

"And she tolerated this?"

"Tolerated it? She loved him all the more! None of us could understand it. And then he demanded money. She gave him what she had. He warned her that he had to have money!"

"How do you know all this?"

"You just find out about such things in the house. His shouting could often be heard through the stairwell, and when he came home drunk at night—sometimes in the daytime too

—he would start his yelling and scolding the minute he got in the door. The poor woman couldn't pay her bills. Sometimes she didn't even have bread. The rest of us helped her out sometimes, though we're none of us rich either. But it only got worse. She seemed to be completely blind to his offenses. She saw them all as boyish pranks. Sometimes she apologized to us after the fellow had staggered up the stairs in the middle of the night, making a lot of noise. That's the kind of son he was, doctor—but to think that it would go this far!" And then she told me the rest of the story: "Today he didn't come home till early morning. I heard him stumble on the steps outside our door. He was singing, too, in that hoarse voice of his. When he got upstairs he must have demanded money again. He left the door open—his raving could be heard as far down as our landing—as far down as here—just think—the fourth floor down to the second. And then suddenly a scream. Then another. People rushed upstairs, and saw what had happened. But he stood there, they said, quite unrepentant, and shrugged his shoulders!"

I left. Behind me I heard heavy footsteps. They were leading the murderer away. Men, women, and children stood in the corridors, staring after him; nobody spoke a word. I turned around in the hallway, went down the stairs and out of the building, and continued my morning's work in a very depressed mood. In the early afternoon I returned to the unlucky house. I found the injured woman as I had left her—unconscious, her breathing labored. The woman who was staying with her told me that the authorities had been there in the meantime and had established the facts of the case. It was so dark in the room that I had a candle lighted and placed on the nightstand at the head of the bed. What infinite suffering there was in that dying face! I asked her a question. She became restless, moaned, and opened her eyes a little. She was unable to speak. After I had prescribed what was necessary, I left. When I came back in the evening, the poor woman seemed somewhat improved. In answer to my question about how she felt, she said "Better . . ." and tried to smile. But then she immediately lost consciousness again.

Six o'clock in the morning!

After midnight, just as I had written the last line in my journal, the doorbell rang loudly. Mrs. Martha Eberlein—that was the name of the gravely injured woman—was asking for me. One of the boys from the house had been sent for me—I was to come instantly. Was she feverish? Was she dying? He didn't know anything—only that it was very urgent.

I followed the boy, my medical bag in hand, and hurried up the apartment-house stairs, while the boy remained below, holding a candle to light my way. The last steps were completely in the dark; only at the beginning of the way did I have a pale, flickering light to guide me. But from the half-open door of my patient's apartment a ray of light shone toward me. I entered and passed through the foyer, which also served as the kitchen, and into the back room. The neighbor woman had stood up as she heard my footsteps and came to meet me. "What is it?" I whispered. "She insists on talking to you, doctor!" said the woman.

I stood at the bedside. The patient lay there motionless. Her eyes were wide open; she was looking at me. Softly she said, "Thank you, doctor, thank you." I took her hand, the pulse was not so bad. I struck the cheerful tone that we doctors must always have ready to use, even when we don't feel like it. "So, I see you are better, Mrs. Eberlein. That's very gratifying."

She smiled. "Yes, better—and I have to talk to you."

"Oh?" I said, "What is it, then?"

"To you alone."

"Why don't you take a little rest." I turned to her companion.

"Outside," the sick woman added.

The woman gave me another questioning look; then she left, closing the door softly behind her. I was alone with my patient.

"Please," she said, glancing toward a chair that stood near the foot of the bed. I lowered myself into it, still holding her hand in mine, and pulled up closer, in order to hear her better.

She spoke rather softly. "I took the liberty, doctor," she began, "because it is very necessary that I speak to you."

"What do you want, my dear?" I asked, "Only, please don't tire yourself too much."

"Oh, no, it's only a few words. You must free him, doctor."

"Whom?"

"My son."

"My dear Mrs. Eberlein," I answered, quite moved, "You know very well that this is not in my power."

"It is in your power—if there is such a thing as justice!"

"I beg you . . . try not to excite yourself. I understand very well that you regard me as a friend, and I thank you for that. But I am also your doctor, so I am allowed to give you orders. Am I not? You must rest. The most important thing is rest."

"Rest . . ." she repeated, and the muscles around her eyes and mouth twitched painfully. "Doctor, you must listen. It weighs so heavily on me!"

She interpreted my silence as an invitation to speak, and, pressing my hand tightly, she began:

"He is not guilty—or at least he is much less guilty than people think. I have been a bad, a miserable, mother."

"You?"

"Yes, I was . . . a criminal!"

"Mrs. Eberlein!"

"You'll understand me right away. I'm not Mrs. Eberlein, I'm Miss Martha Eberlein. People only think I'm a widow. I haven't done anything to deceive them, but I couldn't well tell these old stories to just anyone, either."

"Yes, but, after all this time, that mustn't torment you so much."

"Oh, not that! It is twenty years since I was left alone—alone, even before my son was born—his son and mine. And then . . . it's only by chance that he is still alive, doctor, because . . . I wanted to kill him the first night. Yes, now you see what I am! I was alone and desperate. But I don't want to make excuses for myself. I took blankets and bedsheets and heaped them on top of him, thinking he would suffocate. Then in the morning, full of dread, I took the blankets away . . . and he whimpered! He whimpered, and breathed, and lived!" She wept, the poor woman. As for me, words failed me. But after a short silence she went on:

"And he looked at me wide-eyed and wouldn't stop whimpering! And that little thing, not even one day old yet, made me tremble. I remember clearly that I stared at him for maybe an hour, thinking: What reproach is in those eyes! And maybe he understood what you did and is accusing you. And maybe he has a memory and will always, always accuse you. And he grew bigger, that little thing, and in those big, childish eyes was always the same reproach. Whenever he put his little hands on my face, I would think: Yes, he wants to scratch you, he wants to get even with you, because he remembers that first night of his life, when you buried him under blankets! And he began to babble, to talk. I dreaded the day when he would really be able to talk. But it did come, little by little. And I was always waiting—whenever he opened his mouth, I was waiting: Now he will say it. Yes, now he'll say it—that you can't fool him, that all the kisses, all the caresses, all the love cannot make you into a real mother. He resisted me, he wouldn't let me kiss him. He was unruly, he didn't love me. I let him hit me as a five-year-old child, and later, too, I let him hit me, and smiled. I had a frantic need to be rid of my guilt, and yet I knew that it could never be. Could I ever make up for it? When he always looked at me with those same terrible eyes? As he grew older and went to school it became perfectly clear to me that he saw through me. Contritely I accepted everything he did. Ah, he was not a good child, but . . . I couldn't be angry with him! Angry! I loved him, loved him madly. More than once I went down on my knees to him, kissed his hands, his knees, his feet! But he wouldn't forgive me. Not one loving look, not one warm smile. He became ten years old, twelve years old . . . he hated me! At school he didn't get along. One day he came home and told me defiantly, 'It's all over with at school. They don't want me there anymore.' Oh, how I trembled then! I wanted to have him learn a trade. I begged, I pleaded. But he wouldn't give in. He didn't want to hear anything about work. He just fooled around. What could I say? How could I blame him? One look from him destroyed all my confidence. How I shook when I thought of the day when he would tell me to my face: 'Mother, mother, you have forfeited your right to me!' But he never said it. Sometimes, when he came home drunk, I would think: Now the alcohol will loosen his tongue. But no. Sometimes he would collapse and sleep on the floor until noon. And when he woke up and I was sitting beside him, he would look at me sneeringly—with a knowing little smile on his lips, almost as if to say: Yes, we know where we stand, don't we? He always needed money, too, a lot of money, and I had to get it somehow. But it didn't always turn out the way he wanted, and then he would get angry, bitterly angry. He often raised his hand against me. And when I had collapsed on the bed, exhausted, he would stand over me with that mocking laugh of his, that meant: No, I'm not going to put you out of your misery! This morning, finally . . . he came up the stairs making a lot of noise: 'Money! money!' But, so help me God, I had none. 'What? None?' And I begged him to wait till next week, till tomorrow, till tonight! No! I had to give him money—I must have hidden it. He shouted and searched and tore open the cupboards and the bed, and swore. And then . . . and then . . ."

Then she stopped. After a second she said: "And wasn't it his right?"

"No!" I said, "No, Mrs. Eberlein! You were free of your debt long ago. Your infinite kindness had long ago made up for the bewilderment of a moment in which a delusion held you captive."

"No, doctor," she answered, "it wasn't a delusion. For I

remember that night all too clearly. I wasn't mad—I knew what I wanted! And because of that, doctor, I want you to go before the court and tell what you have heard from me. They will let him go—they'll have to!"

I saw that I couldn't argue with her. "Well," I said, "we'll talk more about it tomorrow, Mrs. Eberlein. Now you must get some rest. You have tired yourself too much."

She shook her head.

"Doctor, a deathbed wish is sacred. You must promise me!"

"You are not going to die, you are going to get well."

"I am going to die, because I want to. Will you testify in court?"

"First of all, listen to me, and remember that I am your physician. I order you to be quiet now and to rest."

With that I stood up and called in the neighbor woman. But Mrs. Eberlein would not let my hand go when I took leave of her. The question burned in her eyes.

"Yes!" I said.

"I thank you!" she answered. Then I gave her neighbor the necessary instructions and left, intending to return as early as possible.

In the morning I found my patient unconscious; by noon she was dead. Her secret still rests with me, hidden in these pages, and it is up to me whether to fulfill her last wish or not. Whether I testify or not—for the miserable son of this wretched mother, it won't make any difference. No judge in the world would admit the mother's mistake as mitigating circumstance in the capital crime committed by the son. It was more than sufficient punishment for this unlucky mother to have to imagine that she saw in her son's eyes an everlasting reproach, a constant reminder of that terrible night.

But what if it were true? Do obliterated memories from the very first hours of our existence remain with us—memories that we can no longer interpret, but that nevertheless do not completely fade? Is perhaps a ray of sunshine coming through a window the very first cause of a happy disposition? And when our mother's first gaze wraps us in boundless love, is it not reflected, sweet and unforgettable, in the fair eyes of childhood? But if this first gaze is one of despair and hatred, doesn't it burn with destructive power into the child's soul, which, after all, receives impressions by the thousands long before it is able to unravel them? And what may go on in the feelings of a child whose first night was spent in the horrible, unconscious fear of losing his life? No human being has yet been able to describe his first hours of life, and none of you—I could say this to the jurors—can know how much of the good and the bad in you can be attributed to the first breath of air, the first ray of light, the first look from your mother's eyes. I will testify in court. I have made up my mind, for it seems to me that it is still far from clear how little we are permitted to will our actions, and how much we are compelled by circumstance.

—Translated by Peggy Stamon

The Judge's Wife

· I ·

In the thirty-second year of his reign and the fifty-seventh year of his life, Karl Eberhard XVI, Duke of Sigmaringen, met a sudden death in the House of the Arbormaidens, and according to all the rumors, in the arms of the very youngest maiden of them all. The House of the Arbormaidens was what the folk thereabout used to call Karolslust, the hunting lodge and summer palace that lay amid spreading woodlands three hours by carriage from the ducal residence in the city and barely one half hour from the little country town of Karolsmarkt. At Karolslust the girls or women who enjoyed the Duke's favor—always ten to fifteen in number—led lives free of common cares but otherwise highly restricted.

The Duke had long since given explicit instructions that should he suffer a precipitate demise, the arbormaidens, provided with sufficient funds, be immediately removed from the palace and transported across the nearby border. The stewards and servants of the court, well trained in obedience, executed their orders faithfully, so that within a few days after the Duke's death, not only the palace in Sigmaringen but also Karolslust stood ready to receive its new master who, it was commonly known, had always disapproved of the customs and conduct of his father. He had been traveling since attaining his majority, and for three years had not set foot in the dukedom he would eventually rule. The sad tidings reached him in Paris, where he had not only enjoyed the hospitality of court and aristocratic circles, but had also cultivated the personal company of scholars and writers, among them the celebrated encyclopedists Diderot and Baron von Grimm, thereby provoking his father's derision even more than his indignation.

The late Duke's subjects had rather detested him in his younger years, but it had been a long time since he had given them any cause for serious complaint. His wife, related by marriage to the Poniatowskis, that princely Polish house of untold wealth, had died young, and the Duke, luxuriating in the considerable income derived from the blessing of his inheritance, could afford not to burden his subjects with inordinate taxes and dues, particularly in recent years. The pleasures of the hunt and the company of his arbormaidens so thoroughly gratified his needs that he had no time to spare for the playing of political and military games. Although this made life more pleasant and less hazardous in his little realm, which a vigorous hiker could cover in a week, than in numerous other German principalities, there was no shortage of malcontents and grumblers, some of whom occasionally expressed themselves more boldly than those with similar views in other dukedoms where an all too free, or even mildly inflammatory, expression of opinion could bring instant reprisal not only to the speaker thereof, but even to anyone foolhardy enough to listen to it.

The man with the reputation for being the most insolent chatterer and, indeed, the most audacious fellow in the entire dukedom was a certain Tobias Klenk. Although the people frequently thought themselves to be rid of him once and for all, he kept managing to turn up again in Karolsmarkt, the little town of his birth where his mother, a locksmith's widow, lived in secluded and penurious circumstances. Her twin daughters, Brigitte and Maria, had enlisted in the ranks of the arbormaidens, not without their mother's consent, when they were but sixteen, and they found their life not disagreeable at all, particularly since conditions of proximity endowed them with frequent opportunities to make themselves scarce for half or whole days at a time and to provide their maternal nest with pastries and wine. Brother Tobias, while unburdening himself of a vast catalogue of sneering insults, did not scorn the chance to nibble and drink right along. A full ten years before the Duke's unexpected death, the twins fled the summer palace as well as the country; they did not bid their mother or anyone else farewell.

Long after their disappearance, an unknown traveler passing through town brought the aging woman greetings and a considerable amount of money from her daughters in Rome where, it would appear, they were living in ambiguous but secure circumstances. This procedure repeated itself several times over the years, except that each time the greetings and attendant gift were delivered by a different stranger; but at last, this too came to a halt, and the twins were never heard from again.

Their brother Tobias, however, kept reappearing in his home town at regular intervals, without anyone ever knowing just exactly where he had come from or why, and he himself preferred to impart only superficial and vague hints about his peregrinations and other activities. In any event, he had seen a good deal of the world and, despite inadequate background had enrolled at various German universities, at each of which he had kicked up a row. Later he fought as a common soldier, though no one seemed to know under whose command or in which war theaters. He also roamed around with a young baron as a traveling companion or private tutor in Spain, Portugal, and England, and was involved in an assortment of activities—honorable to greater or lesser degree—by virtue of which he had reputedly gained considerable familiarity with the police, the courts, and quite likely some prisons. Several years before the old Duke's death, he had surfaced in Karolsmarkt very elegantly, almost aristocratically attired, had brought his mother Dutch linens and fabrics as well as a half dozen silver plates, had taken upon himself the charges for all his acquaintances at the Golden Ox for a full week, and had been called for one evening at that inn by a fine old carriage in whch a richly robed and no longer conspicuously youthful lady could be seen. Since then, however, he would from time to time and only for a brief stay turn up in Karolsmarkt in ever shabbier garb and in ever surlier mood, but nevertheless with ever looser tongue. And so it came to pass that on the very day on which the old Duke was laid to rest in the tomb of his ancestors, Tobias arrived in Karolsmarkt, more ragged and in worse condition than ever before, and now, thirty-three years old, set about living off his aged mother, who had long since had to part with the last of her silver plates and to earn her hard livelihood by sewing and mending in the houses of strangers.

But despite his bad appearance and reputation, Tobias sat at his table in the Golden Ox each evening as if it were his due. Although many a peaceful burgher felt uncomfortable in the presence of his insolent and slanderous remarks, they not only listened to him with mild patience and indulgence, but, with what seemed to be an unspoken understanding, one or the other of them would even pay his bill every night. Though Tobias's benefactors would not admit it to each other, they were secretly terrified of the strange and extravagant man, and after listening to his wild tirades felt him capable of any evil deed, even, perhaps wrongly, of perfidious vengeance.

On occasion, someone or other sitting at the same table would try to appease him with a few playful words masking a basic uneasiness. However, there was one among them who never hesitated to side with him or to support his rebellious statements with arguments of a seemingly historical and philosophical nature. He would also on such occasions sometimes go so far as to utter opinions more offensive and more dangerous than those the assembled were accustomed to hearing even from Tobias Klenk, and even escalated them to the pitch of prophecies and threats. And this man, strangely enough, was none other than the presiding judge of Karolsmarkt, Adalbert Wogelein, Tobias's contemporary and former schoolmate.

Both of their parents had lived in similarly modest though adequate circumstances, but the untimely death of the master locksmith, who left his household unprovided, created a gulf between the two families that grew wider from year to year. Nevertheless, this state of affairs had not the slightest corrosive effect on the tight bond of friendship the two boys shared. In fact, in a strange way it seemed to strengthen the ties between them. Adalbert, a model of gentleness and a student of exemplary diligence, actually fell into an incredible master-slave relationship with the wild and frivolous Tobias, to the extent that he not only put up with all manner of harmless childish pranks but also endured occasional malice and abusive domination with patience and, one might almost say, with pleasure.

Whenever Adalbert offered resistance, perhaps in the form of refusing to provide his crony with the solution to some problem in mathematics or to participate in some sort of youthful mischief, Tobias knew exactly how to punish him. He would not speak a single word to him, indeed appear not even to listen to anything he said, until he left Adalbert no recourse other than to submit or even to beg obsequiously for forgiveness.

Once, shortly after the locksmith's death, Adalbert was moved, during a break between classes, to offer his friend a few coins with which to purchase some bread and sausage. After all, Tobias had fallen into wretched poverty almost from one day to the next. To show his appreciation, Tobias reciprocated by giving Adalbert a vigorous cuff across the ear. Yet, not a quarter of an hour thereafter, Tobias brusquely ordered Adalbert to hand over everything edible that he had with him, as if it were a tribute that was his just due; and while he savored every bite, he mocked his friend who had to stand by and watch on an empty stomach.

On another occasion, while taking a stroll near the outskirts of town, Adalbert chanced to meet Tobias's sisters shortly before Tobias himself happened along—whether also by accident was exceedingly difficult to ascertain. For no reason whatsoever, Tobias insisted that Adalbert had behaved in an unseemly manner toward the girls, who were then fifteen years old, demanded that he leave the scene with utmost haste, and forbade him under threat of dire punishment from ever addressing his sisters again. Several evenings later, Adalbert turned a street corner and inadvertently stood face-to-face with the Klenk trio. He made an immediate move to get as far out of their way as he could, whereupon Tobias called him back with an imperious gesture, and commanded that he kiss Brigitte and then Maria on the mouth. Then he pummeled poor hesitant Adalbert's ribs until he could no longer refuse to submit to his friend's incomprehensible whim. With the burning sensation of the girls' lips still on his own, Adalbert heard Tobias's harsh words warning him that he would be in peril of a sound thrashing if he allowed himself to be seen in their presence in the near future. As Adalbert, with mixed emotions about this bittersweet experience, crept around the nearest corner and away, he was pursued by the sisters' laughter.

It was not too long after this incident that the two girls fulfilled what all their neighbors had prophesied for the longest time by emigrating from their parental home to the House of the Arbormaidens. At first, Tobias took his friend Adalbert into his confidence and told him in dark and menacing tones of the iniquity that had been visited upon his virtuous sisters, but soon he seemed quite willing to adjust to their destiny and his own, as living conditions by his maternal hearth became conspicuously more comfortable. In school, insofar as Tobias actually deigned to honor it with his occasional presence, he demonstrated an ever decreasing inclination to do well in his studies. As for righteous Adalbert, it became downright risky for him to maintain a friendship that would be construed as an inconceivable and, in any case, highly deplorable aberration in the eyes of his teachers, his fellow students, and probably the whole town. One day, shortly before the sisters' flight from Karolslust, Tobias also disappeared. According to his mother, he was temporarily staying in the country with relatives on his father's side who allegedly were good-natured enough to want to look after this lad who had gone astray. Although submitting to this turn of events as if to a self-ordained fate, in resignation, nay joyously, Adalbert surprised himself by breathing a huge sigh of relief.

Henceforth, not very much was known in Karolsmarkt about what ever became of Tobias, and what little information one could glean was quite unreliable, most of it stemming from rumors or whatever Tobias himself found advisable to relate on the occasions of his desultory visits to his home town. On the other hand, the career and work of Adalbert Wogelein were there for anyone with eyes to see. After studying law in Göttingen, during which time his parents died one shortly after the other, he served as assessor in the capital. Then, at the age of twenty-seven, he was appointed judge in the town of his birth, and he discharged the responsibilities of his office with appropriate decorum and with faithful adherence to the letter of the law.

At thirty he married the daughter of the village apothecary who was also its mayor. She was a quiet, happy, refined person who was loyally and respectfully devoted to her learned husband. She maintained an impeccable home in the little house at the edge of town that Adalbert had inherited from his parents, and she spent her days unperturbed in mind or spirit, as do those thousands of other good burgherly daughters who in their provincial existences were raised to have neither any notion of a wider world nor any longing for it. The union had not yet been blessed with offspring; no one came to the house other than her father, a few relatives, and several childhood playmates, some married, some still single. She kept her distance from men, particularly bachelors, because it displeased Adalbert to see anyone directing friendly glances or pleasantries toward the delicate, pretty creature he now called his own, and young men without even the slightest dishonorable intention seem incapable of ever denying themselves that indulgence.

Two or three times a week, his honor would take himself down to the Golden Ox after supper, which Agnes could hardly begrudge him since her father, the mayor, as well as other respected citizens also frequented the inn with regularity, and Adalbert, whose innate frugality made him a scrupulously moderate drinker, never came home any later than midnight.

In all this, it is true, that during the last few days, ever since Tobias Klenk's homecoming on the day of the Duke's funeral, a noteworthy change had taken place that filled Agnes with considerable anxiety. Not only did no single evening go by that could keep Adalbert at home, but the hour of his return also grew progressively later. Furthermore, he would be in a curiously irritable frame of mind which Agnes was inclined, at first, to ascribe to nothing more than an ample partaking of wine. But then she remembered that her husband's personality had temporarily transformed itself in the same unpleasant manner two years ago, the last time Tobias had been in town, and she recalled that the peculiar boyhood friendship of the two men lived on in the town as a half-forgotten legend. At that time Agnes saw Tobias on the street every now and then, but in a completely ingenuous shyness that was even free of any common curiosity, she had hardly paid him any mind at all, let alone ever sought an opportunity to engage him in conversation.

This time, however, Tobias was hardly ever to be seen on the streets, and she knew nothing at all of his presence in town before learning of it from her father, who found it advisable to stop by one morning after his son-in-law had already left the house and to inform his daughter of certain disquieting opinions enunciated by her husband on the previous evening at the inn. Adalbert was obviously under the dangerous influence of his recently returned friend whom he had even outstripped with utterances quite frankly incredible coming from the mouth of an official of the court, and which could generate all sorts of unpleasantness if not far worse consequences. Though the Duke himself may have gone to his eternal reward, the ducal council continued to hold its meeting, decree its ordinances, and pronounce its sentences. And the gamekeeper at Karolslust, as everyone knew, enforced the laws severely, to which poachers and firewood scavengers in particular could attest. Moreover, the young Duke's arrival was awaited any day now, and though no one knew anything unfavorable about him thus far, there was no way of predicting how he would conduct himself in his regency.

That evening when Adalbert came home, he flew into a temper, even before he had finished taking off his coat, and immediately, as had been his wont of late, began to expound on the injustices that townspeople and farmers alike had to suffer in German lands far and wide. He inveighed against the tithes and taxes that princes squeezed out of the toil and sweat of their subjects merely for the gratification of their own appetites, against their hunts that trampled farms and fields, against the shameful traffic that they promoted by selling the young men of their own land as mercenaries in America, and against their disgraceful goings-on with mistresses, the toleration of which meant a constant threat and humiliation to the women and maidens of the country. Agnes nodded in agreement, as was her custom, and also shook her blonde head to indicate how much she deplored these conditions. But as Adalbert, sitting on the edge of the bed, paused in his oration just long enough to pull off his boots, Agnes ventured a faint objection for the first time.

She remarked quite timidly that for as long as she could remember, neither she nor Adalbert, nor their relatives both close and distant, nor anyone in the whole town of Karolsmarkt and, if you think about it, in the entire dukedom, as far back as she could remember, had ever actually had to suffer any of the ills Adalbert had listed. Therefore, she could not quite understand why he was so suddenly incensed about matters which, when all is said and done, did not concern him in the least.

Adalbert, surprised by her unprecedented contradiction, countered caustically that she should surely be aware that he was endowed with the capacity to comprehend issues transcending his own destiny as well as that of relatives, friends, and fellow citizens, and that as long as the subject was raised anyway, conditions in their immediate vicinity were in no way as splendid as Agnes allowed herself to imagine. Furthermore, he found it truly curious that Agnes pretended to know nothing even of the notorious outrage that had spread itself out mockingly for years, yea, even for decades, within sight of her own home. Then suddenly he declared that the day was not far off on which the palace of Karolslust and quite a few other palaces of similar persuasion would disappear from the face of the earth. There would be an end to these pleasure domes that, like the very jaws of hell, devoured honorable women and maidens—for example, the sisters of his old friend, Tobias Klenk.

Startled, Agnes sat up in bed, her abundant blonde hair falling loosely about her shoulders. With ever increasing anxiety, she listened to the words of her husband, who delivered himself of further prophecies more savage than the first while storming about in his flowing dressing gown, with his wig askew and swinging his boots in his hands, so that the peaceful bedroom seemed to fill with the odor of fire and brimstone. At last he threw down the boots, shed the robe and the wig, and when he crammed a white nightcap down over his flushed brow and short, bristly hair, Agnes grasped the opportunity to ask an anxious question: Had his compassion for poor tormented humanity ultimately seduced him into making such fearful predictions in the presence of people who might not be clever enough to understand his noble intentions or who would misconstrue his ideas, or who, given the chance, might even be impelled by spite and envy to exploit them against him?

Adalbert rolled his eyes, flipped his pillow twice for no apparent reason before laying his head on it, turned toward Agnes, and sneeringly answered her question with a question: What do you take me for, a man or a mouse? Then, stretching one arm in front of him as if to ward off any reply, and without bestowing so much as a further glance upon Agnes, he pulled the covers up over his chin, turned his face away, and fell asleep much faster than Agnes expected or even thought possible after such a passionately violent eruption.

• II •

On the following morning he showed not the slightest effect of the previous evening's excitement. After a hasty breakfast, he said goodbye to his wife, who was still resting in bed, casually kissed her forehead, and left the house in his dignified judicial robes, his hat and cane in his hand, and his head held high. He appeared to be a completely different person from the fierce revolutionary whose words and behavior had shocked Agnes into a state of terror during the previous night.

She became increasingly calmer as the day wore on, and when Adalbert returned from his sessions, he seemed to be his old self again. With his customary air of self-importance, he related the various indifferent events of the day in the marketplace and throughout the land, and he told Agnes of all the thoroughly perspicacious judicial decisions he had handed down. When, after the evening meal, he settled back cozily in his easy chair, folded his hands over his stomach, and then drew Agnes close to him with apparent intimation that he was not averse to connubial tenderness, she allowed herself high hopes of actually being able to keep her husband at home today without particular difficulty.

But suddenly, in an instant when she least expected it, he jumped up with a crafty smile, as if he had intentionally lulled his unsuspecting wife into a false sense of security. Without any further explanation and seeming to delight in her disappointment, he picked up his hat and cane, and with hardly a word to her, bounded out the door.

Agnes was still disquieted when Adalbert returned, again long after midnight and, as could easily be seen, in the same or even a fouler frame of mind than on the days before. For all of its inherent rashness, his outburst of yesterday had still managed to preserve a certain decorum and coherence, but today he could bring forth only disjointed and chaotic sentence fragments in the midst of which ominous words would resound all too distinctly through the room. When he burst forth without warning in an almost blasphemous curse the like of which Agnes had never heard cross his teeth, her head shot up from her pillow and she cried out as if suddenly enlightened by a searing insight, "It's all crystal clear to me now, Adalbert; they're trying to destroy you!"

He stood there with his mouth hanging open and babbled something indistinctly, and she, taking advantage of his perplexed state, hurriedly and beseechingly unburdened her heart of all that had lain on it so heavily for so long, and she was surprised by the ease with which her words flowed from her lips. Directly to his face she told him that he had obviously become entangled in a dark, secret plot, and that the conspirators, as whose emissary that horrible Tobias Klenk had reappeared, surely had nothing less in mind than to exploit his courage, his cleverness, and especially his official position in order to attain their nefarious objectives. But she could no longer bring herself to stand idly by and merely watch this self-destructive urge of his. He was an official of the court, a husband, some day maybe a father; it was not his obligation to purge Germany of whatever ills might be besetting it, but of which there were far fewer to perceive in their dukedom than in those elsewhere. This was the work of bachelors or of soldiers of fortune, people with nothing to lose, who were not responsible for the destinies of women and children.

"Have you lost your wits?" Adalbert screamed.

"I wish I had as little cause to doubt your wits as you have to question mine," she replied. "I honestly don't know what sort of wicked spirit has gotten into you of late. There were, of course, all kinds of bad things one could say about the old Duke, even if we, for our part, never had to suffer any evil at all, but for as long as he lived, it never occurred to you to give out with such gruesome, bloodcurdling tirades. And now that we may well have fallen upon better times under a young prince of whom no one has ever heard a damaging word—a man who might make ours the most fortunate dukedom in the realm—you start preaching revolution, arson, and assassination."

Adalbert stood across from her with his eyes opening ever wider, and the uninhibited flow of her words amazed him even more than their boldness. "How do you happen to know that the new Duke has already arrived?" he asked her threateningly.

Her eyes lit up. "Is he here?" she cried out.

"What business of yours is it," he shouted, "whether or not he's here?"

"He *is* here!" And she made it sound like a cheer.

"Who divulged this information to you?"

She laughed. "No one other than you yourself. Is it supposed to be a secret—or only a secret from me?"

"He didn't arrive at the palace until noon," Adalbert screamed. "We didn't get the news at the inn until just before I left. So, how do you explain that you already know?" He sat down next to her on the bed, clasped both her hands, and stared her frighteningly in the eye.

"Why are you in such a rage, Adalbert?" she asked, and wondered why she kept feeling less and less afraid of him. "Shouldn't I be happy about it? Shouldn't all of us be happy that our young ruler has finally arrived?"

"What do you care whether he's young or old?" he spit out to her face.

"Twenty-six," she said quite ingenuously. "The last time he visited the province, he was twenty-one, and that was exactly five years ago."

He glowered at her. "Do you know him, Agnes?"

She burst out laughing merrily. "Just as well as you do—as we all do. Shouldn't I know the Duke's heir?"

"Have you seen him?"

"What's wrong with you, Adalbert? Should I have blindfolded myself when he used to ride through our little town on his way to the hunt? Even that happened seldom enough. His bearing was so noble; his appearance was so gentle; his face was so radiant. Adalbert, a man who looks like that cannot possibly bring us any misfortune."

And once again he shrieked at her. Had she gone completely mad? What made her believe that the young sovereign was cut from different cloth than the rest of the noble gentlemen? Even if some of them did show promise of something better in their youth, once they took the reins they behaved exactly as had their fathers and grandfathers before them. Wasn't that the way it happened hundreds of times? And as far as the new Duke was concerned, what did it matter if he had been the friend of scholars and writers in Paris; he had, at the same time, been carrying on shamelessly with wenches of the worst stripe. And considering the style of life he had been leading, there was no good reason to assume that he had been spared that abomination which is not known for nothing as the "French disease." In any event, his first official act after his investiture would probably be to put the House of the Arbormaidens into operation again. The word was out that Karolslust was feverishly being made ready for its new master, from which one might also conclude that the entire court from the prime minister down to the gamekeeper knew exactly what to expect from the young princeling.

"And haven't you heard that it is once again strictly forbidden to come within a hundred paces of the little summer palace and that no one is to be permitted to show himself as requested

Ungar

250 Park Avenue South, New York, N. Y. 10003

REVIEW COPY

Title THE LITTLE COMEDY AND OTHER STORIES

Author Arthur Schnitzler

Publication Date February 28, 1978

Price Cloth $10.00; Paper $3.95

Five stories by the famous Viennese writer--in English for the first time

acting & death – 198
M. from sickbed to window – 200
yearns for crowds – 201
hated Alfred – 203
well-being – 205
high values – 206
routine – no art, no recovery – 210
a dying man – no homeland – 213
Are you ready? – 219
he senses disappear – 221
I'll take you w. me – 226
peace she possesses in her death – 228
the restoration before death – 229
L thank you – 231
[illegible] – pianist, – 231
dies seeing Marie & a man (Alfred) – alone – 239

SCHNITZLER
~~LEUTNANT~~
DO YOU REMEMBER
VIENNA?

within range of the hunting preserve while carrying a weapon? They're probably already herding together all the game in the area for him and his fine cronies. And as to our poor peasants, may God help them for the duration of the hunting season."

Agnes lay there with childlike, open eyes and listened almost as calmly as a schoolgirl anxious to learn from her teacher, and without revealing the slightest misgiving or even venturing a single contradiction. And so Adalbert might gradually have begun to believe that he had succeeded in convincing her that the facts he had related were true, and also that his opinions were infallible. And in this belief, he calmed himself. The pressure exerted by his hands became noticeably gentler, and what burned within him was no longer his wrath, but a more tender fire whose flame was even more vigorously fanned by those eyes that he had never before seen so brightly aglow.

Yet, when he finally lay down by her side, Agnes seemed already to have fallen into a deep sleep—much to his disappointment. As he tried to wake her with a tender kiss on the forehead, she brushed her hand across her brow and curled up under the covers like a small child whose slumber had been disturbed by a fly. She was still sleeping in that position when Adalbert awoke the following morning, got up, cleared his throat quite audibly, wandered around the room, ate breakfast, and threw on his official garb. And she remained fast asleep when he finally left the house and the door fell shut behind him, not without appreciable noise.

Soon after his departure, Agnes also left the house and proceeded to the marketplace. The streets were as quiet as usual; the young woman's conversations with the acquaintances she chanced to meet and with the shopkeepers she patronized were as bland as ever; and even though the small talk invariably got around to the topic of the young Duke's return, no one seemed to be particularly excited about something that was, after all, an inevitable and natural part of the course of events.

Agnes also stopped in briefly at the apothecary shop, where

she told her father that she had gotten her husband's word of honor that he would henceforth refrain from making provocative statements at the inn. To her complete amazement, she learned that on the evening before, Adalbert had indulged in more than just a little to drink, but that he had not chimed in as heretofore in Tobias Klenk's running chatter, prattle that the Golden Ox regulars were now considering absurd and that was beginning to elicit derisive laughter.

Then Agnes visited one of her friends who, some years ago when she was still a young girl, had confided in her that she could think of no lovelier lot in life than to become an arbormaiden. But shortly thereafter, at about the same time as Agnes, she had married, had since borne two children, and now devoted herself completely to her responsibilities as a wife and mother. Without knowing exactly why, Agnes felt tempted today to bring those harmlessly lubricious adolescent fantasies back into her friend's consciousness by relating Adalbert's stated suspicion of the previous evening that the young Duke would reinstitute Karolslust's former purpose without delay, but she articulated it as if it were an absolute certainty. Her friend seemed hardly able to comprehend exactly what Agnes meant. The judge's wife was embarrassed, felt her cheeks and neck reddening, and only now began to understand what she had expressed and why. All of a sudden, "arbormaiden" was no longer just a word, as it had once been. It was an image that loomed before her, and the sight of it sent an inexplicably pleasant shiver down her spine. Until this moment she had never lamented not yet having any children. All at once, it filled her with pain, and in the next instant, that feeling metamorphosed into a reproach against Adalbert. After a quick goodbye to her friend, she stood in the street again and sensed a trembling of restless anticipation in the air, though it was an early summer's day like many an other that had never given her especial cause for excitement. Why should I be so concerned that the young Duke is back again, she asked herself. Had Adalbert not talked such foolishness about him, I wouldn't give him a second thought. And that also turned into a reproach against Adalbert.

He, however, seemed to be well aware how much his image had dimmed of late in his wife's eyes. During the noonday meal, he showed a less boisterous, an even self-conscious bearing, as if he wanted to wipe out even the memory of the impression his conduct had made in the two foregoing days. Quite abruptly, between the soup and the main course, he made casual mention of a rumor going about that the young Duke would soon announce his engagement to a princess of Württemberg, but the tone of his voice betrayed not the slightest hint that he was speaking about the same man who was the subject of an entirely different conversation between him and Agnes only yesterday. And Agnes replied with only an apathetic, "Oh, really?" and without the slightest change of facial expression.

After dinner, he occupied himself with some documents he had brought home from the office, and Agnes became aware that the possibility of Adalbert's renouncing his customary evening at the inn did not exactly delight her. In fact, when Adalbert did leave the house at dusk, she sighed with relief, and she made up her mind that no matter the hour or with what attendant clatter he came home, she would pretend to be fast asleep.

However, she really did fall asleep, and so she also really awoke when Adalbert stood by her bedside around midnight, and he could not help but notice that she opened her eyes and blinked. He appeared to have been awaiting this moment, and in calm but weighty measures he launched into a report of the incident that was the sole topic of discussion among the patrons of The Golden Ox that day.

Tobias Klenk, in possession of a rifle, was apprehended in the forest adjacent to Karolslust and was taken into custody at the command of the chief gamekeeper for suspicion of poaching. Furthermore, for resisting arrest and for violent assault against the gamekeeper's helpers, he was taken in chains to the

Karolsmarkt prison. Tomorrow he would be brought up before the judge—before *him,* Adalbert Wogelein.

"What are you going to do?" Agnes asked anxiously.

"I can't say, not before I have interrogated the accused."

"But, Adalbert, you yourself just said that Tobias Klenk was poaching and that he conducted himself violently against the authorities. Otherwise they surely would not have taken him to jail in shackles. In any case, you'll be compelled to convict him and hand down a stiff sentence."

"The poaching remains to be proved," Adalbert countered while furrowing his brow. "And as far as violent assault against officers who outnumbered him three to one is concerned, I am not yet convinced it wasn't a matter of self-defense. In any event, I am not about to hand down any decision merely to curry favor with a gamekeeper or even with the Duke himself, nor do I intend to adjudicate according to the letter of an untenable law. I shall dispense true justice. And even if Tobias Klenk had every intention of shooting a stag for his poor mother—yes, even if he did knock down one of the royal lackeys who tried to lay hands on him—the primary investigative question I shall raise is whether those who confiscated his property, the rifle, and physically attacked him, handcuffed him, and put him in leg irons should not also be called to account."

"Adalbert," she cried out, and there was terror in her eyes.

But he interpreted her gaze as something resembling admiration, so he went on imperturbably: "I have just been deliberating whether I should not remove Tobias Klenk's shackles or even order his release forthwith and without further ado, but upon deeper reflection it seems just and proper to me that this case be tried openly and in public."

"What exactly do you have in mind, Adalbert?"

"If you are afraid, Agnes, feel free to remove yourself to the house of your father, the mayor, this very day yet, so that you will not have to bear the possible consequences of my actions with me." He felt himself growing taller by the minute.

"I would never, ever leave you, Adalbert, but," she stretched out her hands imploringly, "I beg you once more to consider—"

"I have considered everything, Agnes, and I have only one regret, namely, that this trial will be held in our little town rather than in the capital, or better yet, before the imperial court in Wetzlar. Nevertheless, it may well come to pass that my pronouncement will spread far beyond here and that my decision will kindle a torch whose flame will illuminate all of Germany."

"Adalbert," she exclaimed, "you're sacrificing yourself to your friendship for Tobias Klenk."

Adalbert extended himself to his full height. "Whether Tobias or another, whether friend or foe, it makes no difference."

"You're rushing headlong into your own ruin, Adalbert, and you're taking me with you."

And yet while she was saying even this, it seemed to him once again that he could discern a ray of shy admiration gleaming from the depth of her gaze, and he was moved to claim the reward for his daring from her lips. He leaned close to her, but she winced and pulled back as the wine fumes greeted her. When he moved closer toward her, she suddenly burst into tears. Adalbert found himself incapable of soothing her, and though it made him sick at heart, he finally had to let her go.

• III •

The courtroom was housed on the ground floor of a spacious old building in the marketplace. When Adalbert entered it the following morning, the clerk gave him the customary schedule of cases set for that day. First, two citizens between whom a claim for payment was pending were called to the bench. After taking the testimony of both parties and three witnesses, Adalbert adjudicated to the best of his knowledge and belief against the plaintiff, whose claim he dismissed because it had outrun the statute of limitations. Next, two youths were brought before him. They had inflicted considerable injury upon each other during a brawl, but having made their peace during their confinement while awaiting trial, they could not understand why nevertheless each of them, according to the judge's sentence, should have to go to jail for several weeks with bread and water.

While they were being led away, news arrived at the courtroom that the young Duke had just appeared in Karolsmarkt unaccompanied by any retinue, had dismounted in front of the schoolhouse, and was now observing a class. Adalbert got his information from the clerk, a middle-aged man who, though not at all well educated, was quite shrewd and with whom he often liked to discuss convoluted cases. The clerk now told the judge that on the preceding day, that is to say, shortly after his arrival at the capital, the Duke had already paid surprise visits to certain state offices and public institutions, which did not sit very well with several councilors and employees.

Adalbert felt a chill go down his back, but without responding in any way whatsoever to the clerk's information, proceeded to the next case.

Standing before the judge was a tramp, a pitiable looking, emaciated, elderly man, who had stayed overnight at a widow's house and was under suspicion of having stolen all kinds of tools belonging to her late husband, as well as some groceries. While he was miserably and tearfully swearing by all that was holy that he had never in his entire life stolen so much as would fit under a single fingernail, the door flew open, a young boy stood there, and he shouted breathlessly, "His Grace, the Duke!"

Adalbert lost not a jot of his composure, ordered the clerk, who had jumped up, to sit back down, and prepared to put another question to the tramp as the Duke entered. He was dressed in black, elegant but without any show of pomp, slim and stately, young, but looking older than his years.

Adalbert Wogelein arose and was about to approach the Duke that he might greet him with the reverence that was his due. He, however, said in a voice that was rather soft but most pleasing to the ear, "I charge you, your honor, to carry on the duties of your office exactly as if I were not present." In like manner he directed the bailiff, who was trying to hold back the pressing crowd, to permit as many people to enter as could find seats. He just allowed the clerk to provide him with a chair, but placed it himself so that he would be sitting at the judge's side and somewhat behind him.

Without a quiver in his voice, Adalbert Wogelein resumed his interrogation. After the tramp continued to deny all the allegations and the widow insisted that no one else could possibly be the culprit, Adalbert handed down his decision: there being no shred of evidence that the accused was in possession of any of the purportedly stolen articles, he was to be released, but he was also to leave the town at once and the province within twenty-four hours. Then, he simply said, "Next," in the same way he always did when he was ready to hear a new case, and thus demonstrated his lack of anxiety at the Duke's presence, while at the same time he felt considerable satisfaction that he had thereby acted according to the Duke's explicitly announced wishes.

Without awaiting the summons of the bailiff, who was still occupied with the tramp, Tobias Klenk stepped forth, dressed in tailor made raiment once fit for a gentleman, but now thoroughly worn out and somewhat incongruous with his high, yellow boots. His dark hair hung in a tangle over his deeply knit brow, his stare was arrogant and not without malice, and he looked bizarre and almost menacing. Completely ignoring the Duke's presence, he stepped right up in front of the judge and said to him in a cutting but not quite rude tone of voice, "First of all, Adalbert, my friend, I would like to be rid of these handcuffs."

Murmuring and muttering filled the tightly crowded room. The people looked toward the Duke, who sat motionless with crossed arms, and only then toward the judge.

And the judge spoke: "The handcuffs would have been removed before your arraignment had you shown the patience to await being called. But your friend, Tobias Klenk, wherever else I may be that, here in this courtroom I am not."

Tobias was released from his fetters at the judge's nod, which simultaneously directed the clerk to read the indictment against Tobias Klenk. The clerk had hardly risen from his chair when Tobias grabbed the sheet of paper from his hand, crumpled it, and threw it on the table. I hope he won't make this too difficult for me, Adalbert thought to himself.

"What do I care about this piece of paper!" Tobias shouted. "Where are those louts who took away my rifle, beat me, and put me in handcuffs and irons? Where are the gamekeeper's helpers? And where is the chief gamekeeper himself? I have business to transact with them, but not with this piece of paper."

"Tobias Klenk," Adalbert Wogelein said, and he hoped that no one would notice the quiet trembling of his voice, "I warn you to be mindful of the dignity of these chambers, all the more so today because they have been distinguished by the presence of His Grace, our most illustrious Duke."

I shouldn't have said that, he thought to himself immediately, and already he heard the Duke's gentle but firm voice: "My presence is irrelevant to the case at issue, your honor." Then with an easy gesture, he rejected the all too deep and plainly sarcastic obeisance with which Tobias Klenk condescendingly bowed as if he had only now taken notice of the Duke.

With a quick glance, Adalbert Wogelein directed that the indictment be read, whereupon the clerk meticulously unfolded the crumpled paper that he had already retrieved, and began:

"While making my official rounds through the ducal hunting preserve this afternoon, I found myself scarcely a hundred paces from the enclosed park when I, the undersigned official ducal chief gamekeeper Franz Sever von Wolfenstein, met Tobias Klenk, citizen of Karolsmarkt in bad repute, born here but usually not in residence—" (At this point, Tobias laughed out loud and Adalbert shook his head with obvious displeasure; no one could tell whether in response to Tobias's laughter or the gamekeeper's remark concerning Tobias's reputation.) "—with hunting rifle in hand. Although empowered and possibly obliged by existing law to relieve the aforementioned Tobias Klenk of his weapon immediately and to take him into custody forthwith, I first gave him fair warning and requested that he depart at once from the game preserve on which he had obviously trespassed only for purposes of poaching. Only after he countered my order with insolent and even threatening words did I whistle for reinforcements, whereupon Kuno Waldhaber and Franz Rebler, gamekeepers who were nearby, rushed to my aid, disarmed the aforementioned Tobias Klenk, and put him in irons because he was swinging his fists, kicking wildly, and generally behaving like a raving lunatic. Thereupon, I ordered that he be taken to the Karolsmarkt jail so that he could be brought before a proper court which would give him the full measure of the law, try him, and sentence him on the following three counts, to wit: (1) unauthorized carrying of firearms in the ducal game preserve; (2) premeditated poaching; and (3) acts of violence against on-duty representatives of the Duke."

As soon as the clerk had finished reading, Adalbert Wogelein turned to question the accused. "Is your name Tobias Klenk?"

"As surely as yours is Adalbert Wogelein."

"Age: thirty-three. Unmarried—"

"And hope to remain so."

"Your profession?"

"Aren't you tired of asking these superfluous questions, Adalbert?"

"My duty is to ask questions, as it is yours to answer them."

"So, let the record state: what he was is nobody's business; what he may some day be, he himself cannot yet predict; what he *is* should be apparent to anyone at first sight—and anyone to whom it is not, won't be helped by an explanation."

"Your wit is somewhat time-consuming," Adalbert Wogelein observed. A sidelong glance at the Duke led him to believe that he had noticed a smile, so he continued lightly: "On my own responsibility, I shall therefore record the following: currently unemployed."

"But why, Wogelein, old friend? I thought *your* job was asking questions and *mine* was answering them. I can't help myself any more than you can; we are both subject to the same legal code. But I almost believe that I feel more comfortable than you do."

Soft murmuring spread through the room. Adalbert Wogelein sat motionless. And in spite of all this, I shall acquit him, he thought, no matter what the consequences. "Do you confess your guilt, Tobias Klenk?" he asked.

"No," Tobias Klenk rejoined.

"So, you deny the accuracy of the chief gamekeeper's signed and sworn testimony that has just been read to you?"

"Not at all, insofar as the factual particulars of the report are concerned, but I dispute the allegation that these facts imply any guilt."

"The first thing with which you are charged is carrying a weapon, specifically a hunting rifle, in the ducal game preserve, whereby you have wilfully and deliberately disobeyed a strict law."

"I know that it is prohibited, but I object strenuously to the notion that a man must subject himself unconditionally to all legal prohibitions, no matter how senseless. Any absolute ruler could suddenly take it in his head to decree that henceforth no one wearing yellow boots may tread upon his gamelands, or that no subject of his may wear a vest with more than three buttons. What is your opinion, Adalbert Wogelein? Would I—or would you—be bound to abide by such a law just because some duke or some chief gamekeeper happened to decree it?"

"Such laws would indeed be senseless," Adalbert replied, "but the assumption that a sovereign would even be capable of ordaining such laws implies, as it were, insult to princely authority. But the point at issue here is the injunction against bearing arms, which is in no way senseless. In fact, as everyone knows, it has the obvious purpose of preventing poaching."

"I declare all prohibitive laws insane," said Tobias, "that arbitrarily restrict the freedom of thousands of enslaved people for the benefit of one mighty overlord. And I want no part of a world in which one person is invested with unlimited power to command while a hundred thousand others are condemned to obey him; a world in which the man who eats roast venison whenever he feels like it, and without paying for it, even has the right to have another man thrown into jail merely for being suspected of desiring roast venison."

The whispering and muttering began to swell all around. Adalbert Wogelein's neck and forehead began to feel uncomfortably warm, for the sentence that Tobias Klenk had just uttered bore enough resemblance to make it interchangeable with one that he himself had pronounced across a table at the Golden Ox only a few days ago. Nevertheless, he kept his composure and commented with a discreet smile: "Tobias Klenk, this is a philosophy you might wish to discuss with scholars and statesmen or with whoever happens to be sitting around a table with you at an inn. In the presence of this court, only the incident at issue is germane, and concerning that, I have no choice other than to equate your answers thus far with a confession that you entered the ducal preserve with your rifle because . . . it was an inexpensive way to provide yourself with a venison roast."

"Don't put words in my mouth, Adalbert. There are all kinds of motives for carrying firearms, sometimes even defending oneself. There is no proof that I was carrying the weapon for the alleged purpose of poaching."

"Regarding this, the court will decide," Adalbert announced quickly, and added: "We come now to the third item in the indictment: that you resisted surrendering your arms and assaulted the ducal gamekeepers."

"I will also admit to that—but that does not in any way make me guilty of a crime. The rifle is my property, and as honestly acquired by me as many a game preserve and adjacent territories were obtained by many a German prince. No man has the right to demand that I give him my property, much less to tear it away from me. But surely I was justified in protecting my own skin when I was attacked by two heavily armed louts who were in no peril of incurring any sort of punishment, even if they had killed me on that occasion."

"We can assume with certainty," Adalbert said softly, "that no harm would have been done you, had you submitted willingly, Tobias Klenk."

"I am not an acquiescent sort of man even when I know I am not completely within my rights. Do you expect me to be one when I am treated with injustice and violence?"

Adalbert Wogelein became uneasy when he realized that the proceedings were drawing to a close and that it was not only Tobias Klenk's destiny that his verdict might determine. "So, therefore you admit," he said, "that you resisted arrest with violent action. Have you anything to state on this count that might vindicate your behavior?"

"I have no need for vindication, because I am not guilty of anything. As a matter of fact, *I* would like to press charges. First of all, I accuse—"

Adalbert interrupted him with urgency. "If you have charges to bring, you should do so at a suitable time and through the appropriate channels and procedures. There are still four cases awaiting my judgment today. This trial must conclude."

Tobias started in all over again. "I accuse—"

"Silence!" Adalbert Wogelein shouted, and thought to himself: there is no way to help him—or myself.

"First of all," Tobias Klenk bellowed, "I accuse the two

deputy wardens, Kuno Waldhaber and Franz Rebler; second, the chief gamekeeper, Franz Sever von Wolfenstein; and finally—"

Go on, keep it up, Adalbert Wogelein mused. He's digging his own grave . . . and that might save me . . .

"—and finally," Tobias screamed, "I charge the sovereign of this state, the Duke—"

"Enough!" Adalbert Wogelein exclaimed, his voice raised, while all eyes turned with intense curiosity toward the Duke, whose expression manifested not the slightest movement. "Charges against the head of state are inadmissible in this court. Nevertheless, any subject who feels that his honor or his well-being has been done injury by anyone whosoever, even by the sovereign of his state, has the right to bring charges in the imperial court at Wetzlar." He breathed a sigh of relief, for now he had gone as far as he possibly could to meet this presumptuous and brazen man halfway. "Now, insofar as the matter to be adjudicated today is concerned,"—he rose—"so say I, Adalbert Wogelein, judge of Karolsmarkt, to you, Tobias Klenk, in the name of his Grace, our most illustrious Duke: In accordance with your own admission, this court finds you guilty on the following three counts: First, for carrying an unauthorized weapon; second, for attempted poaching; and third, for violent assault against officials in the service of His Grace, the Duke. That you were apprehended in the ducal preserve with hunting rifle in hand, you yourself cannot deny. That you were carrying it for any purpose other than poaching is totally unbelievable. That you violently resisted arrest and thereby imperiled both life and limb of individuals exercising their official duty has also been established. Therefore, I sentence you"—he hesitated, because he now realized that he was about to hand down a decision that would seal his own fate—"to prison for one year's duration, thereafter to be banished into exile."

At this moment Adalbert was prepared for numerous possibilities. He thought it just as likely that Tobias Klenk would denounce him as an accomplice in conspiracy as that he would rush at him and physically attack him. He looked piercingly into Tobias's eyes, hoping to keep him in check with his stare, but in Tobias's returning gaze he could perceive nothing other than an expression of boundless contempt. Yet it seemed even more uncanny to him that the Duke still sat as silent and immobile as ever, with his arms crossed over his chest.

Adalbert signaled the bailiff to take away the condemned man. Tobias turned, strode toward the door, and without deeming the judge, the Duke, or any of the onlookers worthy of so much as a single glance, marched out. Everyone else remained in the courtroom and sat as if transfixed by the wordless, motionless bearing of the Duke, and though they looked nervously at one another, no one moved.

Adalbert felt as if he had been isolated in a vacuum, and he uttered his habitual "Next!" almost unconsciously. He picked up a document lying before him, turned to the clerk as if to tell him something pertaining to it, and took advantage of this opportunity to whisper: "Be sure that Tobias is locked in one of the lower, absolutely secure cellar cells." The clerk nodded and got up to leave as a peasant entered, accompanied by his wife who accused her husband of abusing her.

While Adalbert Wogelein was still asking the preliminary questions of the couple, the Duke arose. When Adalbert did the same, the Duke gestured for him to sit down, and he said gently, "Please, do not allow yourself to be disturbed, your honor." He waved farewell all around, departed as he had arrived, and bestowed not even a solitary word which might have expressed his satisfaction or his disapproval. Before leaving, he gestured graciously, though without smiling, toward the judge, who nevertheless could not manage to let himself feel particularly happy about this.

When the crowd began to flock after the Duke, Adalbert reprimanded them, brusquely called the court to order, and resumed his interrogation of the farmer and his wife. The clerk returned and gave the judge a look signifying that his order had been delivered and carried out. Adalbert Wogelein concluded the case of the discordant couple hastily and somewhat peevishly, dispatched the remaining lawsuits with even greater alacrity, recessed the court earlier than usual, obtained the turnkey's assurance that Tobias was being held under maximum security, and warned once again that under no circumstances was any precautionary measure to be overlooked in the guarding of Tobias Klenk, but then added that he should be generously supplied with food and drink.

On the street he learned that the Duke had, in the meantime called on several craftsmen, among them a goldsmith from whom he bought a few ornaments and a turner from whom he purchased a chess set, and that he was currently in the church—not, as it happened, to say his prayers, but to listen to an impromptu recital by the schoolmaster, known far and wide as a highly skilled organist. The mighty resonances thrummed in Adalbert's ears as he passed the church. Except for the Duke's waiting carriage, the street was almost empty, for the crowd had followed him into the sanctuary.

· IV ·

It was an oppressively humid day, more so than was usual this early in the season. Not a breath of air was stirring, and Adalbert was exceedingly uncomfortable in body and spirit. Although he had to affirm to himself that he had conducted himself with as much cleverness and dignity as was at all possible in his unspeakably difficult situation, he not only felt strangely unsure of himself but disconcerted as never before. He called upon his conscience to ask whether he might not have handed down a different verdict had the Duke not attended the trial. And this raised a second question: might not Tobias Klenk, in the first place, have behaved differently?—whether more agreeably or more outrageously was, of course, difficult to say. Well, whatever the case, it was impossible, on the face of the evidence, to let Tobias Klenk go free without some kind of sentence, and it did not make much difference whether he put him under lock and key for a half year or a whole one.

What tormented Judge Wogelein most grievously was that he had boasted to his wife that no matter what, he would let Tobias go scot-free. But then again, did not this intention of his terrify her beyond belief, and would she not be relieved to hear that Tobias Klenk did not in any way deny his guilt, and that his conduct in court had been so outrageously defiant and provocative that it seemed to be his clear purpose to bring the most severe sentence possible upon his head? What kind of hidden reason could lie behind his behavior? Was it only his confounded boastfulness? Or honest and righteous indignation? Or, just nothing more than a malicious impulse to get his old friend and schoolmate, Judge Adalbert Wogelein, into hot water?

The thought chilled him to the marrow. After all, what did he know of the Duke's real character and actual temperament? Had not the clerk, only this morning, dropped all manner of hints about the unpleasantness befalling certain officials in the capital? And whether one was dealing with a kind, possibly even magnanimous sovereign or with a crafty and cruel overlord remained to be seen. And it was by no means outside the realm of possibility that the constables were already waiting outside Judge Wogelein's house to drag him off to some dungeon for conspiring with a brazen rascal who was a clear and present danger to the state. Lulled into an insidiously false sense of security by the inscrutable but affable manner of the Duke, Adalbert had hardly weighed his horrible danger in the balance. Was it not advisable to take the necessary precautions, insofar as that was still a possibility? Should he not seek an immediate audience with the Duke and explain to him that this was not the way in which matters were generally handled in Judge Wogelein's courtroom, as one might have suspected after witnessing the idle chatter and reprehensible conduct of Tobias Klenk? He was an honest and loyal, even if a self-willed, courageously thinking official of the dukedom, one who had never in his entire life been guilty of any misconduct.

And only now Adalbert reached the point of real bitterness. What a terrible lunatic this Tobias was! Whatever could have possessed him to give the impression of being a revolutionary, yea, even to admit to being one, right in front of the Duke? And before the time was ripe for such boldness! Had he not aroused suspicion in the very circles where legal steps could be taken to track down conspiracies, nip them in the bud, and punish the instigators most cruelly? Moreover, what sort of conspiracy was this anyhow that Tobias was always talking about in such dark tones? Who were these comrades who were only waiting for the right signs, and *where* were they? And what were these "right signs" they were supposedly awaiting? Was it not possible that Tobias had ultimately become afraid of the consequences of certain obligations he had committed himself to fulfilling, of oaths he may have solemnly sworn? Did he simply allow himself to be imprisoned that he might be immune to the warnings and orders of his accomplices? And now he, Adalbert Wogelein, had to bear the responsibility alone, having become, so to speak, a conspirator himself—he, of all people, who in essence knew next to nothing about this whole business, and understood little about it.

If Tobias could be believed, these conspirators were even now deployed throughout the entire German empire where they were waiting and hiding in numerous locations. What if they were to show up in Karolsmarkt and call him to account for having thrown Tobias Klenk into prison?

Beads of sweat glistened on his forehead. Danger wherever he looked. It was enough to drive a man mad. He had walked so quickly that he could already see his house, the last at the edge of town. It looked so peaceful and bright, and the blooming lilacs in the garden beckoned to him in the rays of the late afternoon's tranquillity, even though little gray clouds were beginning to appear at the edge of the sky. Well, it certainly didn't look as if any arresting officers were lurking in ambush here.

But then another worry, almost more alarming than its predecessors, suddenly struck him: he had to admit to himself that he was frankly terrified of his impending confrontation with Agnes. When he had left the house in the morning, she was still lying in bed, and an inexplicable embarrassment had come over him when she looked at him with a peculiar gaze which seemed to reflect not the slightest recollection of the previous evening. She had proffered her forehead for his morning kiss and immediately thereafter turned her back and closed her eyes, as if she were not in the least prepared to admit that a new day had begun. How would she receive him now? How would she respond to what he had to tell her?

He found Agnes sitting by the bay window, looking out toward the woods which began only a few paces from the house and extended to Karolslust and beyond. Her crocheting rested in her lap. At other times she would interrupt her work and walk toward him as soon as she heard the sound of his steps, but today she appeared at first not even to notice his homecoming. Then, all of a sudden, she got up, ran toward him, and threw her arms around his neck with an impetuousness to which she was not ordinarily given. At first he was taken aback, but then he felt relieved as he thought: she already knows; she has heard with what honor and dignity I comported myself today, and she is proud of her husband. He handed his hat and coat to the maid, and cheerfully remarked, "I hope dinner is ready. I may say, I brought home a hearty appetite."

Once the maid had left the room, Agnes reached up half playfully to take off her husband's wig, as she had sometimes done before. But he would not put up with that, and he kept it on his head as if, somehow, that would assure his dignity.

"Well, how did everything go today?" he asked good-humoredly. "A lot done around the house and in the garden? Receive any company?"

She said no. He was surprised. If no one had been there, how did she know? And if she did not know, what was making her so happy? So, he asked her cautiously: "What's the matter with you, my dear? I've never known you to be in such high spirits and at the same time so close-mouthed."

"Just think, Adalbert," she said, and her eyes fairly sparkled, "immediately after you left this morning—I had just arisen—the Duke drove by and waved to me in greeting."

Adalbert Wogelein was furious to the point of bursting, but he did not let on. Turning his face away, he said, "There is nothing very remarkable about that. What choice has he other than to drive by our house when he is traveling from the capital to the marketplace by way of Karolslust?"

"And just think, Adalbert, I didn't even recognize him right away. I thought it must be some courtier or attendant, someone like that. It wasn't until he smiled and greeted me that I realized that it must be *he* and none other. And then I made a deep curtsy." Reliving the memory, she curtsied again and remained in that position for some time.

"You did the right thing by curtsying so politely," said Adalbert, still suppressing his fury. "Of course, it must have looked somewhat ludicrous if you blushed as much then, when you did it, as now when you're telling about it."

Restraining himself with great difficulty, he put his arm around her waist, and while she gave him a strange sidelong glance, he led her to the table where soup had just been served.

Agnes ladled it out and said, "It may well be that I looked slightly laughable, because he turned back toward me, smiled, and waved to me again." She raised her hand to demonstrate exactly how the Duke had waved.

"You don't say!" Adalbert exclaimed, vigorously stirring his soup. "He actually waved to you? How gracious and courteous of him! Of course, had it been Aunt Katherine standing in the window, the Duke would never have bothered to turn around; he might barely have greeted her; maybe he wouldn't even have paid that estimable lady any mind at all." And Adalbert laughed, a little too uproariously.

"What are you talking about, Adalbert? Do you really believe he waved only in response to my youth, my blonde hair, and my smooth-skinned face? Surely he greets all his people, women and men, young or old, in the same fashion. Oh, if you had only seen him! Such goodness, such nobility, such cheerfulness in his gaze! It made me feel happy all day long. Not only for myself, Adalbert, but for all of us!"

"Honestly, Agnes, can you really manage to read all that in his countenance? It must be my fault that I find myself incapable of doing likewise. Of course, that may distinctly be possible because I was not treated to that smile of his. All I got to see was the accursed grimacing of his tyrannical face."

Her soup spoon came to a halt between plate and lip. "What are you saying? You saw the Duke, Adalbert?"

"Again I ask you, what on earth is so remarkable about that? Did you think he made himself invisible in the marketplace? Or maybe you believe he visited only the school, the mayor's office, and the church—or that all he bought was a chess set and a few little necklaces and rings, and had the organist play for him? He was also in court, as well he should have been, and he had the special grace to observe me in the execution of my office for a good hour or more."

She grew pale. "And you didn't tell me that at once, Adalbert? What did you mean just a moment ago when you spoke about 'accursedness' and a 'tyrannical face'? Speak, Adalbert! Tell me! I feel as if I no longer have any reason to be happy. Was he there when you presided over Tobias Klenk's case? Tell me, Adalbert! Did you really declare Tobias not guilty?"

Adalbert wrinkled his brow. "If I did not, it was only to protect him from even grimmer consequences." And while pushing his plate away, he said, "You might as well know, Agnes, that it was because of Tobias Klenk that the Duke came to Karolsmarkt."

"What?"

"All the rest was done for show. As a matter of fact, he had been promptly informed of Tobias Klenk's abuse of the chief gamekeeper, and I was given to know—now, not a word of this to anyone, you poor misguided thing—that it was his expressed desire that the most severe punishment be meted out to Tobias. In a word, he wanted him hanged. There is not the slightest doubt that rumors of the conspiracy that is brewing have already reached the Duke."

"For heaven's sake," Agnes cried out, and she touched not a bite of the roast that had just been served. "Does this mean that you are in for it too?"

Adalbert emptied a glass of wine at a single draught. "I am not involved—at least not for the present—but you might as well know what your kind, gracious Duke looks like upon closer examination, what sort of a man he really is. Wants a poor devil hanged for merely wanting to bring his mother something to eat! And you should have seen the oily character who slithered up to me early this morning, even before I entered the courthouse, just to let me know that the loyal execution of my duty would surely not go unrewarded! I cannot help but wonder where the good Lord gets the raw material to forge such faces. And how does it happen that such creatures are always promptly available to a prince? And how do they manage to disappear from the face of the earth right after they recite their little speeches?"

"Tell me everything! Tell me!" said Agnes, her voice choked.

"As if you didn't know enough already," Adalbert countered. "Suddenly, there was the Duke, just sitting there. No one knew how he had come in. His toady had not bothered to tell me that his serene Grace would show up in person. And then, as I saw him sitting in the courtroom, I knew that the Duke had come here all the way from the capital only because of Tobias Klenk who had been denounced to him as the ringleader of the plot. But I did not let that bother me in the least. I continued to carry out my duties exactly as I do every day, and did not order Tobias's case to come up any sooner than was his turn. But he straightaway seemed determined to talk his head into a noose. Not only did he flatly confess to everything of which he was accused, he even appended a gratuitous tirade against princely rule and tyranny, all the while addressing me by my first name, just as if I were his most intimate friend. You would almost think that he had made a bet with someone that he could get me hanged side-by-side with him on the selfsame gallows. I promise you, he did not deserve the lenient treatment I gave him, a sentence of a measly few months. And what he deserves even less is that which I intend to do with him as soon as is humanly possible, maybe even tonight yet: release him from jail and have him safely smuggled across the border to save him from the Duke's vengeance."

"You don't seriously mean that, do you?" Agnes cried out.

"As surely as I am sitting at this table."

"Well," Agnes exclaimed, "since God gave me such an irredeemable fool for a husband, I shall seek an audience with the Duke myself and implore him not to make you do penance for your behavior since, after all, Tobias Klenk and no one else is to blame for all this, including turning you into a madman."

"What are you getting into your head now, you calamity?" Adalbert shouted. "Do you want to deliver me right into the Duke's hands? As of this moment he still hasn't any conclusive evidence against me." He grabbed her by the shoulders and held her tightly, as if he feared that she might make her threat good without delay. "Or maybe you would prefer to have me wasting away helplessly behind the walls of some godforsaken dungeon, while that wretched lecher—"

At that very moment a muffled, crashing sound could be heard coming from the street. Since the sky had, in the meantime, become totally overcast, Adalbert thought at first that it was a clap of distant thunder. But it really sounded like something else, more as if a heavy object had fallen over. Agnes rushed to the window, thrust out her head, and then turned back to face Adalbert who stood there in apprehensive terror with his feet rooted to the floorboards.

"A carriage overturned," said Agnes without a trace of inflection. Adalbert walked toward her. The maid was just running by the window on her way to the site of the accident.

There, on the road, about fifty paces from the house, lay the ducal carriage. The coachman was just getting up from the field into which the crash had thrown him. A half bent-over attendant stretched his hand toward a male shape that emerged, by means of various bodily contortions, from under the carriage. The figure suddenly stood erect and stretched its arms. It was the Duke. They heard his voice without being able to understand his words. He appeared to be turning with calming words to several people who had hurried to the scene, and then seemed to give the attendant an order. The coachman was already occupying himself with the horses. The Duke looked around, and his gaze fell immediately on the nearest house in sight, the judge's, but from where the Duke stood, he could not see the two heads at the window.

After reflecting briefly, he strode toward the house. The maid ran before him; in her haste, she had left the garden gate and the front door open. The maid barged into the room but was unable to utter a single word, pointing helplessly behind her with both arms, and disappeared again. Adalbert and Agnes gave each other blank stares. They heard steps outside. Adalbert, the first to recover his composure, hurried into the entrance hall to meet the Duke whom he greeted with a deep bow.

The Duke recognized him immediately. "So, this is your house, your honor. How fortunate. Will you grant me shelter until the slight damage to my coach has been repaired?"

The first large raindrops were beginning to fall on the threshold.

"Your Ducal Grace," Adalbert began, but seemed unable to form any further words. With a humble gesture, he pointed toward the open door leading into the living room. The Duke entered; Adalbert followed.

Agnes, still by the window, turned her head toward the visitor. She hardly bowed; the pallor of her face, the sparkle of her eyes, and the limpness of her arms were greeting enough.

The Duke casually turned to Adalbert, who, still in bowed posture, was standing behind him. "Your wife, your honor?" And without waiting for any answer, he addressed Agnes: "This morning, as I drove by, I took you for a young girl. What a happy accident that it was in front of this very house that my wheel became disconnected from its axle. For nothing worse than that happened. I shan't be a burden to you for very long. But I have interrupted your meal, which was certainly not my intention, so with your kind permission, I shall join you at your table."

"Your most serene Highness," Adalbert said as he placed a chair for the Duke, "the honor you have brought our modest home is so great that the depth of our gratitude is exceeded only by the intensity with which we feel the good fortune of our lot." He winked quickly toward Agnes in an attempt to make her believe that his abjectly servile words only masked the mockery of his derision.

But Agnes, who was totally enthralled in gazing at the Duke, had hardly heard what Adalbert had spoken. The Duke beckoned to her to sit down. She remained frozen in place. Adalbert's gesture urged her to honor the Duke's request. She noticed nothing of it. Finally, the Duke himself walked over toward her, took her by the hand, and in courtly manner led her to the table. Not until she was seated did the Duke take his own place, directly facing Agnes. All the while, Adalbert just stood there, not knowing what to do next.

"Well, your honor, won't you join us?" the Duke suggested with a smile.

"Your most illustrious Grace," Adalbert answered, "we were already finished with our meal, but I beg your gracious permission, Your Highness, to offer you a light meal and a modest drink."

The Duke replied that he would be delighted to partake of the candied fruits and the pastries before him and happily enjoy a glass of wine. Adalbert brought a plate and a glass, served the sweets, and poured the wine. Then the Duke insisted that Adalbert also sit down, whereupon he toasted his hosts and asked them to toast him in return.

Adalbert did as he was told, but Agnes was able only to clutch her glass firmly, and it was not until the Duke gave her an encouraging look that she could raise her glass to her lips for a small sip. Adalbert refilled his honored guest's glass, and the Duke drank, ate a candied apricot slice, looked around the room with obvious approval, praised its spick-and-span appearance, and admired the lovely location of the house and the charm of its little garden. There was a congenial, innocent flow to his words that made it obvious he was bending every effort to put his lovely hostess at ease. Although Adalbert deeply regretted that the Duke had not broken his neck in the accident, he found himself defenselessly bedazzled by the luster that radiated from the Duke's presence in the house.

The Duke expressed his appreciation of the superb playing of the organist that had brought him such enjoyment in the church, and he praised the skill of the craftsmen whose wares he had purchased. His visit to the schoolhouse had also pleased him greatly, and he described the cleanliness and the industriousness of the little town in the most glowing terms. Furthermore, he was not niggardly in his praise of the mayor, on whom he had called right after his unexpected arrival from the capital quite early in the morning. He had found him in the city hall, hard at work with the affairs of the town.

The judge permitted himself an interjection: "The mayor, Your Grace, is my wife's father."

The Duke nodded and then smiled at Agnes, who had yet to utter a single syllable while hanging on every word the Duke had spoken. "Well, my lovely lady," he said, "you have not only a fine husband but also an exemplary father. It is a joy to know that I have such excellent men in my service." He turned to Adalbert, whose heart had begun to thump furiously, and said, "And why should I conceal that the hour I spent in your courtroom was the oddest of all, thanks in particular to the appearance of that strange fellow in the yellow boots. What was his name again?"

"Tobias Klenk, Your Grace."

"I found it simultaneously amusing and informative. I had hardly thought that there would be such original characters in my little principality."

Adalbert Wogelein held his breath in terrified anticipation as the Duke continued, "Your honor, I find it highly commendable of you not to scorn the opportunity to sit down at the same table with such characters when the occasion arises. Only in this way can men whose profession requires insight into other men's souls gain the knowledge and experience of which they would otherwise be all too easily deprived."

"I realized that early on in my career, Your Grace," the judge remarked while glancing nervously at Agnes who seemed, in her silence, to withdraw ever further from him, and he added, "There are all sorts of dangerous individuals in this country." Actually, he did not mean to say that, but now it was too late.

"You may well be right, your honor," the Duke said, "but it seems to me that Tobias Klenk need not be listed among the ranks of the dangerous. Characters of his ilk do not demand to be taken seriously. At least they have no significance in and of themselves. United with many others who share their views and in the midst of an enraged mob, they might well cause mischief, but in this dukedom there is precious little danger that the swaggering opinions uttered by that crazy man in court today would find any assent among my satisfied and well-disposed subjects. What is your opinion in this matter, Judge Adalbert Wogelein?"

"I too believe I can safely vouch for that, your Grace. Of course, if I may be permitted a comment—"

"Feel free to say whatever you wish, Adalbert Wogelein," said the Duke.

"Your Serene Grace, even as an isolated case, Tobias Klenk should not be thought harmless, as your illustrious Highness was pleased to assume in your princely generosity. He demonstrated this clearly, not only in his behavior toward the chief gamekeeper and his helpers, but even more so in his unwarranted and most regrettable conduct in court in the presence of his most gracious Duke. Furthermore, his past, his reputation, the rumors—"

The Duke interrupted him with mild impatience. "I assure you that such fellows will never be able to make trouble in my dukedom—not so long as, with God's help, it is my good fortune to have such capable and efficient people in my service, be they gamekeepers or judges."

While saying this, he seemed to be looking right past the judge with increasing discomfort. At the same time, Adalbert sensed that Agnes was staring at him with an intensity that grew by the second. He began to wish that the Duke's friendly, pleasant manner of speaking and his kind, gentle demeanor were really only crafty pretense and perfidy. He almost wished that there *were* arresting officers standing at the ready outside the house, awaiting only a signal from the Duke to drag Adalbert Wogelein off to prison. At least this would prove that all those cowardly lies he had told his wife about the Duke were the sad truth. Yet, at the same time that he was thinking all this, he realized that he was involuntarily bowing his head so low in gratitude for the Duke's praise that his face was almost in his plate. And then, to his own utter amazement he listened to himself speak, almost as if the words were coming from someone else's lips, and the meekly submissive voice was saying, "Earning my most gracious and illustrious master's approval will always be my utmost gratification."

The attendant came in and announced that the carriage had been repaired. The Duke rose from his chair, toasted Agnes once again, and spoke: "Accept my thanks for your warm hospitality. I would like to show you my gratitude. Therefore, I beg of you, express any wish the fulfillment of which lies dear to your heart, and do so yet before I take my leave of this hospitable house."

Adalbert answered quickly for her, as if he wished to prevent the Duke from hearing her voice: "That it pleased Your Serene Grace to enter our lowly cottage, to sit at our modest table, and to drink our inferior wine is more than abundant thanks for us."

"Maybe for *you*, your honor," the Duke replied with a chill in his voice, "and since I almost knew that I could expect an answer of this sort from you, I preferred to address my question to your charming wife—also that I might finally hear the tone of her voice, a pleasure that has unfortunately been denied me to this very moment. And so, once again, lovely lady, I ask you to express a wish, and if in any way it lies within my power, I shall grant it."

"Your Grace," Agnes began in a voice soft but clear—and Adalbert felt his entire body begin to tremble—"Our Most Serene Duke, I have but one request, and may it please you, in your benevolence, to look upon it with favor: to pardon Tobias Klenk and to release him from bondage."

The Duke's face suddenly became earnest. Adalbert clutched at the hope, the vague and foolish hope, that the Duke would refuse Agnes's request with harsh words: What? Rescind a sentence of one year that was far too little to begin with? The presumptuousness of it! Now, I see that you are all in league with him! Off to prison with the both of you! And as for Tobias, he hangs!

But the Duke spoke entirely different words. "My good Mrs. Wogelein," he said, "how deeply I regret that of a hundred, or even a thousand wishes that you might have expressed, you have decided upon the one request that I am incapable of honoring." Then, after a slight hesitation: "I cannot give Tobias Klenk the gift of freedom—because for the last hour, he has already been enjoying it." Then to Adalbert, who stood there thunderstruck: "With your kind permission, your honor, I took the liberty of releasing this ludicrous fellow from your jail, and I must confess to you that what I have in mind is to hire him as an assistant gamekeeper in the Karolslust preserve, where he can indulge his desires with far greater ease and comfort than heretofore, and without any danger to himself and to my other hunters."

Adalbert was deathly pale, and a weak, hollow smile contorted his mouth. He did not even dare to look at Agnes. Trying to search for some reply was senseless, so he did nothing more than what he had already been doing so often during the past hour: he bowed deeply, as if he felt compelled, in Tobias Klenk's name, to thank the Duke for his clemency.

This, however, encouraged Agnes to express some other wish, one that was easier to fulfill, so that he would not ultimately be forced, as he put it, to depart from this hospitable house as a debtor.

And in a voice that sounded so distant and unfamiliar to Adalbert that it sent cold chills down his spine, Agnes answered: "Then what I ask of my most illustrious master and Duke is that he choose me as an arbormaiden—and should it not be my lord's pleasure to take me with him to Karolslust at once, I entreat him to have me brought immediately, under his protection, to some other secure spot so that I shall not have to live one hour longer in this house at the side of this man who was once my husband."

Adalbert thought that his shame, his fury, and his despair would make him sink to the ground; but his face grew only paler, his features more contorted; and his lips trembled.

The Duke cast a sympathetic but hardly surprised glance at him. Then, as if to spare him, he diverted his gaze and turned toward Agnes who stood before him motionless, looking in no way like a woman who was about to throw her arms around her beloved's neck with suddenly awakened passion, but rather like one who had set her resolve upon some irrevocable, dismal deed. Slowly shaking his head, as with polite regret, the Duke replied: "Strangely enough, your second wish is also one that I am in no position to fulfill because, my lovely lady, I intend to abolish the institution of arbormaidenhood along with several others in this state—and the palace of Karolslust will serve as a residence during the summer months for me and my future wife, the Princess of Württemberg."

Agnes stood perfectly still, but all the blood had drained from her cheeks.

The Duke looked at her for a long time, and in a gentle, almost kind voice he continued: "Lovely lady, perhaps your wish is not so far-reaching as you imagine it at this moment; so many myths circulate around here concerning the palace, and perhaps you merely feel the enticement of seeing it from up close for once. And therefore I invite you for a little drive to Karolslust; if it pleases you, we will stroll up and down in the park for a while; you will confide your doubts and cares to me, and you will find that they are not so difficult to allay as they might seem to you in this hour. And you will decide for yourself whether you prefer to stay at Karolslust in the safekeeping of the chief gamekeeper's wife, or to return to this house before nightfall—so that you might not do that which you may well rue at a later date."

"From this day forth," Agnes replied, and it seemed to Adalbert that he had never before heard her voice, "I shall rue nothing anymore, no matter what I do, my most gracious Sovereign, be it a drive in the woods or a journey into the wide world." She reached for a light cloak hanging over the back of a chair. "I am ready," she said—and, as if she had always been accustomed to the manner, she extended her hand to the Duke's raised arm. He took it, and led Agnes to the door in the courtly style, as he would any lady of noble blood.

She looked right past Adalbert—or she seemed, rather, not to see him at all, as if, from her point of view, he had been obliterated from the ranks of the living.

The Duke, like someone suddenly overtaken with compassion, turned toward him once again from the door. "Judge Wogelein," he said, "in spite of everything, let us hope that these events will resolve themselves in a satisfactory manner and not completely to your disadvantage. In any case, you may be assured of my favor for the present."

And so he left the house with Agnes. Adalbert, firmly rooted to the spot where he stood, heard their steps on the gravel path in the garden. Immediately thereafter, the sound of murmuring from outside reached his ear, and he knew, without seeing it, that people were standing around the carriage and watching his wife drive off with the Duke.

As the murmuring grew louder, he thought he could understand a disconnected word here and there; then the voices became gradually more distant. All that was left was a dull buzzing in his ear. The room started to revolve about him; his legs felt leaden; his senses whirled. He listened for sounds from the kitchen; it was totally quiet; the maid was gone too. No doubt she had rushed off to the marketplace, straight to his father-in-law, the mayor, to bring him the precious news as quickly as possible. He crept toward the door, which was still open, and locked it without rightly knowing why. Then he let himself sink down on the chair in which the Duke had been sitting before, clenched the tablecloth with both hands so that the plates and glasses rattled, and sat there groaning to himself, his eyes glassy. He picked up a table knife, allowed his fingers to play with it, and thought that the smartest thing he could do would be to slit his throat, but he knew that he had never in the world been cut out for that sort of daring action.

He asked himself what he should actually do now. Sit here and wait until his father-in-law showed up—along with sundry other folk from the town square—to express their sarcastic sympathy for him? Or maybe long enough for Agnes to return home from her little pleasure trip? Ha, ha! Return home! She was never coming back. That was for certain. The Duke wasn't the kind of fool who would not take what was so eagerly offered him. Tonight, in this very hour yet, Agnes would become what she wanted to be—an arbormaiden, the new Duke's very first arbormaiden in the palace of Karolslust. In the moment when the Duke first walked through this door, in fact already this morning when he drove by, she had given herself to him heart and soul. And he, Adalbert, had sensed it, and for that reason only, out of rage and loathing, had prattled all that nonsense about the Duke that ultimately did make very good sense, and had told all those lies that turned out to be truer than the truth. What was it that His Grace, the Duke, had said just before he strolled out the door with that infamous female? "In spite of everything, let us hope that these events will not resolve themselves completely to your disadvantage." That was cunningly anticipated. For the Duke could surely foresee that Agnes was not going to have much to say about her husband that was particularly laudatory.

That wretch! Shame and dishonor was what she had brought down upon him, upon Judge Adalbert Wogelein who, but a few hours ago, was still enthroned in a position of honor, was highly respected in town and country as a just and wise man. Now he could never again dare to show his face on the street; he would be the laughing stock of every boy, every maid, the entire population of Karolsmarkt. And never again into the courtroom, never into the inn, never *any*where *any*one knew him! Holding public office? All over! Living in this town? All over! He could not linger here for one more night. Whatever fate had in store for him, one thing above all was clear: he had to get out, get out, get out, and before anyone came.

He rushed into the adjoining room where he had hidden a small amount of money in a secret place in the clothes closet. It might do for a few months. Get out—get out—but where to? Did he not have to leave primarily to escape the vengeance of Tobias Klenk, set free by this calamity of a Duke, and now likely to be on his way here, and God knows what horrible things he has up his sleeve? All of them had conspired against him: Agnes, the Duke, and Tobias Klenk. And in some fiendish way, they now all seemed to be in league against him. He had to flee from all of them.

And what was to become of this house that was his property?

For whom was he leaving it? That shameless wench who ran off with the Duke? He pictured her at the Duke's side, riding along the road toward the palace in the stately ducal carriage. He saw her alight, saw the Duke reach out his hand toward her, saw how the park gates swung open before her, how attendants bowed deeply to her, how the Duke led her on the walk along the tree-lined path to the palace, how she climbed the broad front staircase with him; he saw the chamber that was prepared for her, the luxurious bed with its blue canopy; he saw her sink into the Duke's arms and heard her cry out with joy as her carnal desires were finally satisfied.

He clenched his fists and banged his forehead against the edge of the open closet door. He felt he must set out for Karolslust immediately and demand the return of the woman who was his and whom he had allowed to drive off with the Duke without lifting a finger, without opening his mouth, standing meekly by the door through which she strode like a lady-in-waiting—yea, even like a princess—on her lord's arm.

The room in which he found himself was almost dark, and outside in the dusk, behind the house, lay the open field. At that very instant, there was a knocking at the windowpane. He recoiled in fear; someone gigantic was standing out there. There he was, like some monstrous specter, Tobias Klenk. He was just then raising his fist as if he wanted to smash the window to bits, but all that came of the gesture was a knock, and not even a particularly forceful one.

Adalbert took the few steps over to the window. He heard Tobias speak, softly, almost gently: "Open up, Adalbert! There's no one in the kitchen or the garden; not your wife, not the maid. Open up! Open up!"

Adalbert hesitated. His eyes searched for a weapon or for something that could pass for one. He picked up an iron lying nearby, but dropped it before Tobias could take any notice.

"Open up, Adalbert!" Tobias called again, and he raised his fist once more, this time so threateningly that one could believe he really did intend to smash the window to smithereens.

And Adalbert opened up. There stood Tobias Klenk, as he had stood in court this morning, in threadbare riding habit with high yellow boots, and with a brown cycling cape thrown over his shoulders. The darkling fields spread out behind him; the slender, pointed church spire of Karolsmarkt thrust itself up into the evening.

"What do you want from me?" Adalbert asked and was seized with horror at the sound of his own voice.

"Why do you want to know?" Tobias answered. "If you had enough courage to let me out of that hole, you must surely have enough courage to give me shelter for a small quarter of an hour. After all, I'm here for your sake more than for mine."

Adalbert's eyes opened wide, but Tobias pushed him aside, swung himself over the sill and into the room without further ado, and locked the window behind him.

What was it Tobias had said? Courage enough to let me out of that hole? Had he understood him correctly? Adalbert fell back and stared him in the face.

"Aha! I see you're not quite so comfortable about it after all," Tobias laughed. "Packing up your things already!" and he pointed to the underwear that was lying around.

"Why am I packing up?" Adalbert stammered. Did Tobias wish to mock him, play with him as a cat with a mouse? Enough courage to let him out of the hole? What was that supposed to mean? Something had happened here that was not yet comprehensible and that could not be clarified until Tobias had spoken further. For the time being there was nothing else for Adalbert to do but remain silent.

"Did you already send your wife ahead? Good thinking, Adalbert; good thinking! Caution never hurts!"

"Come along," Adalbert spoke in consternation, and preceded him into the living room. The plates and still half-filled glasses glittered through the darkening room. "There's some pastry and wine left," Adalbert said. "You probably didn't have much of a noonday meal to enjoy today." He filled the glass from which the Duke had drunk hardly an hour ago, and it made him feel better, as if somehow he were thereby initiating an act of vengeance.

Tobias drank; then he grasped the wine jug himself, poured another glassful, and emptied it at one draught. "I thank you, Adalbert," said Tobias. "And now, let's not waste any time. I have to get across the border right away. Tonight yet. I have friends on the other side. Not far at all. But what will become of you? It won't be kept a secret from the Duke for very long that you released me. Don't trust that jailkeeper, I tell you, and no one else either."

Now Adalbert knew beyond a doubt that the Duke himself had given the order to release Tobias from prison, and that he had done it in Adalbert's name. But why? Out of magnanimity or out of malice? Who could figure that man out? What was he not capable of? Good and evil! And yet, was this not the same man who had just driven off with Agnes? The blood surged to his head all over again. And what if the Duke brought her back after all, and she saw him sitting and drinking at the same table with Tobias, and the Duke must surely already have told her how things had really come to pass. First of all, Tobias had to get out of here, for if *he* ever discovered the truth, everything would be lost. He had to be gotten across the border and never be allowed to return.

"You must get out of here," he said to Tobias. "You must get out! What are you staring at me for? All right, have another glass, for all I care, but then get yourself gone. Or are you just itching to be tossed back into the hole, and into a deeper and darker one than I put you in a few hours ago—for your temporary safety?"

"For my safety?"

"Yes, for your safety, for your rescue. Because if you had any notion of the threat under which you stood in reality, you would know what it feels like to be a man who is destined to become a meal for the vultures."

"Are you in your right mind?" Tobias shouted, and the glass jiggled in his hand.

"The one who is out of his mind is you, Tobias, and you have been from the moment you were led into the courtroom, saw the Duke sitting there, and, in spite of all my winking and blinking, did not want to comprehend that every word I spoke was intended to save your head. As a matter of fact, you did everything you could to be sure to lose it, as if it weren't worth any more than a pumpkin. I was waiting for the Duke to get up at any second so that he himself could decree your sentence that he expected of me—death.

Tobias burst out laughing. "Are you trying to make a fool of me? Or has someone made one of you, insofar as that still needed to be done?"

But Adalbert leaned over the table toward him so that their foreheads almost touched, and said: "Do you really think that the Duke would have driven all the way to Karolsmarkt just to get a closer view of a poacher? He wanted to be face to face with the agitator, the conspirator about whom detailed information had already been reported to him."

"Information about me?"

"And a haggard little man in dark courtly garb, who had a golden chain around his neck and who later vanished without a trace as if the earth had swallowed him, already waylaid me on the way to court today, and he gave me to know that if I were of a mind to shake any nasty suspicions off myself, this would be my only and last opportunity to do it, and to do it by exposing Tobias Klenk in all of his dangerousness and condemning him to the penalty that traitors deserve."

"The stuff you are saying is madness," Tobias screamed. "Who in the world can prove anything against me! If ever I did anything evil, it happened a long time ago and not here in this country."

"I know nothing of your misdeeds committed on foreign soil. Thus far you have prudently kept knowledge of them from me, even if various rumors are flying. But you need not doubt that there are others who know more than I do, and in particular there is a web of information whose threads extend from palace to palace, from prince to prince, from courtroom to courtroom, secret threads of all sorts, and His Grace, the Duke—yes, Tobias my friend, that selfsame Duke who hardly an hour ago sat right on this spot, in the same chair you occupy at this moment, and drank from the same glass from which you are now drinking—he knows full well what to expect from you and your kind. And therefore—"

Then Tobias arose, with one hand on the back of the chair. "The Duke here—at this table—and drank from this glass? Now I really think you've gone mad. For what purpose would the Duke have been here? Was I the topic of conversation?"

"Ha! You?" Adalbert cried out, and stared fixedly.

"When was he here? Why was he here? Are you going to talk or aren't you?"

"Two hours ago, right when it started to rain, he drove up to my house, and a quarter of an hour later, he drove away with Agnes—to Karolslust."

"Away with Agnes? The Duke?"

"Away with my wife to Karolslust, and unless a miracle has occurred in the meantime, the same thing is probably happening to her in this hour that happened to both of your sisters in their time with the old Duke."

With his eyes opened wide, Tobias sat back down, and it sounded more like joy than scorn or anger when he cried out: "Your wife—went off with the Duke? If you're just talking twaddle or trying to make a fool of me, I'll fix you, Adalbert."

"On top of everything else, are you threatening me—you whom I have to thank for all this trouble that has befallen us? My wife, my position, my honor—all gone to ruin just because I saved you from the gallows—and *you* threaten *me?*"

"As long as what you say is true, I have not threatened you. But I cannot make any sense of all this. If it put you in such danger, and you knew it, why did you let me go free, and on the same day yet? Are you the kind of man who would risk that? And furthermore, how could the Duke compel your wife to accompany him to Karolslust so quickly unless she had previously had some understanding with him? And if you let her run off with him, why are you packing your own things as if you had something else to fear and wanted to get away yourself?"

"What are these questions supposed to mean, Tobias? I want to meet your comrades who are of the same opinion as you and I, so that we can exchange our views concerning what we should do to abolish injustice and humiliation from the world and to overthrow the tyrants."

Tobias Klenk placed his hand heavily on Adalbert's shoulder. "Have you given serious consideration to what you are saying? If you go away with me, be assured that there will be no way back for you. Should you ever regret it, be it tomorrow already or not for days or weeks, it will be too late! He who betrays us, in fact, he who only deserts us, will find us relentless in the retribution we exact, as surely as if he had been condemned by the holy fehmic court.* Better to stay at home, Adalbert, because here there is no danger of any kind to threaten you anymore. I am as certain of that as of anything in this life. In fact, I would bet my own neck that in no time you will attain great heights, as many another in your situation has already discovered, and even if some people turn up their noses at you at first, it will not last long. They will all learn to accept it, they will render you courtesy and respect, and soon there will be no one who will not envy you your good fortune."

"Do you take me for a scoundrel?" Adalbert screamed. "If so, then you were not worth what I—"

A carriage stopped in front of the house. Adalbert looked out the window, and his heart froze in his chest. "Get out! Get out, you unlucky fellow!" he shouted in a choked voice. "Duck

* *A secret German medieval court.*

down. Sneak through this door here and then back out the window, the way you came in."

"The Duke?" Tobias whispered as if asking, though he had seen and recognized him for himself.

"Get out, get out, you poor wretch," Adalbert exclaimed, and pushed Tobias into the adjoining room where the window stood open as before, only that the view toward the open field was now obscured by two dark shapes that looked enormous as they stood out against the fading light of the sky.

At the same time, there was a knocking at the front door. Adalbert rushed toward it and, barely in control of his senses, opened up.

The Duke stood there, an attendant with a torch behind him. At his master's nod, he lit the tapers of both the three-armed candlesticks standing on the sideboard. Not a word was spoken while all this happened. At the Duke's repeated nod, the attendant with the torch withdrew and closed the door behind him.

"Shut the other door, Tobias Klenk, and step over here," said the Duke.

Tobias did as he was told. Now the three men were convened in the closed-off room; only the window facing the street stood open, and the candles flickered in the spring evening's wind.

The Duke sat down as if he were at home, and spoke: "How fortunate, Tobias Klenk, that I find you here at your friend's. Has he already made you aware of the plans I have for you?"

Adalbert felt as if someone had knotted a cord around his throat, because the Duke's question could signify nothing other than this: Had Adalbert informed Tobias of the Duke's intention to take him into his service as a huntsman? Tobias, on the other hand, had to believe that the Duke's question alluded to the death penalty for which he had been destined, according to Adalbert's account. Whatever Adalbert answered now, he could only entangle himself anew and in more dreadful ways; he had no choice left other than immediately to admit everything that an interchange of assertions and contradictions would have to bring to light anyway in very little time.

But already he heard Tobias answering for himself: "To what avail is all this, your most illustrious Grace? Here I am, and I know that I am totally within your power. There are two men standing outside—I've seen them—and even if I have not the least desire to say that I submit to my fate contritely, provisions have surely been made to prohibit me from doing anything to evade whatever is intended for me. Therefore, I venture only this one request, Your Grace: that you do not make my lamentable friend pay for having opened the dungeon door for me a bit prematurely. He is more terrified of me than of you, Your Grace. And he has good reason, because the unjust sentence he inflicted upon me would have turned out badly for him. My vengeance would have been far worse than any punishment that Your Illustrious Grace could have meted out to him."

Adalbert lowered his head like a condemned man. He did not dare to look the Duke in the face, and he held his breath as the Duke turned to him again and began to speak. "Before we treat the case of Tobias Klenk with all necessary circumspection, you will surely wish to know with certainty of your wife's destiny. Judge Adalbert Wogelein, you need have no worries about her. Since there was no way to persuade her to return to you for the time being, I have housed her with the chief gamekeeper's wife. I have demanded of her that after one month she be ready to receive you for a thoroughgoing exchange of your views; and this will prove whether you can arrive at some mutual understanding and be reconciled or not. Since I have found you to be a wiser and shrewder man in your profession than in your marriage, although it seems to me you are better able to demonstrate your knowledge of jurisprudence in matters requiring cleverness rather than courage, I will see to it that you are appointed to a position with the imperial court at Wetzlar. As far as the misdemeanor of which you are guilty is concerned, the unauthorized release of Tobias Klenk, we will consider it atoned for by the fear you have endured. But you, Tobias Klenk, should first of all be informed that the two men outside were by no means instructed to take you captive again, but rather to collect you from the jail and bring you to me at Karolslust. I do not exactly mean to say that I approve of you, but since hunting seems to give you pleasure, and since you are not good for much else, I want to enlist your service as an assistant gamekeeper at Karolslust palace. But mark this well, you will be under strict charge and supervision there and will have to do the most severe penance for the slightest rebelliousness or negligence. Most especially, you are urgently warned not to bear any grudge against Judge Adalbert Wogelein or in any way at all to attempt any form of reprisal against him."

In the meantime, Adalbert had cast several anxious glances in Tobias Klenk's direction and became aware of a flashing in his eyes so malicious that Adalbert could have no doubt about what he could expect of Tobias at the very earliest opportunity. And so, fully deprived of his sensibilities by his terror, he fell to his knees in front of the Duke, and even before Tobias was able to answer, Adalbert cried out: "Your Grace, what care I about myself and my poor, miserable life? I can pay my debt of gratitude to Your Gracious Highness only by making an honest confession. My lord, there is a secret brotherhood throughout the states of Germany—Tobias himself has confided this to me; he will not deny it—that is planning criminal attacks against the hallowed heads of our princes. I would become an accomplice were I to stand by silently while knowing of these conditions and to watch Your Gracious Highness allow Tobias Klenk, a member of this secret brotherhood, to remain in your immediate proximity, because the assurances and oaths of such people, though they may be honestly intended at first, are in no instance to be trusted."

"Stand up," the Duke ordered in a stern voice. Adalbert rose and did not venture to look up. And he dared even less to direct his gaze toward Tobias Klenk. The Duke remained silent for some time, then he spoke: "What I said, Tobias Klenk, stands. I accept you as an assistant gamekeeper at the palace of Karolslust. You will report for duty immediately."

"My most illustrious Duke," Tobias Klenk answered, "with all due thanks, I decline Your Highness's gracious offer. If I may be allowed to say so, no matter how utter a scoundrel Judge Adalbert Wogelein may be—and I already recognized him for one in my childhood—it is distinctly possible that I am the worse of the two of us. And he is absolutely right in his warning, Your Grace, and to greater extent than he himself could suspect, for if I was sneaking around in your game preserve with a loaded weapon, it was not with the slightest intention of shooting a stag, but rather to ferret out locations and conditions in the vicinity of Karolslust for a more favorable occasion."

"What do you mean by that?" asked the Duke. "You may be assured of your life and your freedom, in any case. Therefore, speak without any dread."

Tobias hesitated and stared straight ahead.

The corner of the Duke's mouth twitched contemptuously. "If you harbor any fear in spite of my princely word that your life and freedom are secure, you also have the right to remain silent, Tobias Klenk," and he looked as if he would turn away from him.

But then, as if he knew of no greater disgrace than to have anyone imply that he feared for his life, Tobias began in haste: "There is not a word of truth in what this creature here has alleged about any secret brotherhood and all that nonsense, my lord, and I do not want any innocent suspect to have to suffer. But what I, for my part, had in mind to do, your Grace, that was and still is my business and no one else's. And if any man should make a start at bringing about those things that must come to pass one of these days so that order, justice, and equality might be established in the world, I truly believe that I would have been the right man to do it. And you, my lord,"—and he looked him right in the eye with gloomy insolence—"you were the most readily available to me," and he did not lower his gaze.

"Well, Tobias Klenk," the Duke countered after a brief silence, "whether all your babbling be only idle boasting or something worse, or better—I will no longer tolerate having a fellow like you either near at hand or even in my province. The two men waiting outside will take you to the border at once. And I advise you not to bank too heavily on my generosity, of which I have grown weary enough on this one day to last me for a long time. And remember this, Tobias Klenk, if anywhere or anytime you turn up again within the confines of my state, you will hang from the nearest gallows as surely as I am sitting in this chair. And now, open the door by which you are standing, Tobias Klenk."

He obeyed. Outside the window, the two men stood motionlessly in the darkness. "Listen," the Duke called to them. "In a moment a man will jump through the window. Seize him between you and take him to the border at Feldbach. Be sure to watch him closely; and if he makes a move to escape, chase him with your bullets. Once across the border, let him trundle off wherever he pleases so that he may continue to live his silly, fruitless life until his fate catches up with him."

With outstretched arm, he pointed imperiously toward the window. Tobias spun around without farewell, and swung himself over the sill; the two men waiting outside grabbed him firmly by the shoulders and disappeared with him into the night.

Now Adalbert stood there alone with the Duke, who spoke again: "Surely, Judge Wogelein, you have realized by now that it profits no man to play the hero in front of the world, and more particularly in front of his wife, once he was born to be a coward. When such is the case, you cannot accomplish it without a lie, and once you have lowered yourself to one, the succeeding lies will follow without fail until finally they encircle you like vicious enemies you yourself have begotten, and they will smite you to earth so that you may never arise again. This is what happened to you, Adalbert Wogelein, and now I see you before me in such a pitiful state that I should feel sorry for you. But I do not feel sorry for you; and since you seem to me to merit any generosity or the slightest consideration even less than does your friend Tobias Klenk, in fear of whom you have no further need to tremble, you should know that I have no intention whatsoever of driving from here to the capital, but will rather go directly to Karolslust, and that your wife will not sleep in the house of the chief gamekeeper's wife tonight, but in my princely bed, in accordance with her own wish. The position in Wetzlar at the imperial court is reserved for you. . . . And so, farewell, Judge Wogelein."

He departed. The attendant stood outside with the torch. The door fell shut. Footsteps faded away; soon thereafter, so did the rumbling of wheels.

Suddenly, Adalbert collapsed as if he had been shot down. Lying on the floor, he whimpered softly for a while. Then, all at once, he roared like a wild animal. The maid, frightened to death, ran in. "What does she want here?" Adalbert screamed, propped up on his arms. "Where was she all day long?" and he sprang to his feet.

The maid opened her eyes wide in amazement. Then she began to sob timidly. Adalbert stepped closer toward her. Inasmuch as she did not stop moaning, he grasped her shoulders, and as he drew her ever closer to himself, and as hot vapors seemed to rise from her bosom into his nostrils, his monstrous rage metamorphosed, not for the first time, into lustful excitation. And while he was still shouting, "Get her out of here! The devil take her!" he pressed her ever more fervently to himself, so that she finally began to laugh and to submit to his caresses even before she or he himself realized that caresses were actually what she was permitting.

• V •

On the following morning, when Agnes arrived at the house in the ducal carriage, she discovered the front door unlocked, no one in the antechamber or the kitchen, but her maid in Adalbert's arms in the conjugal bedroom. He welcomed her with a sneeringly foolish smirk. She, pale and speechless, slapped the maid in the face. The maid, weeping, jumped out of bed and ran out in her chemise.

Adalbert instinctively pulled the covers over his face. Unassuageable humiliation and empty vindictiveness combined to give him a feeling of bitter lasciviousness surging through his blood.

When he stuck his head out again, he was alone. He got up abruptly, still undecided about what he should do next, but since there was ultimately nothing else left for him, he finally got himself ready for the customary daily routine, as on every other morning. And since he could not very well lock himself in his house and stay in hiding for the rest of his life, he decided to go to the courthouse, albeit somewhat belatedly.

The maid was already attending to her usual morning chores in the kitchen as her master passed by, and she did not look up. But what affected him even more strangely was that Agnes was sitting in the front garden in a bright morning dress and allowing the delicate early sunshine to bathe her blonde hair. For a moment it seemed to him as if everything that had transpired since the previous evening was only a bad dream and nothing more. And he was just about to call out to Agnes to wish her a good morning, but he noticed how her gaze went right through him as though he were a phantom, so that he automatically ran his hands up and down his body to check if he was still there and had not actually turned into an apparition.

As on every other morning on his way to court, he received and returned many a greeting in which no mockery, no disrespect, in fact no awareness of what had happened seemed to be revealed. In the courtroom, the clerk was waiting as always and showed no trace of surprise that the judge was late or, moreover, that he appeared at all; and without further delay, the proceedings began and progressed as they did every day.

Adalbert Wogelein judged strictly but justly, as people had come to expect of him, and while he was carrying out the duties of his office, he became more sharply aware with each passing minute how much better he felt than on the day before at the same time and in the same room. Breathing a sigh of relief, he felt that there was no man on earth who could find any fault with him now; it was as if he were charmed against iniquity and danger from every direction.

He left the courtroom with his head held high. The clerk and the other greater and lesser officials whom he met in the corridor and the entrance hall said goodbye to him humbly and with all due respect. On the way home, he stopped in for a while at the apothecary shop to shake the hand of his father-in-law, who at first could not conceal a certain degree of bewilderment, but then right away pulled himself together. In passing, Adalbert conveyed greetings to him from his daughter, Agnes, exactly as he sometimes used to do. Then, thinking far calmer thoughts than twenty-four hours ago, he strode along the sun-drenched path toward his house.

He did not find Agnes at home. As the maid reported, she had already been called for by the ducal carriage in the early afternoon. He felt more comfortable than if she had been there. And he knew how to pass the time tolerably until the following morning when the carriage bringing Agnes stopped in front of the house again.

And so it went for many an evening, many a night, many a morning. And everybody—Agnes, her husband, her father the mayor, all of Karolsmarkt—became accustomed to the course of events more quickly than anyone might have predicted on that day when the Duke came home again to his province.

Within a short period of time, however, he became a prince whose style very closely resembled that of his ancestors. Not a downright evil ruler, as some of his forefathers reputedly were, but not one of the best either. For a while, he remained in correspondence with Baron Grimm and sometimes invited foreign dignitaries to the palace at Sigmaringen, but over the years he owed his reputation far more to the splendor of his hunts and the exuberance of his drinking parties than to the furtherance of scholarship and the fine arts.

Karl Eberhardt XVII had married a princess of Württemberg, kept many an arbormaiden beside her, and in the course of time sired three legitimate and seven illegitimate children, the first of whom was borne by Agnes and who grew up in her husband's house as a young Wogelein. Three years later, the judge, of whose appointment to the imperial court at Wetzlar no more was ever said, had a second son born to him, but he did not attain any esteem in later life equal to that of his older brother who, around the turn of the century, held the office of master of horses at the palace in Sigmaringen.

The gallows on which Tobias Klenk ended his adventurous life stood in another country.

—Translated by Peter Bauland

Dying

Dusk was already approaching when Marie rose from the bench on which she had been sitting for a half hour, first reading a book but then staring at the entrance to the path on which Felix customarily came. Normally he did not keep her waiting long. It had turned somewhat cooler, but the air still had the mildness of the waning May day.

There were no longer many people in the Augarten, and the procession of strollers was making its way to the gate, which would soon have to be shut. Marie was already close to the exit when she caught sight of Felix. Although he was late he walked slowly, and only when his eyes had met hers did he speed up a bit. She stopped and waited, and when he smilingly pressed her nonchalantly extended hand she asked him with mild annoyance in her voice: "Did you have to work this late?" He gave her his arm and made no reply. "Well?" she asked. "I did, dear," he said at length, "and I completely forgot to look at the clock." She gave him a sidelong glance. He seemed paler than usual to her. "Don't you think," she said tenderly, "it would be better if you started spending a little more time with your Marie? Why don't you stop working for a while? Let's plan on taking more walks. All right? From now on we'll always leave the house together."

"Oh . . ."

"Truly, Felix, from now on I'll never leave you alone."

He gave her a quick, almost frightened look.

"What's the matter with you?" she asked.

"Nothing!"

They had reached the exit and the evening traffic swirled pleasantly around them. The city seemed to be suffused with some of the universal, unconscious happiness that spring usually spreads over it.

"You know what we could do?" he said.

"What?"

"Go to the Prater."

"Oh no, the other day it was so cold down there."

"But look! It's almost sweltering here on the street. We don't have to stay long. Why don't we go!" His speech was choppy and distracted.

"Tell me, why are you talking like that, Felix?"

"What do you mean?"

"What could you be thinking of? You're with *me*, your girl!"

He stared at her distractedly.

"Felix!" she cried in alarm, squeezing his arm.

"Oh yes," he said, pulling himself together. "It is sweltering, sure it is. I know what I'm saying. And even if my mind is wandering, you mustn't get offended." They were walking through little streets in the direction of the Prater. Felix was even more taciturn than usual. The streetlamps were already lit.

"Did you go to see Alfred today?" she suddenly asked.

"Why?"

"Well, you were planning to."

"What do you mean?"

"You felt so tired last night."

"Quite right."

"So you didn't go to see Alfred?"

"No."

"But look, yesterday you still felt sick and now you want to go down to the damp Prater. That's really imprudent."

"Oh, what does it matter."

"Don't talk like that. You are going to ruin your health."

"Oh, please," he said in an almost tearful voice. "Let's go, let's just go. I long to be in the Prater. Let's go where we had such a good time the other day. You know, the outdoor café; it's not that cool there."

"All right, all right."

"It really isn't! And it's warm today anyhow. We can't go home; it's too early. And I don't want to have supper in town because today I don't feel like sitting down between the four walls of a restaurant. The smoke isn't good for me, and besides, I don't want to be among that many people; I can't stand the noise!" At first he talked quickly and more loudly than usual, but he let the last words trail off. Marie clung more tightly to his arm. She was worried and had stopped talking, because she felt tears choke her voice. She now shared his longing for that quiet restaurant in the Prater, for the spring evening amidst peaceful nature. Both were silent for a while, and then she noticed a slow, weak smile form on his lips. When he turned toward her, he tried to make the smile express happiness. But she knew him too well not to realize that the smile was forced.

They reached the Prater. That first tree-lined path off the main road, the one that seemed almost to vanish in the darkness, would take them to their destination. There was the simple inn. The big garden was only dimly lit; the tables had not been set, and the chairs leaned against them. Next to these, dim red lights flickered in globular lamps on slender green posts. A few customers were sitting in the café, the innkeeper among them. When Marie and Felix walked past him, he stood up and raised his hat. They opened the door to the garden salon in which a few turned-down gas flames were hissing. A young waiter sat snoozing in a corner. He quickly roused himself, hurried to turn up the gas lamps, and helped the customers out of their wraps. They sat down in a very dim and cozy corner and moved their chairs quite close together. Without much reflection they ordered food and drink, and they were now alone. Only the blinking dim red lights of the lamps at the entrance were to be seen. The corners of the room blended in with the semidarkness.

Both were still silent, but finally Marie managed some tortured, trembling words. "Tell me, Felix, what is the matter with you? Please tell me."

That smile again appeared on his lips. "Nothing, dear," he said; "don't even ask. Surely you know my moods—or don't you know them yet?"

"Of course I know your moods, oh yes. But you're not in a bad mood. You are out of sorts, I can see that, and there must be a reason for it. I beg of you, Felix: what is the matter? Tell me, I beg of you!"

He scowled, for the waiter was coming in with their order. And when she said again, "Tell me, tell me," he directed her attention to the lad and made a gesture of annoyance. The waiter left. "Now we are alone," said Marie. She moved closer to Felix and took his hands in hers. "What's wrong with you? What's wrong with you? I have to know. Don't you love me any more?" He was silent. She kissed his hand and he slowly withdrew it. "Well? Well?" He looked around as though he were seeking help. "I beg of you, leave me alone; don't ask questions, don't torture me!" She let go of his hand and looked him full in the face. "I want to know." He stood up and drew a deep breath. Then he clasped his head with both hands and said: "You'll drive me crazy yet. Stop asking questions." He remained standing with a fixed gaze for a long time, and she fearfully watched him staring into space. Then he sat down again, took quieter breaths, and a weary gentleness spread over his face. A few seconds later all the terror seemed to have left him, and he gently and amiably said to Marie: "Why don't you eat and drink?"

She obediently took her knife and fork, solicitously asking:

"What about you?" "Sure, sure," he replied, but he remained sitting motionless and did not touch his food. "Then I can't eat either," she said. So he began to eat and drink, but soon he silently put down his knife and fork, propped his head on his hand, and averted his eyes from Marie. For a little while she watched him with pinched lips and then pulled away his arm, which was concealing his face from her. And now she saw something shimmering in his eyes, and the moment she called out "Felix, Felix," he began to cry and sob bitterly. She drew his head to her breast, stroked his hair, kissed his forehead, and attempted to kiss away his tears. "Felix, Felix!" His crying became more and more gentle. "What is the matter with you, sweetheart, my adorable, only sweetheart, do tell me!" Because his head was still against her breast, his words sounded muffled and heavy. "Marie, Marie, I wasn't going to tell you. One more year and then it will be all over." And now he cried violently and loudly. But she, her eyes wide open and deathly pale, understood nothing, refused to understand anything. Something cold and terrifying was choking her, but suddenly she cried out: "Felix, Felix!" Then she flung herself down before him and looked up at his tearful, stricken face, which now had sunk down on his chest. He saw her kneeling before him and whispered to her: "Get up, get up." She stood, mechanically obeying, and sat down opposite him. She was unable to talk, unable to ask. After a few seconds of utter silence, he suddenly burst out in a loud wail, his gaze directed upward as though something incomprehensible were weighing upon him: "Horrible, horrible!"

She regained her voice. "Come! Come!" That was all she managed to say. "Yes, let's go," he said and gestured as though he wanted to shake something off. He called the waiter, paid the bill, and they both quickly left the room.

Outside the spring night silently enveloped them. On the dark path Marie stopped and took her lover's hand. "But now explain to me, at last. . . ."

He had calmed down completely, and what he now told her

sounded simple and matter-of-fact, as though it really were nothing unusual. He freed his hand and stroked her cheeks. It was so dark they could hardly see each other.

"You needn't be frightened, Mitzi, because a year is a long, long time! You see, I've got just another year to live."

She screamed: "But you are insane, you are insane!"

"It is pitiful of me to tell you at all—stupid, in fact. But you know, to keep it all to myself and walk around lonely all the time with the idea—I probably couldn't have endured that for long. Perhaps it's even good for you to get used to it. But come along; why are we standing here like that? I myself am accustomed to the idea, Marie. I haven't believed what Alfred said for a long time."

"So you didn't go to see Alfred? But the other doctors don't know anything."

"You see, dear, the uncertainty has made me suffer terribly these last few weeks. Now it's better. Now at least I know. I consulted Dr. Bernard, and at least he told me the truth."

"No, he didn't tell you the truth. He just wanted to scare you so you'd take better care of yourself."

"My dear, I had a very serious talk with the man. I had to be sure. For your sake, too, you know."

"Felix, Felix," she cried and put her arms around him. "What are you saying! I won't live a day without you, not even an hour."

"Go on," he said quietly, "calm down." They had reached the exit of the Prater. Things around them had become livelier, louder, and brighter. Carriages rattled in the streets, there was the whistling and tinkling of the streetcars, and a railway train rolled heavily over a bridge above them. Marie winced. All of a sudden there was something mocking and hostile about all this life, and it hurt her. She pulled him along with her so that they might avoid the main road and walk home through quiet side streets.

For a moment it occurred to her that he ought to take a carriage, but she could not bring herself to tell him. After all, they could walk slowly.

"You are not going to die, no, no," she said in a soft voice, pressing her head to his shoulder. "But without you I can't go on living."

"My dear girl, you will change your mind. I've thought it all over. Sure. You know, when this borderline was suddenly drawn, I saw things so clearly."

"There is no borderline."

"Of course, sweetheart. It's impossible to believe. Right now I don't believe it myself. It's something so incomprehensible, isn't it? Just think, in one year I, a man who's walking beside you and speaking words, loud words you can hear, will lie there cold and perhaps even decomposed."

"Stop it, stop it!"

"And you will look the way you look now. Just as you do now. Perhaps you'll be a bit pale from weeping, but then there'll be an evening again and a lot of evenings, and it will be summer and fall and winter and then spring again, and I shall have been dead and cold for a whole year. Yes! . . . What's the matter?"

She was crying bitterly and the tears rolled down her cheeks and her neck.

A despairing smile spread over his face, and he whispered hoarsely and harshly between clenched teeth: "Forgive me."

She went on sobbing while they walked along, and he fell silent. Their way led past the City Park through dark, quiet, wide streets over which a gentle, sad fragrance of lilac came wafting from the shrubs in the park. Slowly they walked on. On the other side stood tall houses, monotonously gray and yellow. The mighty cupola of St. Charles's, rising into the blue nocturnal sky, came closer. They turned into a side street and soon reached the house they lived in. Slowly they mounted the dimly lit stairs, and behind the windows and doors facing the corridor they could hear the servant girls chatting and laughing. A few moments later they had closed the door behind them. The window was open, and a few dark roses in a plain vase on the night table filled the room with fragrance. From the street came a gentle hum. They stepped to the window. In the house across the way everything was still and dark. He sat down on the sofa; she closed the shutters and drew the curtains. She lit a candle and put it on the table. He did not see any of this, but sat there absorbed in thought. She approached him. "Felix!" she cried. He looked up and smiled. "What, dear?" he asked. And as he spoke these words in a soft and gentle voice, she was gripped by a feeling of boundless fear. No, she did not want to lose him. Never! Never, never! It wasn't true, anyway. It wasn't even possible. She tried to talk, to tell him all this. She flung herself down before him but did not have the strength to speak. She put her head on his lap and cried. His hands rested on her hair. "Don't cry," he whispered tenderly. "No more, Mitzi." She lifted her head, and a wonderful hope came over her. "It isn't true, is it? Is it?" He kissed her on the lips, long and passionately. Then he said almost harshly, "It is true," and stood up. He went over to the window where he stood completely in the shade, with the candlelight flickering only at his feet. After a while he began to speak: "You have to get used to the idea. Simply imagine that we broke up. You won't even have to know that I am no longer alive."

She did not seem to be listening to him, having hidden her face in the sofa cushions. He continued: "If you consider the matter philosophically, it is not that terrible. After all, we have so much time left to be happy, haven't we, Mitzi?"

Suddenly she looked up with large, tearless eyes. Then she hurried over to him, clung to him, and pressed him to her breast with both arms. She whispered, "I want to die with you." He smiled. "That's childish. I am not as petty as you think. And I don't have the right to take you along with me."

"I can't exist without you."

"How long *were* you without me? When I met you a year ago, I was already doomed. I didn't know it at the time, but I already suspected it."

"You don't know it even today."

"Yes, I do know it, and that's why I am releasing you right now."

She clung tighter to him. "Accept it, accept it," he said. She did not answer, but looked up at him as though not understanding.

"You are so beautiful, and oh, so healthy. What a marvelous right to life you have. Leave me alone."

She screamed. "I have lived with you and I shall die with you!"

He kissed her on the forehead. "You will not. I forbid it. You must get that idea out of your mind."

"I swear to you. . . ."

"Don't swear. You would only ask me one day to release you from your oath."

"Is that how much faith you have in me?"

"Oh, I know that you love me. You will not leave me until . . ."

"I shall never, never leave you." He shook his head. She nestled close to him, took his hands and kissed them.

"You are so good to me," he said, "and that makes me very sad."

"Don't be sad. Whatever may happen, we two share the same fate."

"No," he said gravely and firmly, "forget about that. I am not like other men, and I don't want to be. I understand everything. It would be wretched of me if I tried to listen to you any longer, if I let myself be intoxicated by these words of yours that are inspired by the first moment of pain. I have to go and you must stay."

She had started to cry again. He caressed and kissed her to calm her down, and they remained standing by the window without saying anything more. The minutes passed and the candle burned lower.

After a while Felix went and sat down on the sofa. A great weariness had settled over him. Marie came to him and sat down beside him. She gently took his head and put it against her shoulder. He looked at her tenderly and closed his eyes. Thus he fell asleep.

The morning crept up pale and cool. Felix woke up, his head still on her chest. She, however, was fast asleep. He tiptoed away from her, went to the window, and looked down on the street, which at dawn was deserted. He shivered. After a few minutes he stretched out on the bed in his clothes and stared at the ceiling.

It was bright daylight when he awoke. Marie was sitting on the edge of the bed, having kissed him awake. They both smiled. Had it not all been a bad dream? He now felt so healthy and so fresh, and outside the sun was smiling. Noises came from the street; everything was so alive. In the house across the way many windows stood open. And there on the table breakfast was ready, as it was every morning. The room was so bright; daylight penetrated every nook and cranny. There were shimmering particles of sunlight, and everywhere there was hope, hope, hope!

The doctor was smoking his afternoon cigar when a woman was announced. It was before his office hours, and Alfred was somewhat annoyed. "Marie," he called out in astonishment when the woman entered.

"Don't be angry with me for disturbing you this early. Please go on smoking."

"If you don't mind. . . . But what is the matter, what is wrong with you?"

She stood before him, one hand propped on his desk, the other holding a parasol. "Is it true," she blurted out, "that Felix is so sick? Oh, you are turning pale. Why haven't you told me, why?"

"The very idea!" He walked up and down in the room. "You are being foolish. Please sit down."

"Answer me."

"Of course he is ailing. That's not news to you."

"There's no hope for him!" she shouted.

"Come, come!"

"I know there isn't, and so does he. Yesterday he consulted Dr. Bernard, and he told him."

"Many distinguished doctors have been wrong."

"You have examined Felix many times; tell me the truth."

"In these matters there is no such thing as absolute truth."

"You say that because he is your friend. You simply won't tell me, right? But I can tell by looking at you. So it's true, isn't it? Oh God, God!"

"My dear girl, calm down."

She gave him a quick look. "Is it true?"

"Well, yes, he is sick, but you knew that."

"Oh . . ."

"But why was he told? And then . . ."

"Well? Well? But please don't give me hope if there is no hope."

"One can never predict it with certainty. It can go on like this for a long time."

"I know. For a year."

Alfred pinched his lips. "But tell me, why did he go to see another doctor?"

"Well, because he knew that you would never tell him the truth; it's as simple as that."

"It doesn't make any sense," the doctor burst out, "no sense at all. I don't understand that. As if it were absolutely necessary to tell a person . . ."

At that moment the door opened and Felix came in.

"I thought so," he said when he caught sight of Marie.

"You are certainly being foolish," exclaimed the doctor, "really foolish."

"You can save your breath, dear Alfred," replied Felix. "I thank you for meaning well. You acted like a friend, you were wonderful."

Marie interjected, "He says that the other doctor surely . . ."

"Never mind," Felix interrupted her. "As long as it was

possible you had a right to maintain me in my delusion. From now on it would be a tasteless farce."

"You are being childish," said Alfred. "Vienna is full of people whom the doctors gave up on twenty years ago."

"But most of them are six feet under."

Alfred paced up and down in the room. "First of all, nothing has changed between yesterday and today. You will take it easy, that's all, you will follow my advice more than you have in the past, and that is a good thing. Just a week ago a fifty-year-old man came to see me. . . ."

"I know, I know," Felix interrupted. "This is the famous man of fifty who was given up on as a young man of twenty, but now is the very picture of health and the father of eight healthy children."

"Such things do happen, there is no doubt about it," Alfred interjected.

"You know," Felix said, "I am not the type of person to whom miracles happen."

"Miracles?" exclaimed Alfred. "These are all natural things."

"But just take a look at him," said Marie. "I find he looks better now than he did last winter."

"He just has to take care of himself," said Alfred, stopping in front of his friend. "You will now take a trip to the mountains and relax there, relax completely."

"When should we leave?" asked Marie eagerly.

"But that's nonsense," said Felix.

"And in the fall you'll go south."

"And what about next spring?" asked Felix mockingly.

"I hope you will be well by then," exclaimed Marie.

"Sure, well," laughed Felix, "well! Not ailing any more in any case."

"That's what I always say," the doctor exclaimed; "those great clinicians are no psychologists; none of them are."

"Because they can't see that we cannot stand the truth," Felix interjected.

"I say there are no truths. That doctor thought he had to give you a good scare so you won't do anything foolish. I suppose he thought along those lines. If you get well despite his prognosis, he certainly won't be disgraced. After all, he will only have warned you."

"Let's cut out all the childish talk," Felix interjected. "I had a very serious conversation with the man and was able to make him see that I must have certainty. Family problems! That always impresses such people. And I don't mind admitting that all that uncertainty had become too much to bear."

"As though you had certainty now," Alfred flared up.

"Yes, now I have certainty. Your efforts right now are in vain. Now it's only a matter of spending my last year as wisely as possible. You'll see, dear Alfred, that I am a man who will depart from the world with a smile. Oh, don't cry, Mitzi; you have no idea how beautiful this world will seem to you even without me. Well, Alfred, don't you agree?"

"Oh, come on! You're torturing the girl quite needlessly."

"It's true, it would make more sense to put a quick end to me. Leave me, Mitzi; come on, let me die alone!"

"Give me poison!" Marie suddenly screamed.

"You are crazy, both of you," cried the doctor.

"Poison! I don't want to live one second longer than *he* does, and I want to prove it to him. He won't believe me. Why doesn't he believe me? Why doesn't he?"

"Listen, Mitzi, I will tell you something. If you mention this nonsense once more, just once more, I shall simply vanish from sight and you'll never see me again. I have no right to tie your fate to mine, and I don't even want that responsibility."

"You know, my dear Felix," said the doctor, "you will be kind enough to start your trip without delay. It can't go on like this. I shall take both of you to the station tonight, and I hope the good air and the peace and quiet will bring both of you to reason again."

"I certainly have no objection," said Felix. "I don't care where. . . ."

"All right," Alfred interrupted him; "for the time being there isn't the slightest reason to despair, and you could really stop making all those sad remarks."

Marie dried her tears and gave the doctor a grateful look.

"A great psychologist," smiled Felix. "When a doctor is rude, it makes a person feel so healthy."

"First and foremost, I am your friend. So you know. . . ."

"Leave . . . tomorrow . . . for the mountains!"

"Yes, that's agreed."

"Well, in any case, I thank you very much," said Felix as he shook hands with his friend. "And now let's go. Someone's already clearing his throat outside. Come along, Mitzi!"

"Thank you, doctor," said Marie in parting.

"No need to thank me. Just be sensible and take good care of him. So long, then."

On the staircase Felix suddenly said, "The doctor is a nice person, isn't he?"

"Oh yes."

"And young and healthy, and he probably has forty more years to live—or a hundred."

They had reached the street and were surrounded by people who walked and talked and laughed and lived and had no thought of death.

They moved into a little house right on the lake. It was removed from the village proper as one of the last detached stragglers of the row of houses spread out along the water. Behind the house the meadows extended upward into the hills, and farther up there were fields in the florescence of summer. In the distance, not often visible, were the blurred outlines of faraway mountains. And when they stepped out of their house onto the terrace, which jutted out from the clear bottom of the lake on four brown, moist piles, they faced on the other shore a long chain of bare rocks over whose heights rested the cold gleam of the silent sky.

In the first days of their sojourn a wonderful peace had come over them, a peace they scarcely comprehended. It was as though the common fate had had power over them only in their accustomed surroundings. Here, in the new milieu, nothing that had been inflicted upon them in another world had any validity. In all their time together they had never found such refreshing solitude. There were times when they looked at each other as though there had been between them some small incident, like a quarrel or a misunderstanding, which they could not discuss any more. On the nice summer days Felix felt so well that soon after their arrival he wanted to resume his work. Marie would not permit it. "You are not quite well yet," she smiled. On the little table where Felix had piled his books and papers the sunbeams danced, and through the window came gentle, pleasant lake breezes that carried none of the world's misfortunes.

One evening they had an old farmer row them out on the lake, as was their custom. They used a good, roomy boat with a cushioned seat on which Marie would sit while Felix lay at her feet, wrapped in a warm, gray traveling rug, which doubled as a sheet and a blanket. He rested his head against her knees. A light fog lay over the wide, calm surface of the water, and it seemed as though the dusk were slowly rising from the lake to spread gradually toward the shore. Today Felix dared to smoke a cigar, and he looked over the waves toward the rocks whose domes were bathed in the faint yellow sunlight.

"Say, Mitzi," he started talking, "do you dare to look up?"

"Where?"

He pointed skyward. "Straight up there, into the dark blue. You see, I can't. It gives me the creeps."

She looked upward and let her glance rest there for a few seconds. "If anything, it gives me pleasure," she said.

"Does it? When the sky is as clear as it is today, I can't manage it at all. This distance, this horrendous expanse! When there are clouds up there, I don't find it that unpleasant; after all, the clouds still belong to us, and looking at them I see something akin to us."

"It'll probably rain tomorrow," said the oarsman; "the

mountains seem too close today!" And he rested the oars so that the boat glided over the waves soundlessly and more and more slowly.

Felix cleared his throat. "Strange; cigars don't quite agree with me yet."

"Throw it away, then!"

Felix twisted the glowing cigar between his fingers a few times, threw it into the water, and without turning toward Marie he said: "So I am not quite well yet, am I?"

"Go on," she replied reassuringly and gently moved her hand over his hair.

"What shall we do when it starts to rain? Then you will have to let me work after all."

"You're not allowed to work."

She bent down to him and looked into his eyes. She noticed that his cheeks were flushed. "I will dispel your black thoughts in short order! But shouldn't we head for home now? It's turning cool."

"Cool? I'm not cool."

"Oh, well, you've got the thick traveling rug."

"Oh," he exclaimed, "I'm such an egotist that I forgot all about your summer dress." He turned to the oarsman. "Home, please." After a few hundred strokes of the oar they were close to their house. At that point Marie noticed that Felix was clasping his left wrist with his right hand. "What is wrong?"

"Mitzi, I'm really not quite well yet."

"Go on. . . ."

"I have a temperature. Hmm . . . too bad!"

"I'm sure you are wrong," said Marie, worrying. "I'll go for the doctor right away."

"Sure, sure, that's all I need."

They had reached land and went ashore. Their rooms were almost dark but still contained the warmth of the day. While Marie was preparing supper, Felix sat quietly in his armchair.

"Listen," he said suddenly, "the first week is over."

She quickly walked over to him from the table she had been

setting and clasped him with both arms. "What's bothering you again?"

He shook her off. "Oh, forget it!" He stood up and sat down at the table. She followed him. He drummed with his fingers on the table top. "I feel so defenseless. It suddenly comes over you."

"But Felix, Felix." She moved her chair close to his.

He looked around the room with his eyes opened wide. Then he shook his head in annoyance as though he were unable to grasp something and hissed from between clenched teeth: "Defenseless! Defenseless! No one can help me. The thing itself is not that terrible, but this defenselessness!"

"Felix, I beg of you, don't get excited. I'm sure it's nothing. Just for your peace of mind, would you like me to send for the doctor?"

"Oh, please, don't do that to me. Forgive me for entertaining you with my illness again."

"But . . ."

"It won't happen again. Come, give me something to drink. Yes, yes, something to drink! Thanks. Well, why don't you say something?"

"What shall I say?"

"Anything at all. If you can't think of anything to say, read to me. Excuse me—after the meal, of course. Go ahead and eat. I'm eating too." He helped himself. "I even have an appetite; the food tastes pretty good to me."

"I'm glad," said Marie with a forced smile.

And they both ate and drank.

The following days brought warm rain. They would sit alternately in the room and on their terrace until nightfall. They read or looked out the window, or he watched her do some sewing. Sometimes they played cards, and he even taught her the rudiments of chess. At other times he lay down on the sofa, and she sat beside him and read to him. Those were quiet days and evenings, and Felix actually felt quite well. He was pleased that the bad weather could not harm him. Nor did his temperature return.

One afternoon, when the sky seemed to clear after a long period of rain, they were again sitting on the balcony, and Felix said quite abruptly without referring to any previous conversation: "When you come to think of it, the people walking the earth are all under a sentence of death."

Marie looked up from her sewing.

"Why, yes," he continued; "imagine, for example, that someone said to you: My dear lady, you are going to die on the first of May, 1970. Then you would spend your entire future life in inexpressible fear of the first of May, 1970, though today you surely don't believe you are going to live to be a hundred."

She did not answer.

He continued talking while he looked out on the lake, which was beginning to gleam with the sunbeams now breaking through.

"Others are walking around proud and healthy, and in a few weeks some absurd accident will carry them off. Those aren't giving death a thought, are they?"

"Look," said Marie, "forget those foolish thoughts. Surely you must realize today that you are going to get well again."

He smiled.

"Sure, you are among the very ones who are going to get well."

He laughed out loud. "My dear, do you really believe that I am going to be tricked by fate? You think I shall be deceived by this semblance of well-being with which Nature is favoring me now? I happen to know where I stand, and the thought of my imminent death makes me a philosopher, as it has done to other great men."

"Oh, stop it, will you!"

"Oooh, young lady, I am going to die, and I am supposed to spare you even the little displeasure of hearing me talk about it?"

She flung away her sewing and came to him. "But I feel it," she said in a tone of sincere conviction, "I feel that you are going to stay with me. You yourself can't even judge how much better you are getting. You simply must get it out of your mind, and then the evil shadow will be out of our life."

He looked at her for a long time. "It really seems that you can't grasp it at all. You have to see it with your own eyes. Look at this." He picked up a newspaper. "What does it say here?"

"June 12, 1890."

"Yes, 1890. And now imagine the number one in place of the zero. By that time everything will be over. All right, do you understand now?"

She took the newspaper from his hand and angrily tossed it on the floor.

"It's not the newspaper's fault," he said calmly. And suddenly he rose, seemed to reject all such ideas vigorously and resolutely, and exclaimed: "Look, how beautiful this is! The sun lying on the water—and over there"—he bent over to the side of the terrace and looked to the opposite side, where the land was flat—"how the fields are stirring! I'd like to go out there for a while."

"Won't it be too damp there?"

"Come along, I have to get out into the open."

She did not really dare to give him an argument.

They took their hats, put on their coats, and set out on the road leading to the fields. The sky had cleared up almost completely. Many-formed white mists moved over the distant mountain range. It was as though the green of the meadows blended into the golden white that seemed to hem the landscape. Their path soon led them amidst the wheat, and then they had to walk single file as the stalks rustled under their coats. Soon they branched off into a deciduous forest with foliage that was not too thick and found well-tended paths with benches at short intervals. Here they walked arm in arm.

"Isn't it beautiful here!" Felix exclaimed. "And this smell!"

"Don't you think that after this rain . . ." Marie interjected, without finishing her sentence.

He moved his head impatiently. "Oh, forget it. Does it really matter? It's not pleasant to be reminded of it all the time."

As they walked on, the woods became sparser and sparser and the lake gleamed through the foliage. They were barely a hundred steps away from it. A rather narrow spit of land, on which the forest concluded with a few sparse shrubs, jutted out into the water. On it stood some tables and benches of pine wood, and there was a wooden fence right by the shore. A gentle evening breeze had sprung up and drove the waves to the shore. And now the wind was blowing into the shrubbery and over the trees, so that the moist leaves started dripping again. Over the water lay the faint sheen of the parting day.

"I never suspected how beautiful all this is," said Felix.

"Yes, it is lovely."

"But you don't know," exclaimed Felix. "You can't know it, because you don't have to bid it farewell." And he slowly took a few steps and propped both arms on the slender fence whose narrow supports were laved by the water. For a long time he looked out on the shimmering surface of the lake. Then he turned around. Marie was standing behind him, and her eyes were sad with suppressed tears.

"You see," said Felix in a bantering tone of voice, "all this I am leaving to you. Yes, yes, for it belongs to me. This is the secret of the outlook on life which I have discovered: one has such a powerful feeling of immense possession. With all these things I could do whatever I please. On the bare rock over there I could make flowers bloom, and I could chase those white clouds from the sky. I'm not doing these things, for everything is beautiful just the way it is. My dear girl, you will understand me only when you are alone. Yes, then you will definitely have the feeling that all this has become your property."

He took her by the hand and pulled her close to him. Then

he stretched out his other arm as though he were showing her all that splendor. "All this, all this," he said. Since she was still silent and still had those wide, tearless eyes, he abruptly stopped and said: "Let's head home now!"

Dusk was approaching and they took the shore road, by which they soon reached their habitation. "That really was a nice walk," said Felix.

She nodded mutely.

"We'll take it often, Mitzi."

"Yes," she said.

"And"—he added in a tone of supercilious pity—"I won't torture you any more either."

On one of the following afternoons he decided to resume his work. When he was about to put pencil to paper again, he looked over at Marie with a certain malicious curiosity to see whether she was going to stop him, but she said nothing. Soon he put pencil and paper aside and picked up some unimportant book to read. That provided better diversion for him. He was still incapable of working. He would have to fight his way to an utter contempt for life before he could set down his last will like a sage, calmly facing mute eternity. This is what he was striving for. It was not to be a last will of the kind that ordinary people compose, a will that always betrays a secret fear of dying. Also, this document was not to concern itself with things that can be seen and touched and which, after all, were bound to perish some time after him; *his* last will was to be a poem, a quiet, smiling farewell to a world he had transcended. He said nothing to Marie about this thought. She would not have understood. He felt he was so different from her. It was with a certain pride that he sat opposite her on the long afternoons when, as happened habitually, she had dozed off over her book and her curls had fallen over her forehead. His self-esteem grew when he saw how much he was capable of concealing from her. This made him feel so solitary and so exalted.

On that afternoon, when she had again fallen asleep, he silently stole away and took a walk in the woods. The stillness of the sultry summer afternoon was all around him. And now he clearly realized that it could happen today. He drew a deep breath; he felt so light, so free. He walked on beneath the heavy shade of the trees. The muted daylight flowed over him beneficently. He perceived everything—the shade, the peace, the gentle air—as a boon. He enjoyed it all. The awareness that he was going to lose all this sweetness of life was not fraught with pain. "Lose it, lose it," he muttered under his breath. He drew a deep breath, and as the gentle air flowed into his lungs so deliciously and easily he suddenly could not understand that he was supposed to be sick at all. But he *was* sick, he was lost. And all at once he had something like an illumination: He did not believe it. That was it, and that was why he felt so free and so well and why this seemed to him to be the proper time. It was not that he had overcome his lust for life; he had simply lost his fear of death, because he no longer believed in death. He knew that he was among those who were going to get well. He felt as though something that had lain dormant in an obscure corner of his soul were awakening again. He felt a need to open his eyes wider, to take bigger strides, to draw bigger breaths. The day grew brighter and life became livelier. So that was it; was that what it was? And why? Why did he suddenly have to get so drunk with hope? Ah, hope! It was more than that; it was certainty. As recently as this morning he had felt tortured, his throat had been constricted, and now, now he was well, he was healthy. He cried the word aloud: "Healthy!" He had reached the end of the forest. Before him lay the lake in dark blue smoothness. He sat down on a bench and stayed there in great comfort, his gaze directed at the water. He reflected how strange that would be; the joy of getting well had masqueraded as the pleasure of a proud farewell.

There was a small noise behind him. He hardly had time to turn around. It was Marie. Her eyes shone and her face was slightly flushed.

"What are you doing here?"

"Why did you go out? Why did you leave me alone? I got very frightened."

"Oh, go on," he said and drew her down beside him. He smiled at her and kissed her. She had such warm, full lips. "Come," he said softly and pulled her onto his lap. She nestled close to him and put her arms around his neck. How beautiful she was! A sultry fragrance emanated from her blonde hair, and infinite tenderness for this cuddly, sweet-smelling creature on his bosom welled up in him. Tears came to his eyes, and he reached for her hands in order to kiss them. How he loved her!

A faint hissing sound came from the lake. They both looked up, rose, and approached the shore arm in arm. A steamship could be seen in the distance. They waited for it to come close enough for them to make out the contours of the people on deck; then they turned around and walked homeward through the forest. They linked arms and walked slowly, sometimes smiling at each other. Old words came to them again, the words of their first days of love. They exchanged the sweet questions of doubting tenderness as well as the affectionate words of reassuring blandishment. They were cheerful and like children again, and happiness was there.

A sweltering, scorching summer with hot, blistering days and mild, sensual nights had come. Every day brought back the previous day, every night repeated the previous night; time stood still. And they were alone. They paid attention only to each other; the woods, the lake, the little house—that was their world. A cozy sultriness enveloped them and made them forget to think. Carefree nights of laughter and lazy days of tenderness flew by them.

On one of those nights the candle was burning late and Marie, who was lying in bed with her eyes open, sat up. She looked at the face of her beloved, which expressed the peace of a sound sleep. She listened to his breath. Now, after all, it was as good as certain that every hour brought him closer to a cure. An ineffable feeling of affection surged through her, and she bent close to him in a desire to feel his breath on her cheeks. Oh, how good it was to be alive! And he, only he, was her whole life. Oh, now she had him again, he was restored to her, she had him forever!

One breath of the sleeping Felix that sounded different from the rest startled her. It was a soft, labored moan. His lips had opened slightly and a crease of pain was visible on them. She was horrified to notice beads of perspiration on his forehead. His head was turned slightly to the side. Then his lips closed again, the peaceful expression on his face returned, and after a few labored breaths his breathing became normal and almost soundless again. Marie, however, suddenly felt gripped by torturous anxiety. She felt like waking him up, clinging close to him, and feeling his warmth, his life, his being. A strange consciousness of guilt came over her, and her joyous belief in his recovery suddenly seemed like presumptuousness. Now she tried to persuade herself that it had not really been a firm belief, no, just a slight, grateful hope for which she surely could not be punished so harshly. She vowed not to be so unreflectingly happy anymore. All of a sudden this entire giddy period of rapture seemed to her like a time of frivolous sin for which they had to atone. Of course! But then, what might be a sin under ordinary circumstances, was it not something different with them? A love that might work a miracle? And might it not be those last sweet nights that would restore his health?

A terrible moan came from Felix's mouth. Half asleep, he had sat up in bed with eyes opened wide in fear, and his staring into space made Marie cry out. He became wide awake and blurted out, "What's the matter, what's the matter?" Marie was speechless. "Did you scream, Marie? I heard a scream." He was breathing very rapidly. "I felt as if I was choking. I had a dream, too, though I don't know what it was about."

"I got so frightened," she stammered.

"You know, Marie, now I feel chilly, too."

"Naturally," she replied, "if you have bad dreams."

"Oh, no," he said, darting an angry look upward. "I'm running a fever again, that's what it is." His teeth chattered; he lay down and pulled the blanket over himself.

She looked around in desperation. "Shall I get you . . . do you want . . . ?"

"Not a thing; just go to sleep! I'm tired and shall sleep, too. Leave the light on." He shut his eyes and pulled the blanket up over his mouth. Marie did not dare to ask any more questions. She knew how pity could enrage him when he did not feel quite well. After a few minutes he fell asleep, but she was no longer capable of sleeping. Soon gray strips of dawn came creeping into the room. These first faint signs of morning did Marie a lot of good. She felt as though something friendly and smiling was coming to call on her. She had a strange desire to go out and meet the morning. Very softly she climbed out of bed, quickly put on her robe, and slipped out on the terrace. The sky, the mountains, the lake—they all still coalesced into a dark, uncertain gray. It gave her a special kind of pleasure to strain her eyes a bit so as to recognize the outlines more distinctly. She sat down on the armchair and submerged her eyes in the dawn. An inexpressible sense of well-being suffused Marie as she lounged out there in the profound stillness of the dawning summer day. All around her was so peaceful, so mild, and so eternal. It was so beautiful to be alone for a while in the midst of the great stillness, away from the narrow, steamy room. And suddenly this realization flashed through her: she had gladly left his side, she was glad to be out here, all alone!

All day long the thoughts of the previous night kept coming back to her—no longer as torturous or uncanny as they had been in the darkness, but all the more distinct and forming the basis for decisions. Her first decision was to tone down the ardor of his love as much as possible. She could not understand why she had not thought of that the whole time. Oh, she would be so gentle and so clever that it would not look like a rejection but only like a new and better kind of love.

But she did not need any particular cleverness or gentleness. Since that night his ardor seemed to have cooled, and he treated Marie with a weary tenderness that at first reassured and finally alienated her. During the day he read a lot or just seemed to be reading, for often enough she saw him stare into space over his book. Their conversation touched on a thousand everyday matters and nothing of importance, but without Marie's gaining the impression that he was no longer initiating her into the secret of his thoughts. Everything happened in an entirely natural way, as though this subdued, indifferent element in his manner were only the cheerful weariness of a convalescent. In the morning he would lie in bed for a long time, while it had become her custom to rush out into the open air at the first sign of daybreak. She either remained sitting on the balcony or walked down to the lake where she sat in a boat and let the gentle waves rock her without leaving the shore. Sometimes she took a walk in the woods, and usually she was already returning from her little morning outing when she stepped to his bed to wake him up. She was happy about his sound sleep, for she regarded it as a good omen. She did not know how often he awoke during the night, and she did not see his look of immense sadness that rested on her while she was enjoying the deep sleep of a healthy young person.

One morning she had boarded the boat again and the day was spraying its first golden sparks over the lake when she was gripped by the desire to venture farther out into the shimmering clear water. She went out a good distance, and since she was not an experienced oarswoman, she overexerted herself while rowing, though this only increased her enjoyment of the ride. Even at such an early hour one could not be all alone on the water. Several boats passed Marie's, and she seemed to notice that some came intentionally closer to her. A small, elegant keelboat operated by two young men came very close to hers and passed her very quickly. The two gentlemen shipped their oars, raised their caps, and greeted her politely and smilingly.

Marie gave them a surprised look and said an automatic "Good morning." Then she followed the two young men with her eyes without being quite aware of what she was doing. They turned around as well and greeted her once more. Suddenly she realized that she had done something wrong, and she rowed toward her house as quickly as her modest skill permitted her. It took her almost a half hour to go back, and she arrived heated and with disheveled hair. From the lake she had seen Felix sitting on the balcony, and now she rushed into the house. Quite confused, as though she were conscious of some guilt, she hurried out on the balcony, embraced Felix from behind and asked jocularly and with exaggerated jollity: "Guess who!"

He slowly detached himself and calmly gave her a sidelong glance. "What's the matter with you? Why are you so exuberant?"

"Because I have you again."

"Why are you so hot? You're burning up!"

"Oh, Lord! I'm so happy, so happy, so happy!" She frolicsomely pushed the blanket from his knees and sat on his lap. She was annoyed first at her embarrassment, then at his peevish expression, and kissed him on the lips.

"What is it that makes you so happy?"

"Don't I have any reason? I'm so happy that . . ."—she stopped and then continued—"that you have been freed from it."

"From what?" There was something resembling suspicion in his voice.

She had to keep on talking, there was no remedy for it.

"Well, the fear."

"Do you mean the fear of death?"

"Don't come right out and name it."

"Why do you say that *I* have been freed from it? *You* have been freed from it, too, haven't you?" He said it with a searching, almost malicious expression in his eyes.

Instead of answering, she burrowed in his hair with her hands and brought her mouth close to his forehead. He bent his head back a little and continued, inexorably and coldly: "Wasn't it once at least your intention? *My* fate was supposed to be *your* fate?"

"And it will be, too," she interjected animatedly and cheerfully.

"No, it will not be," he interrupted her, seriously. "Why are we lulling ourselves? I have not been freed from 'it.' I can feel 'it' coming closer and closer to me."

"But . . ." She had imperceptibly moved away from him and was now leaning against the railing of the balcony. He got up and started pacing up and down.

"Yes, I can feel it. I think it is my obligation to inform you. If it happened suddenly, it would probably scare you too much. That's why I am reminding you that almost a quarter of my time is up. Perhaps I'm only deluding myself that I have to tell you—and only cowardice is causing me to do it."

"Are you angry with me," she said, full of anxiety, "for leaving you alone?"

"Nonsense!" he quickly replied. "I wouldn't mind seeing you cheerful; I know myself well enough to say that I shall await that certain day cheerfully myself. But your jollity—frankly, I can't understand it. For this reason I want you to feel free to separate your fate from mine within the next few days."

"Felix!" She stopped his pacing with both hands. He freed himself from her again.

"The most miserable period is coming. Up to now I have been an interesting patient: a bit pale, a slight cough, a bit melancholy. Well, this sort of thing can still be rather attractive to a woman. But what is coming now, my dear, I had better spare you. It could poison your memories of me."

She vainly sought an answer and stared at him quite helplessly.

"You think it is hard to accept this. It might look unloving, perhaps even vile. I hereby declare to you that there can be no question of that, that you will even perform a very special service to me and my vanity if you accept my proposal. Because the very least that I want is that you remember me with sorrow, that you weep real tears for me. But what I don't want is that you sit bending over my bed for days and nights on end, wishing it were all over, since it has to be over some day, and that you feel released by my departure."

She was struggling for something to say. Finally she blurted out: "I shall stay with you forever."

He paid no attention. "Let's not talk about it any further. In a week's time, I think, I shall go to Vienna. I'd like to put a number of things in order. Before we leave this house I shall ask you my question—no, make my request—once more."

"Felix! I . . ."

He interrupted her vehemently. "I forbid you to speak another word on this subject until the time I mentioned." He left the balcony and turned toward the room. She wanted to follow him. "Let me go," he said very gently. "I want to be alone for a bit."

She remained on the balcony and stared with tearless eyes at the glistening surface of the lake. Felix had gone into the bedroom and had flung himself down on his bed. For a long time he stared up at the ceiling. Then he pinched his lips and clenched his fists, and with a scornful movement of his lips he whispered: "Surrender! Surrender!"

From that moment on something alien stood between them, while at the same time they had a nervous need to speak a great deal with each other. They treated the most ordinary matters with great prolixity and always became worried when they stopped talking. There were long conversations about the origin of the gray clouds that covered the mountains, what kind of weather could be expected for the next day, and why the water displayed various colors at different times of the day. When going for a walk, they would leave the immediate vicinity of the house more often than they had previously done and chose the road leading to the more densely inhabited shore. This gave them various opportunities to discuss the people they encountered. When it happened that young men crossed their path, Marie showed particular reserve, and when Felix passed some remark about the summer attire of some boatsman or mountain climber, she was apt to go so far in her hardly conscious insincerity as to reply that she had not even noticed the persons, and then it took an effort to induce her to look them over carefully when they encountered them again. The sidelong glances that he gave her on such occasions made her uncomfortable. At other times they walked alongside each other in silence for a quarter of an hour. They would sit together on the balcony without exchanging a word—until Marie frequently hit upon the idea (without being able to conceal its intentionality) of reading to him from the newspaper. She went on reading even when she noticed that he was no longer listening, because she was glad of the sound of her voice, glad that there was not utter silence between them. And yet, despite all these strenuous efforts, both of them were absorbed only in their own thoughts.

Felix acknowledged to himself that he had put on a ridiculous act for Marie that time. If he had been serious about his desire to spare her the impending misery, the best thing he could have done would have been to disappear from her side. He would have been able to find a quiet place to die in peace. He was surprised that he could think about these things with complete equanimity. But when he began to reflect seriously about the execution of this plan, when one terribly long, sleepless night he searched his soul for the details (he was planning to clear out at dawn on the next day and go to his solitude and his death, neglecting to bid Marie goodbye and leaving her in the midst of the sunny, laughing life that was lost to him), he became aware of his whole impotence and felt deep down that he would never be able to go through with it. What, then, was he to do? After all, the day was inexorably coming closer when he would have to go and leave her behind. His entire existence was waiting for that day, nothing but a torturous respite worse than death itself. If only he had not learned in his youth to observe himself! All the symptoms of his illness could have been overlooked or at least minimized. His memory recalled the image of people he had known who had been consumed by the same mortal illness and who had faced the future cheerfully and hopefully weeks before their deaths. How he cursed the hour when his uncertainty had taken him to the doctor whom he had pestered with lies and false dignity until he had been told the full, unmerciful truth! And so he was now lying there, damned a hundred times over, no better off than a condemned man who might be approached any morning by the hangman come to take him to the place of execution, and he understood that he could at no time realize the full horror of his existence. In some corner of his heart there lurked the hope, insidious and blandishing, that would never completely leave him. But his reason was stronger and it gave him clear and cold advice, kept giving it to him, and in the endless nights in which he lay awake and on the monotonous days which yet passed all too quickly he heard it ten and a hundred and a thousand times that there was only one way out and one salvation for him: to wait no longer, not an hour or a second more, and end his own life, for that would be less pitiful. And it was almost a comfort that he was under no compulsion to wait. He could put an end to it at any moment he chose.

But she, she! Especially during the day, when she walked beside him or read to him, it often seemed to him as though it was really not so hard to part from this creature. To him she was no more than a part of existence generally. She was part of the life around him that he would have to leave, not part of *him*. At other moments, however, particularly at night when she rested beside him in her youthful beauty, sound asleep with her lids shut tight, he loved her beyond measure, and the more quietly she slept, the more secluded from the world her slumber was, the more remote her dreaming soul seemed to his wakeful torment, the more madly did he adore her. And once —it was the night before they were going to leave the lake—he could barely suppress his desire to rouse her from this delicious sleep, which seemed to him like a spiteful act of unfaithfulness, and scream into her ears: "If you love me, die with me, die now." But he let her go on sleeping; tomorrow he would tell her, tomorrow—maybe.

In those nights she felt his eyes resting on her more often than he suspected. More often than he suspected she only pretended to be asleep, because a paralyzing fear kept her from opening fully the lids from between which she sometimes peered into the semidarkness of the bedroom and at his figure sitting up in bed. She could not get that last serious conversation out of her mind, and she dreaded the day on which he was going to ask her that question again. Why did it make her shudder when she saw the answer so clearly? She would stay with him to the last second and not leave his side, kiss every sigh from his lips and every tear from his lashes! Did he have no confidence in her? Was any other answer possible? Which one? Perhaps this one: "You are right. I will leave you. I will only preserve the memory of the fascinating sick man. I am now leaving you alone so as to be able to love your memory more." And then? She could not keep from imagining everything that was bound to follow this answer. She could see him before her, cool and smiling. He would extend his hand to her and say, "I thank you." Then he would turn away from her and she would rush off. It would be a summer morning, sparkling with a thousand burgeoning delights. And she would hurry on and on into the golden morning, trying to get away from him as fast as possible. And suddenly the spell would be lifted from her. She would be alone again, freed from pity. No longer would she feel those sad, querying, dying eyes rest upon her that had tormented her so frightfully all those final months. She would belong to joy and to life, she would be permitted to be young again. She would hurry off, and the laughing morning breezes would come chasing after her.

Oh, she felt doubly miserable when this image of her tangled dreams became submerged again. The very fact that it had appeared made her suffer.

And how her pity for him gnawed at her heart, how she shuddered when she thought of his awareness, his hopelessness! How she loved him, loved him more and more ardently the closer the day came on which she would have to lose him. Oh, there could be no doubt about her answer: Stay by his side, suffer with him—how little that was! To watch him wait for death, to endure these months of fear of dying—all this was so little. She would do more for him, her best, her utmost. If she promised him to kill herself on his grave, he would depart doubting whether she would really do it. She would die with him—no, *before* him. When he asked her the question, she would have the strength to say: "Let us put an end to the torment! Let us die together, and right away!" And as she became intoxicated with this idea, that woman appeared to her whose image she had just seen: a woman hurrying through the fields, caressed by the morning breeze, rushing toward life and joy. She herself was that woman—contemptible and vile.

The day of their departure dawned—a wonderfully mild morning, as though spring were returning. Marie was already sitting on the balcony and breakfast was ready when Felix came out of the living room. He drew a deep breath. "Oh, what a wonderful day!"

"Isn't it?"

"I have something to tell you, Marie."

"What is it?" And she quickly continued, as though she wanted to take the answer out of his mouth: "We're staying here, are we?"

"No, we're not, but we won't go back to Vienna right away. I am feeling pretty good today, not bad at all. Let's stop somewhere on the way."

"As you like, sweetheart." Suddenly she felt good inside, better than she had in a long time. He had not spoken so naturally all week.

"My dear, I think we shall stop in Salzburg."

"Whatever you say."

"We'll get back to Vienna soon enough, won't we? And the train trip is too long for me, anyway."

"All right," said Marie animatedly, "we aren't in any hurry."

"Everything is packed, isn't it, Mitzi?"

"Sure, we could leave right away."

"I think we'll go by carriage. It's a four or five hours' trip, and much more pleasant than by train. Yesterday's heat would still be in the compartments."

"Just as you like, sweetheart." She urged him to drink his glass of milk, and then she drew his attention to the beautiful silvery sheen on the crests of the waves. She spoke a great deal and with exaggerated jollity, and he gave her friendly and innocuous answers. Finally she offered to order the carriage in which they wished to leave for Salzburg at noon. He smilingly agreed; she quickly put on her wide straw hat, kissed Felix on the lips a few times, and then ran out in the street.

He did not ask her, and he wasn't going to either. This could be clearly seen from his cheerful facial expression. Nor was there anything lurking in his friendliness, as there sometimes was when he intentionally slashed a harmless conversation with some harsh words. When anything like that was on the way she always knew ahead of time, and now it seemed to her as though he had done her a great favor. In his gentleness there had been something giving and conciliatory.

When she returned to the balcony, she found him reading the newspaper that had arrived during her absence.

"Marie," he exclaimed, motioning to her with his eyes to come closer, "there is something strange, something strange."

"What is it?"

"Here, read! That man—well, Dr. Bernard—died."

"Who?"

"Well, the one at whose . . . oh, the one who gave me such a bleak prognosis."

She took the newspaper out of his hand. "What, Dr. Bernard?" She was about to say, "Serves him right!" but she did not utter these words. Both of them felt as though this event had a great significance for them. Yes, the man who with all the supercilious wisdom of his robust health had deprived a man seeking help of all hope had himself been carried off within a few days. Only at that moment did Felix realize how he had hated that man, and the fact that the vengeance of fate had overtaken him seemed like a most propitious omen to the sick man. It was as though a sinister ghost had disappeared from his orbit. Marie put the newspaper down and said: "Well, what do we human beings know about the future?"

He eagerly picked up that thread. "What do we know about tomorrow? We know nothing, nothing!" After a short pause he suddenly switched to another subject. "Did you order the carriage?"

"Yes," she said, "for eleven o'clock."

"That would give us time to go out on the water for a while, wouldn't it?"

She took his arm and they walked toward the boathouse. They felt as if they had received a well-deserved satisfaction.

They arrived in Salzburg in the late afternoon. To their surprise they found most houses in the city beflagged. The people they encountered were in their best clothes and some wore cockades as a decoration. In the hotel where they rented a room with a view of the Mönchsberg they were told that a big choral festival was being held in town, and they were offered tickets to the concert that was to take place in the park amidst magnificent festive illumination at eight o'clock. Their room was one floor up, and under their window they could see the Salzach river flowing by. They had both taken naps on their trip and felt so fresh that they stayed at the hotel for only a short time and went down to the street again before dusk.

The whole town was joyfully astir. All the inhabitants seemed to be in the streets, and the singers, wearing their badges, strolled among them in lighthearted groups. Many tourists were to be seen also, and farmers from the surrounding villages wearing their Sunday best wove in and out of the crowd. Flags with the city's colors waved from the gabled roofs, and in the main streets there were flower-bedecked triumphal arches. The restless stream of people surged through every lane, and a fragrant summer evening bathed this crowd in comfortably mild air.

Starting out from the banks of the Salzach, where they had been surrounded by blissful quiet, Felix and Marie joined the hustle and bustle of the city. After the monotony of their stay on the lake they found the unaccustomed noises almost disconcerting. But they soon regained the aplomb of experienced city dwellers and were able to take the goings-on in their stride. Felix did not find the gaiety of the crowd very agreeable; he never had. Marie, however, soon seemed to be in her element, and like a child she stopped to watch some people who strolled by: women in the folk costume of Salzburg or some tall singers wearing sashes. At other times she looked up and admired an especially magnificent decoration on a building. Felix walked by her side rather apathetically, and when she turned to him with a lively "Look, how beautiful!" a mute nod of his head was the only answer she received.

"Tell me honestly," she finally said, "wasn't it a good thing we came here?"

He gave her an enigmatic look. Finally he spoke: "I suppose you'd really like to attend the concert in the park."

She only smiled, and then she replied: "Well, we can't start going on binges."

Her smile annoyed him. "I wouldn't put it past you to ask me to go."

"Oh, the very idea!" she said, frightened, and immediately

looked over to the other side of the street where an elegant and good-looking pair, evidently honeymooners, was walking by in smiling conversation. Marie strolled along next to Felix, but she did not take his arm. Not infrequently they were briefly separated by the crowd, and then she found him slinking along the walls of the houses, evidently loath to establish any closer contact with all those people. In the meantime it grew darker; the street lights were lit, and in some places of the city, particularly along the triumphal arches, Chinese lanterns had been put up. Most of the crowd now moved in the direction of the concert hall, for the time of the concert was approaching. At first Felix and Marie were pulled along, but then he suddenly took her arm and they turned into a narrower side street. Soon they found themselves in a quieter, less brightly illuminated part of town. After walking along silently for a few minutes, they came to a rather remote part of the Salzach bank where the monotonous rustling of the river below reached their ears.

"What are we doing here?" she asked.

"Looking for quiet," he said almost imperiously. And when she made no reply, he continued in a tone of nervous irritability: "We don't belong there. The colorful lights and the singing gaiety and the people who are laughing and being young—these are no longer for us. *This* is the place for us where we don't hear any of that jubilation and where we are by ourselves; this is where we belong." Changing from an anguished tone to one of cold scorn, he added: "At least *I* do."

When he said that, she felt that she was not as profoundly moved as she had previously been. But she accounted for this by reflecting that she had often heard him say this, and besides, he was obviously exaggerating. And she said in a gentle, conciliatory tone of voice: "What have I done to deserve this?"

As he had done so often before, he replied maliciously: "Pardon me." Grasping his arm and pressing it tightly to her, she said: "Neither of us belongs here."

"Yes, we do!" he almost screamed.

"No," she replied gently. "I don't want to go back to that crowd either. It would revolt me as much as it does you. But what reason do we have to flee as if we were outcasts?"

At that moment the full sound of an orchestra came through to them in the calm, pure air. It was possible to hear almost every note clearly. "Music from the distance—that makes me sadder than anything else in the world."

"Yes," she agreed, "it sounds very melancholy."

They quickly walked toward the city. Here the music was less distinctly audible than it had been out there by the river bank, and when they had reached the illuminated streets with their milling throngs again, Marie felt the old tenderness of compassion for her beloved return. She understood him again, and she forgave him for everything. "Shall we go home?" she asked.

"No, why should we? Are you sleepy?"

"Oh, no."

"Let's stay out in the open a bit longer, shall we?"

"Gladly; as you like. But isn't it too cool for you?"

"Oh, it's humid. It's positively hot," he replied nervously. "Let's eat at an open-air restaurant."

"I'd love to."

They were near the park. The orchestra had finished its opening number, and the multifarious murmurs of people chatting and having a good time could be heard from the brightly illuminated park. Some people were still hurrying by on their way to the concert. Two singers who had been delayed rushed past them. Marie followed them with her eyes and then quickly looked at Felix with some anxiety, as though she had some offense to atone for. He gnawed at his lips, and his forehead bespoke laboriously suppressed anger. She thought he was going to say something, but he kept silent. He averted his gloomy gaze from her and again looked at those two singers who were now disappearing from sight at the entrance to the park. He knew what he was feeling. Here in front of him was the object of his deadly hatred, part of what would still be here when *he* was no more, something that would still be young and alive and laughing when he would no longer be able to laugh or cry. And here beside him, now guiltily pressing against his arm more tightly than before, there was another piece of laughing, living youth that felt an unconscious kinship with those others. And *he* knew this, and it gnawed away at him with excruciating pain. For a long time neither of them spoke. Finally a deep sigh came from his mouth. She wanted to look in his face, but he kept it averted. Suddenly he said: "Here it would be pretty nice."

At first she did not know what he meant. "What?"

They were in front of an outdoor restaurant in the immediate vicinity of the park, with tall trees whose tops overspread the white tablecloths and dim lamps. Business was slow that day. Felix and Marie had their choice of tables and finally sat down in a corner of the garden. There were barely twenty people there in all. Close by sat the young, elegant couple they had encountered earlier. Marie recognized them immediately. Over in the park the chorus started singing. The voices sounded a bit faint but perfectly mellow, and the leaves of the trees seemed to be agitated by the powerful sound of gay voices. Felix had ordered a good Rhine wine, and he sat there with eyes half closed, savoring the wine on his tongue and surrendering to the magic of the music without reflecting whence it came. Marie had moved up close to him, and he could feel the warmth of her knee next to his. After the terrible excitement of the last moments a soothing nonchalance had suddenly come over him, and he was pleased that he had been able to will this nonchalance into being. For right after they had sat down at the table he had firmly resolved to overcome his piercing pain. He was too weary to investigate how much his will power had contributed to this act of conquest. But now he was mollified by a number of considerations: that he had given a worse interpretation to that look of Marie's than it deserved, that she might not have looked any differently at anyone else, and was now looking at the pair of strangers at the next table in the same way she had earlier looked at those singers.

The wine was good, the music sounded seductive, and the summer evening was intoxicating. When Felix looked over at Marie, he saw that her eyes reflected infinite kindness and love. He wanted to immerse his entire being in that moment and made one last claim on his will power: to be rid of everything that was the past and the future. He wanted to be happy, or at least intoxicated. And suddenly, quite unexpectedly, he felt an entirely new sensation that was something marvelously liberating for him: that it would now hardly require a decision on his part to take his own life. Yes, instantly. And this would always be available to him; it would be easy to reproduce an atmosphere like the present one. Music and a mild intoxication and such a sweet girl at his side—oh, it was Marie. He reflected. Perhaps any other girl would have been just as welcome at this moment. She, too, was sipping the wine with great pleasure. Soon Felix had to order another bottle. He had not felt such contentment in a long time, and he explained this to himself by reflecting that all this was actually due to a bit more alcohol than he was accustomed to. But what did that matter as long as such a feeling was possible at all? Truly, death had lost its sting for him. Oh, everything was so unimportant.

"Isn't that right, Mitzi?" he said.

She nestled close to him. "Isn't what right?"

"Everything is so unimportant. Isn't it?"

"Yes, everything," she replied, "except the fact that I shall love you forever and ever."

When she said this so seriously, it seemed quite peculiar to him. Her personality was almost a matter of indifference to him; it coalesced with everything else. Yes, that was it, that was how one had to deal with things. Oh, no, it was not the wine that was conjuring this up for him; wine only relieves us of something that at other times makes us cumbersome and cowardly. Wine takes the importance away from things and from people. How simple it would be to take a little white powder and put it in this glass! As he reflected on this, he felt a few tears welling up in his eyes. He was a little touched by himself.

The chorus over there stopped singing. Now they could hear applause and shouts of bravo followed by muted noise, and soon the orchestra started in again with the solemn gaiety of a polonaise. Felix beat time with his hand as this thought occurred to him: "Oh, I have a bit of life left and will live it as well as I can." There was nothing horrifying about this idea; if anything, there was something proud and royal about it. What? Timidly await the final breath, which, after all, is in store for everyone? Sour his days and nights with vapid brooding when he felt in his bones that he was still sound and vigorous enough for any kind of enjoyment, when he felt that the wine tasted great to him and that he would like best to take this flower of a girl on his lap and cover her with kisses? No, it was still a bit too early to let his mood be spoiled. And when the time came when there no longer was any rapture or desire for him, then let there be a quick end, proud and royal. He took Marie's hand and held it in his for a long time while he let his breath slowly move over her.

"Oh," whispered Marie with an expression of contentment.

He gave her a long look. She was beautiful, so beautiful. "Come," he said.

She replied unaffectedly: "Shouldn't we listen to another song?"

"Oh, yes," he said. "We'll open our window and let the wind carry it into our room."

"Are you tired?" she asked, a bit uneasy.

He jestingly caressed her hair and laughed: "I am."

"Let's go, then."

They got up and left the garden. She firmly linked arms with him and pressed her cheek against his shoulder. On the way home they were accompanied by the choral selection, sounding fainter and fainter, which the singers had just intoned. It was a gay waltz tune with a rollicking refrain, and it compelled them to take easier and freer strides. The hotel was only a few minutes away. As they walked up the stairs, the music was no longer audible. But no sooner had they stepped into their room than the refrain of that waltz tune could be heard again in all its boisterousness.

They found the window wide open, and the blue moonlit night gently flooded the room. Opposite them the outlines of the Mönchsberg and its castle were clearly visible. It was not necessary to light a lamp; a wide strip of silvery moonglow lay on the floor, and only the corners of the room remained in darkness. In one corner by the window stood an armchair. Felix plunked himself down in it and violently pulled Marie close to him. He kissed her, and she returned his kisses. The chorus in the park had finished, but there had been so much applause that they repeated the selection. Suddenly Marie rose and went to the window. Felix followed her. "What are you doing?" he asked.

"No, no!"

He stamped his foot on the floor. "Why no?"

"Felix!" She folded her hands imploringly.

"No?" he said with clenched teeth. "No? Am I supposed to make dignified preparations for death instead?"

"But Felix!" She flung herself down before him and clasped his knees.

He pulled her up to him. "You are a child," he whispered. And then, into her ear: "I love you; do you know that? Let us be happy while we still have a little life left. I'd rather not have a year of misery and fear; all I want is a few weeks, a few days and nights. But I want to *live* them, I don't want to deny myself anything, anything—and after that, down there, if you are willing"—and while he held her embraced with one arm, he pointed with the other out the window past which the river flowed. The singers had ended their song, and the gentle rushing of the river could be heard.

Marie made no reply. She had firmly clasped his neck with

her hands. Felix drank in the fragrance of her hair. How he adored her! Yes, a few more days of happiness, and then . . .

It had become still around them, and Marie had fallen asleep at his side. The concert had ended long ago, and under their window the last stragglers of the festival went past loudly talking and laughing. And Felix reflected how strange it was that these shouting people were probably the ones whose singing had so deeply moved him. Finally even those last voices died away completely, and now he could hear only the plaintive rushing of the river. Yes, a few more days and nights, and then . . . But she enjoyed life so much. Would she ever dare to do it? But she did not need to dare anything, or even know anything. Some day she would fall asleep in his arms, as she had just now—and not awake anymore. And when he was entirely certain of that—well, then he too could go. But he would not tell her anything; she enjoyed life too much. She would grow frightened of him, and then he would have to go alone—horrible! The best thing would be to do it right away . . . She was sleeping so soundly! Some firm pressure here on her neck and it would be done. No, it would be stupid! He still had many hours of happiness ahead of him; he would know which hour had to be the last one. He looked at Marie, and he felt as though he was holding his sleeping slave in his arms.

The decision he had finally made calmed him down. On the following days, when he walked about the streets with Marie and occasionally saw a man give her an admiring glance, a smile expressive of spiteful glee played about his lips. And when they took a ride in a carriage, when they sat in a garden in the evening, when she was in his embrace at night, he had a proud feeling of ownership such as he had never had before. Only one thing disturbed him sometimes: that she was not to depart with him of her own free will. But there were indications that he would succeed in this respect as well. She no longer dared to resist his tempestuous desires; she had never surrendered as dreamily as she had in the last few nights, and with tremulous joy he saw the moment approaching when he could venture to tell her: "Today we shall die." But he postponed that moment. Sometimes he could see an image in romantic colors: He was plunging a dagger into her heart and, breathing her last sigh, she was kissing his beloved hand. He kept wondering whether she had reached that point yet, but he had reason to doubt it.

One morning, when Marie awoke, she got terribly frightened: Felix was not by her side. She sat up in bed and saw him sitting by the window, deathly pale, with his head sunk down and his shirt open over his chest. Gripped by a raging panic, she rushed up to him. "Felix!"

He opened his eyes. "What? What is it?" He touched his chest and moaned.

"Why didn't you wake me?" she cried, wringing her hands.

"I'm all right now," he said. She hurried over to the bed, took the blanket, and spread it over his knees. "Tell me, for heaven's sake, how did you get here?"

"I don't know. I must have been dreaming. Something seized me by the throat. I wasn't able to breathe. I wasn't even thinking of you. Here by the window I felt better."

Marie had quickly slipped on a dress and closed the window. A nasty wind had risen up, and from the gray sky a thin rain began drizzling down, bringing an atmosphere of insidious dampness into the room. The room had suddenly lost all the coziness of the summer night and was now gray and alien. Suddenly a bleak autumn morning had dawned and mocked away all the magic they had dreamed into their abode.

Felix was completely calm. "Why do you have such frightened eyes? What's wrong, anyway? I used to have bad dreams even when I was still healthy."

She would not calm down. "I beg of you, Felix, let's go back, let's go to Vienna."

"But . . ."

"The summer is over, anyway. Just take a look out there—how bleak and cheerless it is. It's turning cold now, too, and that's dangerous."

He listened attentively. To his own astonishment he felt quite comfortable at that moment, like a weary convalescent. He was breathing with ease, and in the fatigue that enveloped him there was something sweet and relaxing. Leaving this town made perfect sense to him. There was something rather attractive about the idea of a change of scenery. He looked forward to lying in the railway compartment on that cool rainy day with his head propped on Marie's breast.

"All right," he said, "let's leave."

"This very day?"

"Yes, today. On the noontime express, if you like."

"But won't that exhaust you?"

"Oh, not a bit! The trip won't be much of a strain, will it? And you'll take care of everything that I dislike about traveling, won't you?"

She was delighted to have found it so easy to induce him to leave. She immediately set about packing, took care of the hotel bill, ordered a carriage, and had a train compartment reserved. Felix soon dressed, but he did not leave the room and lay on the sofa all morning long. He watched Marie rushing up and down the room and sometimes smiled. But most of the time he dozed. He was so weary, so weary, and when he looked at her he was glad that she was going to stay with him everywhere, and as in a dream he kept thinking of how they were going to rest together. "Soon, soon!" he thought. And it had actually never seemed so far off to him.

And just as he had imagined it that morning, in the afternoon Felix lay comfortably stretched out in the train compartment covered by the traveling rug and his head against Marie's breast. Through the closed windows he stared out into the gray day; he watched the rain trickle down and immersed his glance in the fog from which nearby hills and houses occasionally emerged. Telegraph poles flitted past, and the wires danced up and down. Now and then the train stopped at a station, but in his position Felix could not see the people who might be standing on the platform. He heard only muted steps, voices, bells, and bugle signals. At first he had Marie read to him from the newspaper, but it was too much of a strain on her voice and they soon gave it up. Both were glad to be on their way home.

It was getting dark and it continued drizzling. Felix felt a need for perfect clarity, but his thoughts refused to assume sharp outlines. This is what he reflected about: Here lies a gravely ill person. . . . He has been to the mountains, because that is where the seriously ill go in the summer. . . . And this is his sweetheart who tended him faithfully and now is tired. . . . She is so pale, or is it only the light? . . . Oh yes, the lamp up there is already burning. But it's not quite dark outside. . . . And now autumn is coming. . . . Autumn is so sad and so quiet. . . . Tonight we shall be in our room in Vienna again. . . . Then it will feel as though I have never been away. . . . Oh, its a good thing that Marie is asleep; I wouldn't want to hear her talking now. . . . Wonder whether any of the people from the choral festival are on the train. . . . I'm just tired, I'm not sick at all. There are people on the train who are much sicker than I. . . . Oh, it's so good to be alone. . . . How did we spend the whole day? Was it really today that I lay on the sofa in Salzburg? It seems so long ago. . . . Yes, time and space—what do we know about them? The riddle of the universe—perhaps we'll solve it when we die. . . . And now a tune came into his head. He knew that it was only the noise of the train. . . . And yet it was a melody. . . . A folksong . . . Russian . . . monotonous . . . very nice. . . .

"Felix, Felix!"

"What is it now?" Marie was standing before him and stroking his cheeks.

"Did you sleep well, Felix?"

"What's going on?"

"We'll be in Vienna in fifteen minutes."

"No, it can't be."

"That was a sound sleep. I'm sure it did you good."

She got their luggage together while the train rattled on

through the night. At short intervals there was the prolonged sound of a high-pitched whistle, and through the windowpanes flashed a shimmer of light that soon disappeared again. They were traveling through the stations on the outskirts of Vienna.

Felix sat up. "All this lying has made me tired," he said. He sat down in a corner and looked out the window. In the distance he could see the shimmering city streets. The train slowed down. Marie opened the window and leaned out. They were entering the station. Marie stretched out her hand and waved. Then she turned to Felix and cried: "There he is, there he is."

"Who?"

"Alfred."

"Alfred?"

She kept waving her hand. Felix got up and looked over her shoulder. Alfred quickly approached their compartment and extended his hand up to Marie. "Greetings! Hello, Felix."

"What are *you* doing here?"

"I sent him a wire," said Marie quickly, "telling him of our arrival."

"A fine friend *you* are," said Alfred; "I suppose letter writing is an unknown invention to you. But come along now."

"I slept so much," said Felix, "that I'm still quite groggy." He smiled as he climbed down the stairs of the carriage, a bit wobbly.

Alfred took his arm, and Marie quickly took the other one as if she wanted to link arms with him.

"I suppose you're both quite tired, right?"

"I'm really done in," said Marie. "Don't you think, Felix, that those stupid train rides tucker you out?"

They slowly descended the stairs. Marie sought eye contact with Alfred, but he avoided her eyes. In the street he hailed a carriage. "I'm very glad to have seen you, dear Felix," he said. "Tomorrow morning I'll stop by for a longer chat."

"I'm quite groggy," repeated Felix. Alfred tried to help him into the carriage. "Oh, but it isn't that bad!" He got in and held out his hand to Marie. "You see!" Marie followed him inside.

"Till tomorrow, then," she said as she held out her hand to Alfred through the carriage window. Her eyes expressed so much doubt and anxiety that Alfred managed a forced smile. "Yes, tomorrow," he said. "I'll have breakfast with you." The carriage rode off. For a while Alfred remained standing with a serious face.

"My poor friend!" he whispered to himself.

Alfred came very early the next morning, and Marie received him at the door. "I have to speak with you," she said.

"Better let me see him first. After I have examined him, everything we have to talk about will make more sense."

"I'd just like to ask you for one thing, Alfred. No matter how you find him. I implore you not to tell him anything."

"The very idea! Well, it surely won't be that bad. Is he still asleep?"

"No, he's up."

"How was the night?"

"He slept soundly till four. Then he grew restless."

"Let me see him alone first. You must put a little peace in your pale little face. You can't go in to him like this." He smilingly squeezed her hand and went into the bedroom by himself.

Felix had pulled the blanket over his chin and nodded to his friend. Alfred sat down on the bed and said: "So you're home again, safe and sound. You've certainly had a wonderful rest, and I hope you left your depression in the mountains."

"Oh, I have!" answered Felix without moving a muscle.

"Don't you want to get up a little? You see, I make such early calls only as a doctor."

"All right," said Felix indifferently.

Alfred examined the patient, asked a few questions and received curt answers, and finally said: "Well, so far so good."

"Oh, stop the flimflam," replied Felix peevishly.

"*You* are the one who should stop the foolishness. Let's tackle this thing vigorously. You have to have the will to get well and not play the role of the person resigned to his fate. You see, you're not very good in this role."

"What do I have to do, then?"

"To start with, you're going to stay in bed for a few days. Got that?"

"I don't feel like getting up, anyway."

"All the better."

Felix became more animated. "Tell me just one thing. What was the matter with me yesterday? Seriously, Alfred, you've got to explain that to me. Everything is like an obscure dream to me: the railway trip and our arrival, how I got up here and into bed. . . ."

"What is there to explain? You're not exactly a giant, and when a person is overtired, these things can happen."

"No, Alfred. A fatigue like yesterday's is something quite new for me. I'm still tired today, but I have regained my mental alertness. It wasn't that unpleasant yesterday, but the memory of it is horrible to me. When I think that something like that could befall me again. . . ."

At that moment Marie stepped into the room.

"Say thank you to Alfred," said Felix. "He is appointing you my nurse. Starting today I have to stay in bed, and I herewith have the honor of introducing to you my deathbed."

Marie looked horrified.

"Don't let this fool befuddle you," said Alfred. "He has to stay in bed for a few days, and you will be good enough to take care of him."

"Oh, if you only knew, Alfred," exclaimed Felix with ironic enthusiasm, "what an angel I have by my side!"

Alfred now gave them detailed instructions on the dos and don'ts of Felix's bed rest, and finally said: "Please be informed, my dear Felix, that I shall make a doctor's visit only every other day. That's all that is needed. On the other days your condition will not be discussed. On those days I shall come to chat with you in the customary way."

"My God," cried Felix, "what a psychologist this man is. But please reserve your charming bedside manner for your other patients, particularly the very simple ones."

"My dear Felix, I am talking to you man to man. Listen to me. It's true, you are ill. But it is just as true that you will get well if you receive the proper care. I can't tell you any more or any less than that." With that he rose.

Felix's eyes reflected mistrust. "One would almost be tempted to believe him."

"That's up to you, dear Felix," replied the doctor curtly.

"Well, Alfred, now you've done it again," said the patient. "This brusque manner with seriously ill patients—a well-known trick."

"Till tomorrow," said Alfred, turning to the door. Marie followed him to show him out. "Stay," he whispered imperiously. She closed the door behind him.

"Come to me, my little one," said Felix when she, feigning a cheerful smile, busied herself with sewing gear on the table. "Yes, here. Fine, you are a nice, nice, very nice girl." He spoke these tender words in a harsh, sharp tone of voice.

On the next days Marie stayed close to his bed full of kindness and devotion. Her manner reflected a calm and unaffected cheerfulness which was intended to comfort the patient and at times did comfort him. But at other times he was irritated by the gentle cheerfulness that Marie sought to spread about him. When she began to chat about some news item she had read in the paper, or said she noticed he was looking better, or talked about the life style they would adopt as soon as he was fully recovered, he sometimes interrupted her and asked her please to leave him alone and to spare him such talk. Alfred came every day, sometimes twice daily, but he hardly ever seemed to concern himself with his friend's physical condition. He spoke about mutual friends, told stories about the hospital, and also carried on conversations about artistic and literary matters, taking care that Felix did not have to do too much talking. Both Felix's sweetheart and his friend acted so natural that Felix sometimes had trouble warding off the bold hopes that would come crowding in upon him. He told himself that it was only the duty of these two to put on for his benefit the kind of act that had always been put on with varying success for gravely ill people. But even though he thought he was only going along with their charade and participating in it, he repeatedly caught himself chatting about the world and people as though he were destined to walk in the sun among the living for many years to come. Then he remembered that precisely this kind of euphoria among patients like him was often regarded as a sign of imminent death, and so he angrily rejected all hope. He even got to the point where he interpreted vague feelings of anxiety and moods of depression as good omens and came close to rejoicing at them. But then he discovered again how absurd this kind of logic would be, and finally he realized that in this area there was neither knowledge nor certainty. He had started to read once more but he got no enjoyment from novels; they bored him, and some, particularly those that opened broad vistas into a vibrant and eventful existence, profoundly depressed him. He turned to the philosophers and asked Marie to get him Schopenhauer and Nietzsche from the bookcase. But their wisdom brought him peace for only a short time.

One evening Alfred found him lowering a volume of Schopenhauer to his blanket and gloomily staring into space. Marie was sitting next to him with her needlework.

"Listen, Alfred," Felix called out to his friend in an almost excited voice. "I shall start reading novels again after all."

"What has happened?"

"At least novels contain honest fabrications. They may be good or bad, by masters or dilettantes. But these gentlemen here"—and he looked at the volume on his blanket—"are wretched poseurs."

"Oh?"

Felix sat up in bed. "To despise life when one is as healthy as a god and to look death in the face calmly when one goes for a ride in Italy and all around one life blooms in the brightest colors—that's what I call a pose. Take such a gentleman and lock him up in a room, condemn him to run a temperature and gasp for breath, tell him that he will be dead and buried between the first of January and the first of February of next year—and then let him philosophize for you."

"Oh, go on!" said Alfred. "What kind of paradoxes are these!"

"You don't understand. You can't understand that! I find it downright disgusting. They're poseurs, all of them."

"What about Socrates?"

"An actor. It is natural for a human being to be afraid of the unknown; at best he can conceal this fear. Let me tell you this quite frankly. The psychology of dying people is falsified because all the greats of world history whose deaths we know about have felt obligated to put on an act for posterity. And what about me? What am *I* doing? What do *I* do when I talk with you calmly about all sorts of things that no longer concern me?"

"Oh, stop talking so much, especially such nonsense."

"Even I feel obligated to dissimulate, and in reality I feel an immense, frenzied fear that healthy persons can't imagine; and yet they all feel fear, even the heroes and the philosophers. It's simply that these are the best actors."

"Oh, calm down, Felix," Marie begged him.

"I suppose you two also believe," continued the patient, "that you are calmly facing eternity. This is only because you don't know what it is. You have to be under a sentence like a criminal, or like me, before you can talk about it. The poor devil who walks up to the gallows with composure; the great sage who invents aphorisms after draining the cup of hemlock; the imprisoned freedom fighter who smiles when the guns are aimed at his chest—*I* know that they are all hypocrites, and their composure and their smiles are all a pose, for they are all afraid, horribly afraid of death. Such fear is as natural as dying itself."

Alfred had quietly sat down on the bed, and when Felix had finished he replied: "In the first place, it is unwise of you to talk so much and so loudly. In the second place, you are being as absurd as can be and an awful hypochondriac."

"But you are feeling so well these days," Marie exclaimed.

"Could she really believe that?" asked Felix, turning to Alfred. "Go ahead and tell her the truth at last, won't you?"

"My dear friend," replied the doctor, "*you* are the only one here who needs to be told the truth. But today you are being obstreperous, so I can't do it. In two or three days you will be back on your feet, provided you don't make any long speeches before then, and then we will have a good discussion of your mental condition as well."

"If only I weren't able to see through you so completely!" said Felix.

"All right, all right," responded Alfred. "Don't look so sad," he said to Marie. "Some day even this gentleman will see the light. But now tell me, why is there no window open? Outside it is the most beautiful autumn day one can imagine."

Marie got up and opened a window. It was beginning to get dark, and the air that came in was so refreshing that Marie felt a desire to be caressed by it for a while longer. She remained standing at the window and stuck her head out. It suddenly seemed to her as though she had left the room itself; she had not had such a pleasant sensation in days. When she turned back to the room, the whole mustiness of the sickroom rushed in upon her in an oppressive way. She watched Felix and Alfred converse; she could not fully make out the words, but she had no desire to participate in the conversation. Again she leaned out the window. The street was rather quiet and deserted, and only from the nearby boulevard could the muted rolling of carriages be heard. On the pavement opposite a few strollers were sauntering by. In front of the doorway across the street stood a few servant girls chatting and laughing. A young woman in that house was looking out the window, just as Marie was. At that moment Marie could not comprehend why the woman was not going out for a walk. She envied all people who were more fortunate than she.

Mild, comfortable September days came. Night fell early, but it remained warm and calm.

It had become Marie's custom to move her chair away from the sick man's bed as often as possible and to sit by the open window. There she would remain for hours, particularly when Felix was dozing. A profound weariness had come over her, an inability to gain complete clarity about the situation, even a downright aversion to thinking. There were hours on end when there were neither memories nor future plans for her. Then she would daydream with open eyes and was content when a fresh breeze from the street touched her forehead. When a soft moan from the sickbed reached her ears, she would give a start. She discovered that she had gradually lost the gift of commiseration. Her compassion had turned into nervous strain and her pain into a mixture of fear and indifference. She surely had nothing to reproach herself with; and when the doctor in all seriousness called her an angel, as he recently had, she had hardly any reason to feel ashamed. But she was tired, tired beyond measure. She had not left the house for ten or twelve days now. Why hadn't she? Why not? She had to reflect. Well—so it suddenly flashed through her mind—because it would have displeased Felix. And she liked to stay with him, yes, she did. She adored him no less than before. But she was tired, and this was only human. Her longing for a few hours in the open air became more and more overpowering. It was childish of her to deny herself the gratification of this longing; even he would finally have to see that. And now she again realized how boundless her love for him must be if she wanted to spare him even the semblance of a hurt. She let her needlework slip to the floor and looked over to the bed which was already in the darkness of the wall. It was dusk, and the patient had dozed off after a quieter day.

Now she could even have left without his noticing it. Oh, down the stairs and around the corner, and among people again in the City Park and on the Ringstrasse and past the Opera House where the electric lights were glowing, among the crowds, and it was the crowds that she yearned for so much. But when would this kind of life return? It could happen only when Felix was well again; and what did the streets and the park and the people mean to her, what did all of life mean to her, without Felix?

She stayed home and moved her chair close to his bed. She took the hand of the slumbering man and shed quiet, sad tears on it. She went on weeping long after her thoughts had strayed far from the man on whose pale hand her tears now fell.

When Alfred called on Felix the following afternoon, he found him more alert than on the preceding days. "If things stay the same," he told him, "I shall let you get out of bed in a few days." Like everything that was said to him, the patient received this statement with distrust and responded with an ill-humored "Yes, yes." Alfred turned to Marie, who was sitting at the table, and said: "*Your* appearance could stand a bit of improvement, too."

These words made Felix take a closer look at Marie, and he noticed that she was especially pale. He was accustomed to banishing in short order the thoughts that he sometimes had about her self-sacrificing devotion. At times her martyrdom seemed to him not to be quite the genuine article, and he was annoyed at the patient air that she displayed. Sometimes he wished she might become impatient. He watched for the moment when she would betray herself with a word or a glance and he could maliciously tell her to her face that he had not let himself be deceived for a moment, that her hypocrisy disgusted him, and that she ought to let him die in peace.

Now that Alfred had referred to her appearance, she blushed a bit and smiled. "I feel quite well," she said.

Alfred stepped up to her. "No, it isn't as simple as that.

Your Felix won't enjoy his recovery very much if you are going to be sick."

"But I really feel quite well."

"Tell me, don't you ever get any fresh air?"

"I don't feel any need for it."

"Tell me, Felix, doesn't she stir from your side?"

"But you know," said Felix, "that she is an angel."

"Forgive me for saying so, Marie, but this is just plain stupid. It is useless and childish to wear yourself out in this way. You have to get some fresh air. I prescribe it as a necessity."

"But what do you want from me?" said Marie, smiling weakly. "I have absolutely no desire to get out."

"That doesn't matter. The very fact that you have no desire is a bad sign. You'll go out this very day. Sit on a bench in the City Park for an hour. Or, if you don't like that, hire a carriage and go for a ride—in the Prater, for example. It's wonderful down there now."

"But . . ."

"No buts. If you continue to carry on like this and be an angel, you will ruin your health. Go and look in the mirror. You are ruining yourself."

As Alfred spoke these words, Felix felt a sharp pain in his heart. A pent-up rage gnawed at him. He thought he could discern in Marie's features an expression of conscious martyr-like suffering that demanded pity. And like a truth that it would be presumptuous to challenge it flashed through his mind that this woman was, after all, obliged to suffer and die with him. She was ruining her health, but that was natural. Was it perhaps her intention to keep her red cheeks and bright eyes while he was rushing to his doom? And did Alfred really believe that this woman, who was his sweetheart, had the right to think beyond the hour that would be his final one? And did she herself perhaps dare . . .

With eager rage Felix studied Marie's facial expression while the doctor made an ill-humored speech in which he kept repeating what he had already said. Finally he made Marie promise him that she would go out that very day and explained to her that the fulfillment of this promise was just as important a part of her nursing duties as anything else. "Because I don't count any more," thought Felix; "because a person who is a lost cause they let perish anyway." When Alfred finally left, he limply shook hands with him. He hated him.

Marie escorted the doctor only as far as the sickroom door and immediately returned to Felix. He lay there with pinched lips and a deep wrinkle of anger on his forehead. Marie understood him, she understood him completely. She bowed down to him and smiled. He drew a deep breath and was about to speak, to fling some outrageous insult in her face. He thought she deserved it. She, however, stroked his hair and with that weary, patient smile on her face she bent quite close to his face as she whispered: "I'm not going, you know."

He made no reply. All evening long and deep into the night she remained sitting by his bed and finally fell asleep in her chair.

When Alfred came the next day, Marie tried to avoid talking with him. Today, however, he did not seem to be interested in her appearance and concerned himself only with Felix. But he said nothing about his being able to get out of bed soon, and the patient was reluctant to ask him. He felt weaker than he had on the preceding days. He had an aversion to talking such as he had never had before, and he was glad when the doctor left. To Marie's questions he also gave curt and peevish answers. And when after hours of silence she asked him in the late afternoon, "How do you feel now?" he replied, "Well, what difference does it make?" He folded his arms over his head, closed his eyes, and soon dozed off. Marie stayed next to him for a while and looked at him, but then her thoughts became blurred and she started daydreaming. When after a while she snapped out of it, she felt a strange relaxation in her limbs, as though having awakened from a sound sleep. She rose and opened the curtains. It was as though the fragrance of late blossoms had strayed into the narrow street from the nearby park. The air that now flooded the room had never seemed more magnificent. She turned around and looked at Felix, who was lying there asleep and breathing calmly. At other moments like this she had felt a compassion that had held her transfixed in the room and suffused her entire being with a torpid melancholia. Today she remained calm, was pleased that Felix was asleep, and decided without any inner struggle, as naturally as though it were an everyday occurrence, to go out for an hour. She tiptoed into the kitchen, instructed the cleaning woman to stay in the sickroom, quickly took her hat and umbrella, and fairly flew down the stairs. There she was out in the open, and after a quick walk through some quiet streets she reached the park and enjoyed seeing beside her shrubs and trees and above her the dusky blue sky for which she had yearned for so long. She sat down on a bench; on the benches next to her sat nursemaids and governesses. Children were playing on the tree-lined paths. But since it was already growing dark, these activities were coming to an end; the maids called the little ones, took their hands, and left the park. Soon Marie was almost alone; a few people were still walking by, and now and then a man turned around to look at her.

So now she was out in the fresh air. Well, how did everything actually stand? She thought the time had come to survey the situation with untroubled eyes. She wanted to find clear words for her thoughts, words that she could pronounce inwardly: I am with him because I love him. I am not making any sacrifice, for I can't help doing it. And what will happen now? How much longer will it take? There is no saving him. . . . And what will happen afterward? And what then? Once I wanted to die with him. . . . Why are we such strangers to each other now? He only thinks of himself now. . . . Does he still want to die with me? And at that point she felt certain that he did. But the image that appeared to her was not that of an affectionate young man who wished to bed her down by his side for eternity. No, it seemed to her as though he were pulling her down to him, willfully, jealously, because she simply belonged to him.

A young man had sat down next to her and made a remark. She was so distracted that she first asked, "What?" But then she got up and quickly walked away. The glances of those encountering her in the park began to bother her. She walked out to the Ringstrasse, hailed a carriage, and went for a ride. Night had fallen. She comfortably leaned back in a corner of the carriage and enjoyed the agreeable, effortless motion and the shifting images that moved past her, bathed in the dusk and the flickering gaslight. The beautiful September evening had lured a crowd out onto the streets. When Marie rode past the Volksgarten, she heard the bright notes of a military band, and she could not help thinking of that evening in Salzburg. In vain she tried to persuade herself that this whole life around her was something empty and transitory, that departing from it was a matter of no consequence. She could not banish from her senses the well-being that gradually began to take hold of her. She simply felt good. That the festive theater stood there with its arc lamps gleaming white; that people came sauntering out onto the street from the paths of the City Hall Park; that people were sitting outside that café; that there were people of whose cares she knew nothing, or who might not even have any; that the breezes blew about her so gently and warmly; that she would be allowed to experience many more such evenings, a thousand more wonderful days and nights; that a feeling of life-affirming health was flowing through her veins—all these things did her good. What?! Was she perhaps going to reproach herself for finding herself, so to speak, for one minute after countless hours of deathly weariness? Was it not her right to become aware that she was alive? After all, she was healthy, she was young, and from everywhere, as though from a hundred sources at once, joy of life came flooding over her. This was as natural as her breath or the sky above her—and was she going to feel ashamed of it? She thought of Felix. If a miracle happened and he got well, she would certainly go on living with him. She thought of him with a gentle, conciliatory pain. Soon it would be time to return to him. Did he approve of her only when she was with him? Did he appreciate her tenderness? How harsh his words were! How piercing his eyes! And his kiss! How long had it been since they had kissed each other? She had to think of his lips, which now were always so pale and so dry. Henceforth she was going to kiss him only on the forehead. His forehead was cold and damp. How ugly illness was!

She leaned back in the carriage and deliberately averted her thoughts from the sick man. To avoid having to think of him she eagerly looked out on the street and watched everything so intently as though she had to imprint it on her memory.

Felix opened his eyes. A candle burned beside his bed and diffused a dim light. Next to him sat an old woman, impassive, her hands in her lap. She gave a start when the patient called out to her: "Where is she?" The woman explained to him that Marie had gone out and would be back soon.

"You can go!" answered Felix. And when the woman hesitated, he added: "Go, I don't need you."

He remained alone. An unrest, more painful than any before, befell him.

Where was she, where was she? He could hardly stand staying in bed, but he did not dare to get up. Suddenly it flashed through his mind: Maybe she is gone! She wanted to leave him, leave him alone forever. She could not endure life by his side any longer. She was afraid of him. She read his thoughts. Or he had once spoken in his sleep and said aloud what had rested in the depths of his conscious forever, even if for days on end he could not clearly grasp it himself. And she simply did not want to die with him. . . . The thoughts rushed through his mind. The fever that came every evening was there. He had not spoken any kind words to her for such a long time; perhaps it was no more than that. He had tortured her with his moods, his distrustful looks, his bitter speeches, and what she needed was gratitude. . . . No, no, only justice! Oh! If only she were here! He had to have her. With a piercing pain he realized that he could not do without her. He would beg her for forgiveness if he had to. He would again look at her with eyes of affection and speak words of profound tenderness to her. He would not betray with one syllable that he was suffering. He would smile when his chest felt crushed. He would kiss her hand while he was struggling for breath. He would tell her that he was dreaming nonsense and that the things she heard him say in his sleep were delirium. And he would swear to her that he adored her, that he did not begrudge her, and wished for her, a long, happy life. She should only stay with him and not stir from his bed; she must not let him die alone. He would surely face the terrible hour in prudence and peace if he only knew that *she* was with him! And that hour might come so soon; it could come any day. That is why she had to stay with him always, for he felt fear when he was without her.

Where was she? Where was she? The blood whirled through his head, his eyes grew dim, his breathing became more labored, and nobody was there. Oh, why had he sent that old woman away? She was, after all, a human soul. Now he was helpless, helpless. He sat up in bed; he felt stronger than he had thought, except for his breath, his breath. . . . It was terrible how this tormented him. He could not stand it any longer. He jumped out of bed, and almost naked as he was he rushed to the window. There was air, air. He drew a few deep breaths: how good that was! He put on the wide robe that hung over the bedpost and sank down into a chair. For a few seconds all his thoughts became tangled, and then one thought, always the same thought, came flashing through: Where was she? Where was she? Had she left him on other occasions while he had been asleep? Who knows? Where might she have gone on such occasions? Was she simply trying to escape from the stuffy sickroom for a few hours, or did she want to escape from *him* because he was sick? Was his nearness repugnant to her? Was she afraid of the shadows of death that already hovered there? Was she longing for life? Was she looking for life? Did he himself no longer mean life to her? What was she seeking? What did she want? Where was she? Where was she?

And the flitting thoughts turned into whispered syllables, into loud words of moaning. And he cried, he screamed: "Where is she?" And he could see her hurrying down the stairs, with a smile of liberation on her lips, rushing off somewhere, to places where there was no illness, no disgust, no slow dying, to something unknown, to some place of fragrance and flowering. He could see her vanish, submerge herself into a light-colored mist which concealed her and from which her rippling laughter emerged, a laughter of happiness and joy. And the mists parted and he saw her dancing. And she whirled on and on and disappeared. And then came a muffled rumbling, came closer and closer and suddenly stopped. Where was she? He gave a start and hurried to the window. It had been the rolling of a carriage, and now it had stopped in front of his house. Yes, of course, he could see it. And from the carriage—yes, it was Marie! It was she! He had to go and meet her, so he rushed into the hall, which was completely dark. He was not able to find the door knob. A key turned in the lock, the door opened, and Marie entered, bathed in the dim gaslight from the corridor. She bumped into him in the darkness and cried out. He grabbed her by the shoulders and dragged her into the room. He opened his mouth but could not speak.

"What's the matter with you!" she cried out in horror; "have you gone mad?" She freed herself from his grasp, and he remained standing. It was as though he were growing taller. Finally he regained his voice.

"Where have you been? Where?"

"For heaven's sake, Felix, get a hold of yourself. How could you . . . ! I beg of you, at least sit down."

"Where have you been?" He said it more softly, as though he had lost all hope. "Where? Where?" he whispered. She took his hands and found them burning hot. He readily, almost apathetically, let her lead him to the sofa and slowly press him down in its corner. He looked around as though he had to regain his senses gradually. Then he repeated, quite audibly but in the same monotonous tone of voice: "Where you have been?"

Having regained some of her composure, she threw her hat on a chair behind her, sat down on the sofa next to him, and blandishingly said: "Sweetheart, I only was in the fresh air for an hour. I was afraid I was going to be sick myself. What good would I have been to you then? And I even took a carriage to be back with you sooner."

He was lying in his corner in complete exhaustion. He gave her a sidelong glance and said nothing.

She went on, caressing his hot cheeks. "Tell me you're not angry with me! By the way, I told the cleaning woman to stay in your room until I returned. Didn't you see her? Where is she, anyway?"

"I sent her away."

"Why, Felix? She was simply supposed to stay until I came back. I missed you so much. What good does the fresh air outside do me if I don't have *you*?"

"Mitzi, Mitzi!" He put his head against her chest like a sick child. As in days of yore, he brushed his lips against her hair. Then he looked up to her with a supplication in his eyes. "Mitzi," he said, "you must always stay with me, always, do you hear?"

"Yes," she replied and kissed his tangled, damp hair. She was heartsick, absolutely heartsick. She would have liked to cry, but her emotions were curiously dried up and withered. She could not derive comfort from any source, not even from her own pain. And when she saw tears running down his cheeks, she envied him.

All the succeeding days and nights she sat by his bed again, brought him his meals, gave him his medicine, and read to him from the newspaper or a chapter from some novel when he was alert enough to ask for it. The morning after her outing it had begun to rain, and a premature autumn set in. And now those thin, gray streaks drizzled past the window-panes almost continuously, for hours and days on end. Of late Marie had sometimes heard the patient talk incoherently in his sleep. On such occasions she would mechanically stroke his forehead and hair and whisper: "Sleep, Felix, sleep, Felix!"—the way one calms a restless child. He grew weaker and weaker, but he did not suffer much, and when the brief attacks of shortness of breath that were a severe reminder of his illness were over, he usually sank into a state of torpor which he could no longer account for. At times, to be sure, it seemed to him that he was a bit surprised: "Why is it that I have stopped caring about anything?" When he saw the rain drizzling down outside, he thought, "Oh sure, it's autumn," and did not pursue the connection any further. He actually gave no thought to any possible change—his end or his recovery.

And in those days Marie, too, completely gave up any prospect of a possible change. Even Alfred's visits had become routine. Of course, for him, the man who came from the outside, for whom life rolled on, the appearance of the sickroom changed every day. He had given up all hope. He noticed that for both Felix and Marie a certain phase had begun, a stage occasionally reached by people who have gone through extreme excitement, one in which there is no hope and no fear and the perception of the present itself becomes blurred and unclear because there is no vision of the future and no review of the past. Alfred always entered the sickroom with a feeling of great discomfort and was very pleased when he found the two just as he had left them. For the time was bound to come again when they would be compelled to think of what was impending.

One day, when he had ascended the steps once again with such thoughts, he found Marie standing in the hall with pale cheeks and wringing her hands. "Come quick, come quick!"

she cried. He followed her. Felix was sitting up in bed; he gave them both angry looks and cried: "What is it you're planning to do with me, anyhow?"

Alfred quickly stepped up to him. "What's the matter with you, Felix?" he asked.

"I'd like to know what you are planning to do with me."

"What a childish question!"

"You're letting me perish, perish miserably!" Felix almost screamed.

Alfred stepped quite close to him and tried to take his hand, but the patient quickly withdrew it. "Oh, leave me alone; and you, Marie, stop wringing your hands. I want to know what you are planning to do with me, how much longer this is supposed to go on."

"Things would go on much better," said Alfred calmly, "if you didn't get so needlessly excited."

"Well, I've been lying here for heaven knows how long. You look on and leave me lying there. What are you planning to do with me anyway?" He suddenly turned toward the doctor.

"Oh, don't talk nonsense."

"But nothing is being done for me, nothing at all. It's coming over me, and no one is lifting a finger to help me."

"Felix," began Alfred in a firm voice as he sat down on the bed and again tried to take Felix's hand.

"Well, you're simply giving me up. You let me lie there and take morphine."

"You must be patient for a few days longer . . ."

"But you can see that it isn't doing me any good! I know how things are with me. Then why do you let me perish so hopelessly? You can see that I am being ruined here. I can't stand it any longer! There must be something you can do, some possibility of a remedy. Think hard, Alfred, you're a doctor and it's your duty."

"Of course there is a remedy," said Alfred.

"And if there is no remedy, perhaps there is a miracle. But

no miracle will happen here. I have to get away, away from here."

"But you're going to get out of bed as soon as you're a bit stronger."

"Alfred, I'm telling you, it's getting too late. Why should I stay in this horrible room, anyway? I want to get away, get out of the city. I know what I need. I need spring, I need the South. When the sun shines again, I'll get well."

"All of this makes some sense," said Alfred. "Of course you will go south, but you must have some patience. You can't travel today or tomorrow. As soon as it is at all possible."

"I *can* go today, I feel it. Just as soon as I'm out of this horrible death chamber, I'll be a different person. Every additional day that you keep me here is a danger."

"My dear friend, you have to keep in mind that I am your doctor—"

"You are a doctor and make stereotyped judgments. Patients know best what they need. It is inconsiderate and irresponsible to leave me lying there and let me perish. In the South miracles sometimes happen. As long as there is a glimmer of hope left you don't twiddle your thumbs, and there is always some hope left. It is inhuman to leave a person to this fate, and that's what you are doing with me. I want to go south, I want to go back to spring."

"But this is what you *should* do," said Alfred.

"We can leave tomorrow," Marie interjected hastily, "can't we?"

"If Felix will promise me to relax for three days, I shall let him go. But to go today, right now—that would be a crime. I can't permit that under any circumstances. Look at this weather," he said, turning to Marie. "It's stormy and rainy; I wouldn't advise a person in the best of health to go traveling today."

"Tomorrow, then!" exclaimed Felix.

"As soon as it clears up a bit," said the doctor. "In two or three days; I give you my word."

The patient gave him a firm and searching look. Then he asked: "On your word of honor?"

"Yes!"

"You heard him!" Marie exclaimed.

"So you don't believe," said the patient, turning to Alfred, "that there is any remedy for me? You wanted to let me die in my homeland? That is misguided humanitarianism. When a man is dying, there is no homeland any more. Being able to live—that is homeland. And I don't want to die so helplessly."

"My dear Felix, you know that it is my intention to let you spend the entire winter in the South. But I certainly can't let you leave in this weather."

"Marie," said the sick man, "get everything ready." She looked at the doctor with an anxious question in her eyes.

"Well," the doctor said, "there's no harm in that."

"Get everything ready. I want to get out of bed in an hour. We'll leave as soon as the first sunbeam appears."

In the afternoon Felix got out of bed. It almost seemed as if the idea of a change of scene had a beneficial effect on him. He lay on the sofa the whole time, awake, but there were no outbursts of despair, nor did he sink into the torpor and apathy of the previous days. He took an interest in the preparations that Marie was making, he made suggestions, gave directions, designated books from his library which he wanted to take along, and even took out of his desk drawer a big stack of manuscripts that were to go into the suitcase. "I want to look over my old writings," he said to Marie, and later, when she tried to fit this material into the suitcase, he adverted to it again. "Who knows whether all this rest hasn't done my mind a lot of good! I can virtually feel myself grow mature. Sometimes I feel that there is a wonderful clarity about everything I have thought up to now."

The day after that rainstorm the weather cleared up. And on the following day it was so warm that they were able to open the windows. Now the floor of their room was aglow with the warm and friendly autumn afternoon, and as Marie knelt in front of their suitcase, the sunbeams nestled in her wavy hair.

Alfred arrived just as Marie was carefully putting the papers in the suitcase, and Felix, lying on the sofa, began to speak about his plans.

"Am I supposed to permit you that also?" asked Alfred smilingly. "Well, I hope you are apprehensive enough not to start working too soon."

"Oh," said Felix, "that won't be any effort for me. A thousand fresh lights are now illuminating trains of thought for me that used to be shrouded in darkness."

"That certainly is nice," drawled Alfred as he watched the patient stare into space.

"Don't misunderstand me," Felix continued. "I really have no very clear idea. But it is as if something is brewing."

"Hmm, hmm."

"You know, I feel as if I heard the instruments in an orchestra tuning up. This always impressed me greatly in real life. And any moment now all the instruments will come in correctly and there will be pure harmony." And suddenly changing the subject, he asked. "Did you reserve a carriage?"

"Yes," replied the doctor.

"So we're leaving tomorrow morning," cried Marie good-humoredly. She constantly busied herself, walking from the dresser to the suitcase, from there to the bookcase, then back to the suitcase, arranging things and packing them. Was Alfred among gay young people who were preparing a pleasure trip? Today the atmosphere in this room seemed so buoyant, so untroubled almost. When he was ready to leave, Marie saw him out. "My goodness," she exclaimed, "it's such a good thing that we are going away! I'm so happy. And he's practically a changed person since it's become definite."

Alfred did not know what to reply. He shook hands with her and turned to go. But then he turned around again and said to Marie: "You must promise me . . ."

"Promise you what?"

"I mean, a friend surely is more than a doctor. You know that I'm always at your disposal. Just send me a wire."

Marie was frightened. "Do you think it might be necessary?"

"I'm telling you just in case." And with that he left.

She remained standing for a while lost in thought; then she quickly stepped into the room, worried that Felix might be concerned about her leaving him alone for minutes on end. But he only seemed to have waited for her return to continue his earlier train of thought.

"You know, Marie," he said, "the sun always has a good effect on me. When it gets colder, we'll go farther south, to the Riviera, and after that—what do you say to Africa? All right? Below the equator I would manage to produce a masterpiece for sure."

So he chatted on until finally Marie stepped up to him, stroked his cheeks, and smilingly said: "But now enough of that. Don't get carried away. Besides, you have to go to bed now, because we've got to get up early tomorrow." She saw that his cheeks were quite red and his eyes almost shiny. And when she took his hands in order to help him up from the sofa, they were burning hot.

Felix awoke at the crack of dawn. He felt the joyous excitement of a child going on vacation. Two full hours before they were to leave for the station he was sitting on the sofa ready to go. Marie, too, had been ready for a long time. She had on her light duster and her hat with the blue veil, and thus attired she stood by the window to watch for the arrival of the carriage that had been ordered. Every five minutes Felix asked whether it was here. He grew impatient and spoke of sending for another carriage when Marie exclaimed: "Here it is, here it is."

"Felix," she added, "Alfred has come, too."

Alfred had turned the corner at the same time as the carriage and waved up a friendly greeting. Right afterward he stepped into the room. "You're all ready," he cried. "What are you going to do at the station so early, especially since you've already had your breakfast, as I can see?"

"Felix is so impatient," said Marie. Alfred stepped up to him, and the sick man gave him a cheerful smile. "Wonderful traveling weather," he said.

"Oh yes, you'll have a marvelous time," said the doctor. He took a piece of zwieback from the table. "May I?"

"Don't tell me you haven't had your breakfast!" Marie exclaimed, appalled.

"Sure I have. I drank a glass of cognac."

"Wait, there's some coffee left in the pot." She insisted on pouring the remaining coffee into a cup for him and then went out to give some instructions to the cleaning woman in the hall. Alfred kept the cup close to his lips for a long time. It was embarrassing for him to be alone with his friend, and he would have been unable to talk. Now Marie came in again and told them that they were ready to leave the apartment. Felix rose and walked to the door. He was wearing a gray inverness and a soft, dark hat, and he carried a cane. He wanted to be the first to walk down the stairs, too. But he had hardly touched the banister when he began to reel. Alfred and Marie were right behind him and supported him. "I'm a bit dizzy," said Felix.

"Oh, that's quite natural," said Alfred, "when you're out walking for the first time after a number of weeks." He took the patient by one arm, Marie took him by the other, and they led him down. The coachman took off his hat when he caught sight of the sick man.

Some women's faces expressing compassion became visible at the windows of the house across the street. And when Alfred and Marie lifted the deathly pale man into the carriage, the janitor of the building came running and offered his help. As the carriage drove off, the janitor and the compassionate ladies exchanged understanding, emotional glances.

Standing on the steps of the train compartment, Alfred chatted with Marie right up to the last signal. Felix had sat down in a corner and seemed apathetic. Only when a whistle sounded from the locomotive did he seem to regain his alertness and nodded farewell to his friend. The train started moving. Alfred remained standing on the platform for a while and followed it with his eyes. Then he slowly turned to leave.

No sooner had the train left the station than Marie sat down quite close to Felix and asked him whether there was anything he wanted. Should she open the cognac bottle, get him a book, or read to him from the newspaper? He seemed to be grateful for all this kindness and squeezed her hand. Then he asked: "When do we arrive at Merano?" Since she did not know the exact time of arrival, he had her read to him all the pertinent data from the travel guide. He wanted to know where the lunch stop was going to be, where they would be at nightfall, and showed an interest in a lot of unimportant matters to which he normally paid no attention whatever. He tried to figure out how many people might be on the train and wondered whether any newlyweds were among them. After a while he asked for cognac, but it made him cough so much that he angrily told Marie never to give him cognac again, even if he asked her for some. Later he had her read to him the weather report from the newspaper and nodded contentedly on hearing a favorable forecast. They were crossing the Semmering. He attentively watched the hills, forests, fields, and mountains, but his comments were limited to a gentle "pretty" or "very nice," words that completely lacked the intonation of joy. At lunchtime he ate some of the cold food with which they had provided themselves and became very angry when Marie denied him cognac. She finally had to give him some. It agreed with him fairly well, and he became more alert and began to evince interest in all sorts of things. He had been talking about what flitted by the windows of their compartment and what he saw at the stations, but soon he reverted to himself. He said: "I read about somnambulists who dreamed of some remedy that no doctor had discovered and that made them well. I say that a sick person should follow his yearnings."

"Of course," responded Marie.

"The South! Southern air! They think the only difference is that it is warm there and that there are flowers all year and perhaps more ozone and no storms and no snow. Who knows what floats in that southern air! Secret elements that we don't even know about."

"You'll certainly get well there," said Marie, taking the sick man's hand between hers and pressing it to her lips.

He continued talking about the many painters that one could meet in Italy, about the longing which had impelled many artists and kings to go to Rome, and about Venice which he had visited once, long before he met Marie. Finally he grew tired and desired to stretch out full-length on the seats of the compartment. Thus he remained, most of the time lightly dozing, until evening came.

She sat opposite him and watched him. She felt calm, though she harbored a gentle regret. He was so pale. And he had aged so much. How this handsome face had changed since spring! It was a different kind of pallor from the pallor that was now on her own cheeks. Hers made her look younger, almost virginal. How much better off than he she was! She had never had this idea with such clarity. Why was this pain not more excruciating? Oh, it certainly was not lack of sympathy; it simply was profound fatigue, a weariness that had not left her for days even though at times she might seem more vigorous. She was glad of her fatigue, for she dreaded the heartache that would come when she ceased to be tired.

Marie suddenly started up from her sleep. She looked around; it was almost completely dark. She had put her veil over the light that glimmered above them, and so only a faint greenish gleam came into the compartment. And outside, in front of the windows, there was night, night! It was as though they were traveling through a long tunnel. Why had she given such a start? The quiet was almost absolute now; only the monotonous rattling of the wheels continued. Gradually she became accustomed to the dim light, and she was now able to make out the patient's features once again. He seemed to be sleeping quite soundly and lay there motionless. Suddenly he gave a deep, uncanny, moanful sigh. Her heart started pounding. Of course, he had moaned like that a while ago, and that is what had awakened her. But what was that? She took a closer look at him. He was not sleeping! He was lying there with his eyes opened wide, wide; she could now see it quite clearly. She was afraid of those eyes that were staring into space, into the distance, into the darkness. And again a moan, even more plaintive than the previous one. He moved, and now he heaved a sigh again, a sigh more savage than painful. And suddenly he sat up, propped both hands on the pillows, kicked the gray coat that was covering him on the floor, and tried to get up. But the motion of the train did not permit this and he sank back into the corner. Marie had jumped up and wanted to remove the veil from the lamp. But suddenly she felt his arms clasping her and he drew the trembling girl down onto his knees. "Marie, Marie!" he said in a hoarse voice.

She tried to free herself, but she could not manage. All his strength seemed to have returned and he violently pressed her to himself. "Are you ready, Marie?" he whispered, with his lips quite close to her neck. She did not understand, but only felt immense fear. She was defenseless and wanted to scream. "Are you ready?" he asked again, clasping her less convulsively, so that his lips, his breath, and his voice were not quite so close to her and she was able to breathe more freely.

"What do you want?" she asked fearfully.

"Don't you understand?" he replied.

"Let go of me, let go of me!" she screamed, but her voice was drowned out by the noise of the rolling train.

He paid no attention to her scream. He dropped his hands; she rose from his knees and sat down in the opposite corner.

"Don't you understand?" he asked again.

"What do you want?" she whispered from her corner.

"I want an answer," he responded.

She was silent; she trembled and longed for the dawn.

"The hour is coming closer," he said more softly, bending forward so that she could hear his words more distinctly. "I am asking you whether you are ready."

"What hour?"

"Ours! Ours!"

She understood what he meant. Her throat was constricted.

"Do you remember, Marie?" he continued, and his tone of voice was now gentle, almost supplicating. He took her hands in his. "You have given me a right to ask you this," he whispered. "Do you remember?"

She had now regained some of her composure, for even though the words he was speaking were horrible, his eyes had ceased to stare and there was no longer a threat in his voice. He seemed to be a supplicant. And again he asked, almost weeping: "Do you remember?" By now she had the strength to reply, though her lips were still trembling: "But you are being childish, Felix!"

He did not seem to hear her. In an even tone of voice, as though half-forgotten things were coming back to him with fresh clarity, he said: "Now the end is coming, and we have to go, Marie; our time is up." Whispered though these words were, there was something spellbinding, peremptory, and ineluctable in them. If he had threatened her, she would have been better able to defend herself. When he moved still closer to her, the enormous fear came over her for a moment that he might pounce upon her and strangle her. She was already thinking of fleeing to the other end of the compartment, smashing the window and calling for help. But at that moment he released her hands from his and leaned back as though he had nothing further to say. At that point she spoke:

"The things you are saying, Felix! Now that we are going south where you are supposed to get completely well." He was leaning on the other side and seemed lost in thought. She got up and quickly pushed the veil from the lamp. Oh, how much good that did her! Suddenly it was light, her heart began to beat more slowly, and her fear vanished. She sat down in her corner again, and he raised his eyes from the floor and looked at her. Then he said slowly:

"Marie, I won't be deceived by the morning any more, and not by the South either. Today I know."

Why is he speaking so calmly now? thought Marie. Is he trying to lull me? Is he afraid that I shall attempt to save myself? And she resolved to be on her guard. She watched him ceaselessly, hardly listened to his words, observed his every movement and glance.

He said: "But you are free, you are not even bound by your oath. Can I compel you? Won't you give me your hand?"

She gave him her hand, but in such a way that her hand was on top of his.

"If only it were day!" he whispered.

"Let me tell you something, Felix," she said. "Try to get a little more sleep. Morning will be here soon, and in a few hours we shall be in Merano."

"I can't sleep any more," he replied, looking up. At that moment their eyes met. He noticed the mistrustful, watchful look in hers, and in that instant everything became clear to him. She wanted to get him to sleep so she could get off unnoticed at the next station and escape from him. "What is it you are planning to do?" he screamed.

She gave a start. "Nothing."

He tried to get up. No sooner did she become aware of this than she fled from her corner into another corner far from him.

"Air!" he screamed. "I need some air!" He opened the window and stretched his head out into the night air. Marie felt reassured: it was only a breathing difficulty that had suddenly forced him to rise. She went up to him again and gently pulled him back from the window. "This can't be good for you," she said. He sank down into his corner again, his breath labored. She remained standing in front of him for a while, supporting one hand on the window's edge, and then resumed her former seat opposite him. After a while his breathing became more normal and a gentle smile appeared on his lips. "I shall close the window," she said. He nodded. "The dawn! The dawn!" he exclaimed. Gray-reddish streaks had appeared on the horizon.

Now they sat opposite each other for a long time without saying anything. Finally he spoke, with that smile flickering about his lips again: "You are not ready!" She was going to reply in her usual manner—that he was being childish, or something of that sort. But she was not able to say it; that smile repelled any answer.

The train slowed down. A few minutes later it made a breakfast stop. Waiters ran up and down the platform with coffee and rolls. Many travelers left the train; there were shouting and noises. Marie felt as though she had awakened from a bad dream. The triviality of this station scene soothed her. With a feeling of complete security she rose and looked out on the platform. Finally she beckoned to a waiter and had him hand her a cup of coffee. Felix watched her sip the coffee, but shook his head when she offered him some.

Soon thereafter the train was in motion again, and when they left the station, it was bright daylight and a perfect day. The mountains towered there bathed in the redness of early morning. Marie resolved never to be afraid of the night again. Felix intently looked out the window and seemed to be trying to avoid her eyes. It seemed to her as though he was a bit ashamed of what had happened during the night just past.

The train now stopped several times at short intervals, and it was a wonderful, summery morning when they arrived at the Merano station. "Here we are," exclaimed Marie, "at long last!"

They hired a carriage and went house hunting. "We don't have to economize," said Felix, "I have enough money." They asked the coachman to stop at certain villas, and while Felix remained in the carriage, Marie inspected the living quarters and the gardens. They soon found a suitable house. It was quite small, of medium height, with a little garden. Marie asked the caretaker, a woman who also acted as rental agent, to come out and explain to the young man sitting in the carriage the various merits of the villa. Felix agreed to everything, and a few minutes later the pair moved in.

Felix withdrew to the bedroom without paying attention to Marie's bustling about the house. He gave the room a cursory inspection. It was spacious and friendly, with very light, greenish wallpaper and a large window that was open, so that the whole room was flooded with the fragrance of the garden. Opposite the window were the beds. Felix was so exhausted that he stretched out on one of them.

Meanwhile Marie had the caretaker show her around, and she was particularly happy about the little garden that was surrounded by a high lattice fence and could be entered through a little door on the other side without any need to come into the house. At the back of the garden there was a wide path that offered a more direct and shorter access to the railway station than the road on which the house was situated.

When Marie returned to the room in which she had left Felix, she found him lying on the bed. She called out to him, but he did not answer. She came closer and saw that he was even paler than usual. She called his name again; no answer, he did not stir. A horrible fright came over her; she called the caretaker and asked her to send for a doctor. No sooner had the woman left than Felix opened his eyes. But the moment he was about to talk he sat up with a face distorted with fear, immediately sank back again, and breathed stertorously. Some blood trickled from his lips. Marie bent over him helplessly and desperately. Then she hurried to the door again to see whether the doctor was coming, only to rush back to Felix and call his name. If only Alfred were here! she thought.

Finally the doctor arrived, an elderly gentleman with gray whiskers. "Help him, help him!" Marie called out to him.

Then she told him about the patient as best as her excitement would permit her. The doctor looked at the sick man and felt his pulse, said that he could not examine him immediately after a hemorrhage, and gave the necessary instructions. Marie saw him out and asked him what she had to expect. "I can't tell yet," replied the doctor. "Be patient; let's hope for the best." He promised to return that evening, and when he was seated in his carriage he waved such a friendly and unaffected greeting to Marie, who was standing inside the house, that one might have thought he had paid her a social call.

Marie stood there in perplexity for only a moment. The next moment she had an idea that seemed to promise succor to her, and she hurried to the post office to send a telegram to Alfred. After it was dispatched, she felt relieved. She thanked the woman, who had taken care of the patient during her absence, begged her to excuse the trouble they had caused her on the very first day, and promised that they would show their appreciation to her.

Felix was still lying stretched out on the bed in his clothes; he was unconscious, but his breath had become normal. While Marie sat down at the head of the bed, the caretaker consoled her by telling her about the many gravely ill persons who had recovered in Merano. She told her that she herself had been ailing in her youth and, as was plain to see, had made a wonderful recovery. And this despite all the misfortune that had befallen her: her husband had died after two years of marriage, her sons had gone out into the world—well, everything could have been different, but now she was quite pleased to have the position in this house. One could not really complain about the owner, because he lived in Bolzano and came over twice a month at most in order to see whether everything was all right. Thus she kept rambling on and was friendly in a gushy way. She offered to unpack their suitcases, an offer which Marie gratefully accepted, and later she brought their dinner to their room. The milk for the patient was ready, and gentle movements indicated that he was about to awake.

Finally Felix regained consciousness, turned his head back and forth a few times, and fixed his gaze on Marie who was bending over him. He smiled and feebly pressed her hand. "What happened to me?" he asked. When the doctor came in the afternoon, he found him much better and permitted Marie to undress him and put him to bed. Felix submitted to everything with equanimity.

Marie did not stir from the sickbed. What an endless afternoon that was! Through the window, which had remained open on doctor's orders, the gentle odors of the garden came in, and it was so quiet! Marie mechanically watched the glimmering of the sunbeams on the floor. Felix held her hand clasped almost uninterruptedly. His was cool and damp, and this gave Marie a disagreeable sensation. At times she broke the silence with a few words she actually had to force herself to speak. "You're feeling better, aren't you? . . . Well, you see! . . . No talking! . . . You're not allowed to! . . . In a couple of days you will go out in the garden!" And he nodded and smiled. Then Marie tried to figure out when Alfred might arrive. He could be there tomorrow evening—one more night and one day, then. If only he were there!

It seemed the afternoon would never end. The sun disappeared and the room began to grow dark, but when Marie looked out into the garden, she could see the yellowish sunbeams glide over the white gravel paths and the bars of the fence. While looking out, she suddenly heard the voice of the sick man: "Marie." She quickly turned her head toward him.

"I'm feeling much better now," he said quite loudly.

"You shouldn't talk so loud," she gently admonished him.

"Much better," he whispered. "This time it went well. Perhaps it was the crisis."

"Sure!" she agreed.

"My hope is the good air. But such an attack must not come again, otherwise I am lost."

"Oh, but you see that you're already feeling stronger again."

"You are good, Marie. I'm grateful to you. But take good care of me. Be careful, be careful!"

"Do you need to tell me that?" she replied, a bit reproachfully.

He continued in a whisper: "Because if I have to go, I shall take you with me."

When he said that, mortal fear shot through her. Why was that? Surely there was no danger from him; he was too weak to use violence. She was now ten times stronger than he. Whatever could he have in mind? What did his eyes look for in the air, on the wall, in space? He was not able to get up, and he had no weapons on him. But perhaps he did have poison. He could have obtained poison; perhaps he had it with him and was going to put some drops in her drinking glass. But where could he be keeping it? She had helped to undress him herself. Perhaps he had a powder in his wallet? But his wallet was in his jacket. No, no, no! These were words caused by his delirium and by his desire to torment her, nothing more. But if a fever could cause such *words* and *thoughts,* why not *deeds* as well? Perhaps he would utilize a moment in which she was asleep to strangle her. It did not take much strength for that. This might make her faint right away, and then she would be defenseless. Oh, she was not going to sleep that night . . . and tomorrow Alfred would be there!

The evening progressed and night came. Felix had not spoken another word, and even the smile had completely disappeared from his lips. He stared into space with a uniformly gloomy seriousness. When it grew dark, the caretaker brought in burning candles and prepared to make up the bed next to Felix's. But Marie motioned to her with her hand that this would not be necessary. Felix noticed the signal. "Why not?" he asked, and immediately added: "You are too good to me, Marie. You should get some sleep; I'm feeling better, after all." It seemed to her that there was mockery in these words.

She did not go to bed, but spent the long, lingering night by his bedside without shutting an eye. Felix lay there quietly almost the whole time. Now and then she wondered whether he was perhaps only pretending to be asleep in order to lull her. She took a closer look at him, but the uncertain light of the candle simulated twitching movements around the patient's lips and eyes, and these confused her. At one point she went to the window and looked out into the garden. It was bathed in a dim bluish gray, and when she bent forward a little and looked up, she could glimpse the moon which seemed to be floating right above the trees. Not a breeze was stirring, and in the infinite stillness and motionlessness that enveloped her it seemed as if the fence bars, which she could quite clearly discern, slowly moved forward and then stopped again.

After midnight Felix awakened. Marie smoothed out his pillows, and obeying a sudden impulse she took this opportunity to feel with her fingers whether he had hidden something among them. She remembered his words "I shall take you with me! I shall take you with me!" But would he have said that if he had meant it seriously? If he were even capable of concerning himself with a plan? The first thing then to occur to him would have been not to give himself away. She was certainly quite childish to let the trivial ravings of a sick man frighten her. She grew sleepy and moved her chair far away from the bed—just in case. But she did not *want* to fall asleep! Only her thoughts began to grow indistinct, and from the bright consciousness of the day they fluttered into the twilight of gray dreams. Memories welled up of days and nights of radiant happiness, memories of hours in which he had held her in his arms while over them a breath of early spring moved through the room. She had an indistinct sensation that the fragrance of the garden did not dare to enter here. Again she had to go to the window to drink in this fragrance; the damp hair of the sick man seemed to exude a stale, sweetish odor which nauseatingly permeated the air in the room. What now? If only it were over! Yes, done with! She no longer shrank back from the thought, and she remembered the insidious words that turn the most horrible of all wishes into hypocritical compassion: "If only he were released!" And what then? She could see herself sitting out there in the garden on a bench under a tall tree, her face pale and tear-stained. But these signs of mourning were only on her face. In her soul there was a blissful peace such as she had not known for a long, long time. And then she saw the figure that was herself rise and step out on the street and slowly walk off. For now she was free to go wherever she wished.

But in the midst of this reverie she remained alert enough to listen to the patient's breath, which at times turned into a moan. Finally the morning hesitantly approached. At the crack of dawn the caretaker came to the door and made the friendly offer to relieve Marie for the next few hours. Marie accepted with genuine joy. After a brief final glance at Felix she left the room and went into the adjoining chamber where a sofa beckoned her to a comfortable rest. Oh, how wonderful that felt! Without undressing she lay down on it and closed her eyes.

It was many hours later that she awoke. A pleasant semi-darkness enveloped her. Through the crevices of the closed shutters came only narrow strips of sunlight. She quickly rose and immediately grasped the situation clearly. Today Alfred was bound to come! This made her face the gloomy atmosphere of the coming hours with greater courage. Without hesitating she went into the next room. When she opened the door, she was dazzled for a second by the white blanket that covered the sick man's bed. But then she caught sight of the caretaker who put a finger over her mouth, rose from her chair, and tiptoed toward Marie. "He's fast asleep," she whispered, and then told Marie that a high fever had kept him awake until an hour ago and that he had asked for her a few times. The doctor had come early in the morning and found the patient's condition unchanged. She had wanted to wake the lady of the house, but the doctor would not permit it. He was going to come back sometime that afternoon.

Marie listened attentively to the good old woman, thanked her for her solicitude, and then took her place.

It was a warm, almost sultry day. It was close to noon. Over the garden lay the still and heavy gleam of a blazing sun. When Marie looked in at the bed, the first thing she saw were the two narrow hands of the sick man lying on the blanket and at times lightly twitching. His chin had sunk down, his face was deathly pale, and his lips were slightly opened. His breathing stopped for seconds on end, and then he drew some shallow, wheezing breaths. "Perhaps he will die before Alfred comes," Marie thought. The way Felix now lay there, his face had again assumed the expression of ailing youthfulness, and in his features was etched a limpness as after unspeakable pain, a surrender as after hopeless struggle. It was suddenly clear to Marie what it was that had so horribly changed those features in recent days and what they lacked at that moment. It was the bitterness that was etched in his face when he looked at *her*. Now there surely was no hatred in his dreams, and he was handsome again. She wished he would wake up. As she looked at him now she felt full of an unspeakable grief, of a fear for him that was consuming her. The man she was watching die was, after all, her beloved again. Suddenly she understood what that really meant. The whole misery of this inescapable and dreadful fate came over her, and she again understood everything, everything: that he had been her happiness and her life and that she had wanted to join him in death, and that the moment was now terrifyingly close when everything had to be over beyond recall. And the rigid coldness that had laid hold of her heart and the indifference of days and nights on end coalesced for her into something obscure and incomprehensible. And now, at this moment, things were still all right. He was, after all, still alive and breathing, perhaps dreaming. But later he would lie there stiff and dead, he would be buried and would rest deep in the earth in a quiet cemetery over which the days would uniformly pass while he decayed. And she would live, she would be with people while still aware of a silent grave out there in which he rested, he, the man she had loved! There was no stopping the flow of her tears, and at length she sobbed loudly. He stirred, and as she quickly dried her cheeks with her handkerchief, he opened his eyes and gave her a long questioning look, though he said nothing. After a few minutes he whispered, "Come!" She rose from her chair, bent over him, and he raised his arms as though he wanted to hug her around the neck. But he dropped his arms again and asked:

"Were you crying?"

"No," she quickly replied, brushing her hair from her forehead.

He again gave her a long and solemn look, then turned away from her. He seemed to be pondering.

Marie reflected on whether she ought to tell the sick man about her telegram to Alfred. Should she prepare him for his arrival? No, what for? The best thing would be if she pretended to be surprised at Alfred's arrival. The rest of the day passed in the torpid tension of expectation. Outward events moved past her as in a fog. The physician's call was soon done with. He found the patient utterly apathetic, only infrequently waking from a moanful semislumber to ask some trivial questions or make some routine requests. He asked what time it was and requested water. The caretaker came and went, and Marie spent the whole time in the room, usually sitting on a chair next to the patient. At intervals she stood by the foot of the bed, resting her arms on the footboard; at other times she went to the window and looked out into the garden in which the trees gradually cast longer shadows until finally the dusk settled over meadows and paths. It was a humid evening, and the light of the candle that stood on the night table by the patient's head scarcely flickered. Only when it was completely dark and the moon came out over the gray-blue mountains that were visible in the distance did a light breeze begin to stir. Marie felt very refreshed when it blew about her forehead, and it seemed to please the patient, too. He moved his head and turned his wide open eyes toward the window. And finally he drew a deep, deep breath.

Marie took his hand which was hanging down the side of the blanket. "Is there anything I can get you?" she asked.

He slowly withdrew his hand and said: "Marie, come!"

She came closer and moved her head quite close to his pillow. He put his hand over her hair as if to bless her and kept it there. Then he said: "I thank you for all your love." Her head was now resting next to his on the pillow, and she again felt her tears flow. It became quite still in the room. The whistling of a distant train became audible and faded away, and then there again was the stillness of the sultry summer evening—heavy, sweet, and incomprehensible. Suddenly Felix sat up in bed, so quickly and vigorously that Marie was frightened. She lifted her head from the pillow and stared in Felix's face. He took Marie's head with both hands, as he had often done in the heat of passion. "Marie," he cried, "now I want to remind you."

"Of what?" she asked and tried to wrest her head from his hands. But he seemed to have regained all his strength and held her fast.

"I want to remind you of your promise," he said hastily, "to die with me." As he spoke these words he came quite close to her. She could feel his breath move over her mouth and was unable to draw back. He was so close to her when he spoke that he seemed to be forcing her to drink in his words with her lips. "I'm taking you with me; I don't want to depart without you. I love you and won't leave you behind!"

She was almost paralyzed with fear. A hoarse scream, so muffled that she could hardly hear it herself, issued from her throat. Her head was motionless between his hands, and he convulsively squeezed her temples and her cheeks. He talked on and on, and his hot, damp breath singed her.

"Together! Together! It was your will, wasn't it? I'm afraid of dying alone. Will you? Will you?"

She had kicked the chair away from under her, and finally, as though it were a matter of freeing herself from a steel ring, she wrested her head from the clasp of his two hands. He continued to keep his hands up in the air as though her head were still between them and stared at her as though he could not comprehend what had happened.

"No, no," she screamed, "I won't!" and she ran to the door. He rose as though he wanted to jump out of bed. But now his strength gave out, and like a lifeless mass he sank back on his bed with a dull thud. But she could not see this; she had flung the door open and was running through the adjoining room into the hall. She did not know what she was doing. He had tried to strangle her! She could still feel his fingers moving down her temples, her cheeks, her throat. She rushed out the front door; no one was there. She remembered that the caretaker had gone out to get some supper. What was she to do now? She rushed back and through the hallway into the garden. As though pursued, she ran along over paths and lawns until she reached the other end. Turning around, she could see the open window of the room from which she had just come. She saw the flickering candlelight, but nothing else. "What was that? What was that?" she kept saying to herself. She did not know what she was supposed to do, so she walked aimlessly up and down on the paths next to the fence. Now she remembered: Alfred! He was coming! He was bound to be coming now! She looked through the bars onto the moonlit path that led there from the railway station. She hurried to the garden gate and opened it. The path lay before her, white and deserted. Perhaps he was taking the other road. No, no—over there a shadow was approaching, coming closer and closer, walking faster and faster, a man's figure. Was it he? She took a few steps toward him: "Alfred!" "Is it you, Marie?" It was he. She could have wept with joy. When he had reached her, she wanted to kiss his hand. "What's going on?" he asked. And she only pulled him after her without answering.

Felix had lain there motionless for only a moment, then he had risen and looked around. She was gone; he was alone! A constricting fear seized him. He knew only one thing: he had to have her there, there with him. At one leap he was out of bed. But he could not stay erect and again fell backward on the bed. There was a buzzing and roaring in his head. He leaned on the chair and managed to move forward by pushing it ahead of him. "Marie, Marie!" he mumbled. "I don't want to die alone, I can't!" Where was she? Where could she be? Pushing the chair ahead of himself, he had reached the window. There lay the garden, covered with the bluish gleam of the humid night. What shimmering and whirring! How the grasses and trees were dancing! Oh, that was a spring which would make him well. That air, that air! Whenever such air surrounded him, there had to be a recovery. Oh, there! What was that over there? From the fence which seemed to be in a deep abyss he saw a female figure coming over the white, shimmering gravel path, bathed in the bluish glow of the moon. How she floated, how she flew, and yet she was not coming any closer! Marie! Marie! And right behind her there was a man. A man with Marie—of enormous size. Now the fence began to dance and danced after them, and so did the black sky behind it, and everything, everything danced after them. And from the distance came sounds and singing and ringing—so beautiful, so beautiful. And it grew dark . . .

Marie and Alfred came running, both of them. When they got to the window, Marie stopped and anxiously peered into the room. "He isn't there!" she cried. "The bed is empty." Suddenly she let out a scream and sank back, into Alfred's arms. Gently pushing her out of the way, he bent over the balustrade and saw his friend lying on the floor right by the window, in his white nightshirt, stretched out with his legs spread far apart, next to him an overturned chair whose back he held clasped with one hand. Blood was trickling from his mouth onto his chin. His lips and his eyelids seemed to be twitching. But when Alfred took a closer look, it was only the illusive moonlight that played about his pale face.

—Translated by Harry Zohn